D0844136

LIGHTSHIP

ARCHIE BINNS

LIGHTSHIP

BINFORDS & MORT, *Publishers*
PORTLAND, OREGON

CONTENTS

7

LIGHTSHIP

I

Graveyard Watch

THE lightship rolled its high sunken sides easily in a profound swell coming from half-way round the world, out of the distant stretches of the Pacific. The swell had risen in eastern sunlight and now heaved past the moored ship in darkness and broke on the stone-jawed reef a few miles farther inshore. *Lightship 167* was there because of the reef, and its name was painted in eight foot letters on her tumbled red sides. The sea was calm, and the Indian village on the shore was calmer still, sleeping in darkness. The reef divided the two silences with its low, menacing thunder. Captain Lindstrom, who was an unabashed philosopher, had once remarked to Ole that the reef was the tumult of death between the living, who are peaceful enough when given the opportunity, and the dead whose opportunity for peace is infinite.

Ole respected his captain and saw the thought was appropriate, though the way it was put had a flavor of hymn books and varnished pews, which he scorned. But there was no denying the reef was death, and *Lightship 167* lay there as a reminder for other vessels to pass by at a distance.

Just now Ole was walking the deck with folded arms,

taking quick rolling strides and turning abruptly at each
end of his short promenade. Now and then he glanced
up critically at the two circles of oil lamps burning with
deceptive feebleness under the white turrets of the day-
marks aloft. Adjusting the quid in his left cheek, he
swept the horizon with shrewd eyes, from north through
west to the south. Until four o'clock that arc of the sea
was in his keeping. To the northwest the range lights
of a freighter were disappearing over the hill of the
world. To the west the *President*, glowing with many
lights, steamed towards the south, ahead of her schedule.
When he had come on watch at twelve, Ole commented
on the log slate that the weather was fine.

The pulse of the ocean continued evenly, answered
by the low, recurring thunder from the reef, and the
lights swung endlessly in their slow arc. The range
lights of the out-bound freighter disappeared, too
quickly, but the *President* was still a glowing constella-
tion, west by south from the lightship. Ole turned and
went down the companionway with brisk gravity. The
'tweendecks were deserted, but from the head of the
engine room ladder he made out the young fireman, Ben,
sitting asleep on a box before the fire-doors.

"Start the bell," the seaman called down.

"A'right." The boy rose in his sleep, turned his shut
eyes in the direction of the steam gauge, and climbed the
iron ladder. Ole watched him opening the valves of the
delicate little engine on the bulkhead by the carpenter's
bench. With an eager whine the mechanism started and
clicked out the number of the ship: one beat on the
sunken bell, pause, six beats, pause, seven beats, long

pause; then one, six, seven over again. Navigators with submarine telephones could hear the bell clanking in the sea from a distance of fourteen miles. (When Ben had first come on station, he attempted to polish the bell machine while it was running. A wisp of cotton waste, fouled in the lugs, caused the mechanism to sound off the number of another lightship, three thousand miles away. Ole had been scandalized, and Captain Lindstrom jumped out of his sleep and ran forward.)

The seaman wrote on the log slate in a neat round hand: "2:46: distant fog. Started the bell." Then he went on deck. The lights of the *President* softened and went out with gentle abruptness. He turned to the companionway again. The fireman had opened the drains and exhaust of the red whistle engine and stood with his hand on the throttle, waiting the inevitable order.

"Start the whistle."

Ben cracked the valve, then opened it slowly. The fly-wheel revolved and the vessel shuddered with the roar of the great whistle. In the respite that followed, someone forward turned over in his sleep and answered the whistle with a groan. At the second blast Ole was writing on the slate: "2:52: fog. Started the whistle."

On deck he found the fog bank alongside. Another minute and it boarded the ship and surrounded her. The stars disappeared and the dark shore to leeward. Nothing was left in the world but the ship, rolling its lights aloft mistily, beating out its number on the sea-muffled bell and wracked at two minute intervals with the spasm of its whistle, like the recurring pain in some monstrous travail. Below there was the clash of a shovel on the floor plates of the fire room; the whistle engine was notorious for its devouring of coal.

With the ship producing its utmost of light and noise, Ole went below and forward to the dark galley for coffee. Before filling a mug, he fed the range a shovelful of coal from the wooden box. Through some obscure tradition of the service, the seamen and not the firemen tended the galley fire in the night watches. Perhaps it was assumed that a fireman above the level of the water was too much out of his element to perceive the connection between coal and fire. No one knew, exactly.

While Ole was sugaring his coffee, Ben came into the galley. Ben was not his first name, but a corruption of his last. Full names did not survive on the lightship—except in the case of Jimmy Gill, "Mr. Gill," the four-to-eight fireman. One name per man was the proper allotment, and if it was not already simple and precise it suffered a sea change. At the Eagle Harbor shipyard Ole had once spent half an hour convincing a stranger there was no Larsen on board. That evening he recounted the incident to Karl, who had shared the same room with him for two years. Karl was sorrowful when he heard the description of the man who had been sent away.

"That must have been my brother," he said. "Didn't I ever tell you my family name is Larsen? You must tell me your family name, too, in case anyone asks for you."

Ole thought a moment and then said, "Hanson." No one ever asked for him.

Ben filled a mug from the pot on the range and rummaged for food. Since the big cook started going insane the night lunches had suffered. The fireman and seaman were friends, but they exchanged no comments. They

14

shared the same watch, and therefore the same information: fog, bell, whistle. There was nothing to say. The boy had found the pilot bread and was munching a disc along with his coffee. Ole took nothing with his, but knew the young are always hungry. He remembered how he had eaten as a boy of sixteen in the bark *Stadsholmen*, which never arrived at any port.

The lightship rolled steadily, the bell clanked monotonously in the sea, and at two minute intervals the whistle bellowed, vibrating everything loose in the ship. Ole washed his cup and spoon at the sink, dried them and found their proper places in the dark. "An hour more," he observed.

"That's good."

On his way out he heard the fireman searching for more food. Even the graveyard watch did not seem long to the seaman, who had spent fourteen years in the lightship, but he knew how Ben looked forward to the end of his watch.

At twenty minutes of four Ole was lighting the lamp in the little stateroom forward of the one he shared with Clark. The lightship had no foc'sle, but double staterooms on each side of the mess room.

"Twenty to four," he said, shaking the occupant of the lower berth.

Fat Oscar opened his little, suspicious eyes. He opened them craftily to spy on someone who might be spying on him. "What you want?" he grunted.

"It's twenty to four."

"*Ha*!" Oscar commented loudly, like a blast of escaping steam. Then he settled back to injured repose.

"Twenty to four." Ole shook him again.

"*Ha!*" Oscar sat up with surprising quickness, his little eyes blazing with hatred and suspicion. "*Ha!*" Suddenly he began to dress, as if the statement about the time, the place, everything, was a damned lie and he was going to prove it and poison someone for the fraud imposed upon him. Oscar had been with the lightship seventeen years, but his disgust for life dated back forty. As far as the companionway Ole heard him grunting and snorting and exclaiming "*Ha!*" as he fought with his clothes. Then the bellowing whistle triumphed over the lesser human protests and Ole walked alone on deck under the deep tide of fog, with the lights swimming in lazy unison ten fathoms above.

In the cubbyhole across the mess room Ben summoned "Mr." Gill to prepare for his watch. The oil lamp was still burning, and a pair of spectacles and a three months' old copy of *The Literary Digest* shared the narrow upper bunk with the ponderous old fireman. In repose, Mr. Gill was reminiscent of the moon, with his large face, too full for wrinkles, and his perfectly bald head.

Mr. Gill was a personage. After thirty-odd years of the life usual to a fireman, he had quit drinking, without apparent cause or effort, and saved his money. Later, he quit the sea to live in a respectable room on First Avenue, Seattle, where he subscribed to the "*P.I.*," voted, paid visits to former shipmates in the Marine Hospital and enjoyed the reputation of a solid citizen. He only went on the lightship occasionally, as a holiday, and he was amused by landsmen who referred to it as "going to sea." Ashore, he was the beau-ideal of Seattle firemen; afloat, he gave the lightship a flavor of gracious dignity.

No one ever quite thought of him as a member of the crew: he was more of a welcome guest—helpful and unobtrusive, yet conscious of his own worth.

Waking him was a simple matter.

"Twenty to four," Ben said quietly.

Mr. Gill opened his eyes. "Right, my boy," he answered, and was fully awake, without effort. Sleep had come upon him while he was reading, and now it went away from him with the same ease, like a cloud floating away from the face of the full moon. "How is everything, Ben?" he asked with placid heartiness, sitting up to put away his magazine and spectacles.

"All right," the boy answered sleepily, with the shattering roar of the whistle punctuating his remark. When it had finished he added: "I cleaned the fires a little while ago."

From the shelf beside his berth Mr. Gill collected a black pipe, tobacco and safety matches. With gravity he completed dressing by pulling a padded black sateen cap over the nakedness of his head. He slept fully clothed, which was only appropriate for one who treated sleep so lightly. "Turn in when you like, Ben." He slid his two hundred and fifty pounds to the floor with careful ease. "I'll have a cup of coffee, and then a look at the fires. Turn in, boy."

Mr. Gill was having his coffee in the unlighted galley when Oscar came in. His soft gaiters made no sound in the alleyway or on the galley floor, but wherever he went he gave his course away by puffing and hissing and muttering to himself. At night he sounded like an angry spirit or a disembodied voice of protest wandering through the ship. Fumblingly he found a mug and fumblingly filled it, muttering his everlasting resentment against a maimed hand. Turning from the range, he collided unexpectedly with the fireman. The galley was over-small for two men of such girth. At the touch of a human body in the dark, Oscar started violently with an agonized "*Ha!*"

"Why did you jump?" Gill asked.

"I didn't know anybody was there," Oscar mumbled. "Is that Mr. Gill?"

On being told it was, he muttered his doubts and drank hastily, with vocal and digestive rumblings between swallows. In the dark Gill felt the boring, suspicious little eyes questioning the identity and even the reality of his bulky shadow.

When he had made his leisurely descent to the fire room, Mr. Gill settled himself on the box before the Scotch boiler with a sigh of contentment. There was nothing to do, and he did nothing. The bell clanked its numbers monotonously in the sea and the whistle engine above alternated two minutes of rumbling to itself with half a minute of blasphemous roaring at the fog. The steam pressure was still high. Five minutes more or less would make no difference.

To Ben, whom he had relieved, going off watch was one of the events of the day. To Gill they were all harbor watches, rest after a lifetime of savage toil. He enjoyed the quiet dusk of the fire room, deserted except for himself and a gently-laboring auxiliary pump, and the honest, familiar smells of coal and waste and oil; the fidelity of half-banked fires drowsing behind the eyes of the fire-doors. In the unaccountable years of his past he had heard the call of the quiet fire room in port, when its furnaces had ceased raging. Instead of answering that call, he and countless others like him had stampeded up the iron ladders and ashore to drunkenness and love-making with women of strange hues and voices and infections. There had been senseless brawls, too, and sometime sudden death, and always the quick separation of a man and his money.

Those years and their passions had become unreal. They were clouded in the smoke of fires that consumed them, and Mr. Gill had come home at last to the peace of an idle stokehold. It was for others to decide, if they cared to, whether it was the dross that had been burned away, or whether it was the ashes and clinkers that remained. In Seattle a well-meaning officer in the forces of salvation had once spoken familiarly to Mr. Gill of his "lost years," and the old fireman suggested with dignity that in the end all of us lose everything.

He had no regrets for the past. What he had done he had done, and where there was a penalty attached he paid like a gentleman. If he had learned anything, he had learned respect for others and himself. Now he never raised his voice or hand to any man. Neither did he raise his hat. He was at honorable peace with himself and his peers.

In the grimy little cabin which he shared with Allen Ross, the eight-to-twelve fireman, Ben sat on the wooden bench and pulled off his shoes. Close beside him, Allen's homely red face frowned in sleep. That was strange because the boy had never seen him anything but pleasant when he was awake. More than anything else, it was his roommate's cheerful courtesy that made life bearable. But now, as always, he frowned at some dark menace which faced him in sleep. Ben kicked off his last shoe, puffed out the lamp and climbed into the upper berth, where he immediately fell asleep: a big, obstinate boy of eighteen who held good cards in a face that might never be played.

Across the mess room Ole undressed, folding his clothes away neatly. The room he shared with Clark (first name unknown) was ordered like the parlor of a maiden lady. In thirty-odd years at sea Ole had learned that neatness is the foundation of seamanship, just as beauty is the secret of a ship's seaworthiness. The truth was beyond dispute. It was beyond dispute, also, that the life founded on neatness and dedicated to beauty was two-thirds ugliness and dirt.

Before turning in Ole looked gravely at his sleeping roommate. Clark was a tall man, large-boned, with coarse, iron-gray hair. When his eyes were open, they were dark and rather sad. Ole had thought deeply and arrived at a dislike of that quality. People ought not to look sad any more than they should be unpleasantly cheerful. They should be gravely hopeful, remembering they will get very little themselves and looking forward to the time when their kind will learn all the secrets of the world.

Clark was a good seaman though, and a model room-mate—quiet, thoughtful and orderly. He seemed to have learned that two people are always two and not one, and therefore cannot live together. He lived by himself in the stateroom, and Ole lived there by himself. They did not knock their heads together in any brotherly attempt to join forces, and so never quarreled. Ole respected Clark for that, but saw no reason for his looking sad. Like himself, Clark had come of decent people. He had gone to sea at nineteen, and joined the lightship when he tired of deep water. That was a reasonably complete history, but it did not explain everything about the man.

Once something odd happened. At breakfast Ole looked up and saw tears in Clark's eyes. First he thought his roommate, who was new to the service, had taken some of the Government horseradish. But the bottle was on the revolving shelf about the foremast, undisturbed. Then he wondered if they were going to have another case. One of the men who had gone insane on the lightship cried almost incessantly, and another at intervals until he jumped overboard and was drowned on the way in from station. But Clark showed none of the other symptoms.

The messman in the galley was whistling—a foolish thing to do in a ship—long drawn out and piercing, "Down by the Old Mill Stream." He whistled well. Perhaps that was it. The tune reminded Clark of something, his boyhood home, perhaps. But that would be foolish. A home has done its duty when a boy is old enough to break away. Or a woman. But that, too, would be foolish. One class of women bore children for men who lived ashore. Sailors had nothing to do with them. The other class amused sailors and others whose calling did not allow them to marry. They were a necessity, but a man did not cry about them. No one should cry about anything. People only did that when they looked back, which they should never do. They must look forward to the time when people will learn the meaning of life.

Another incident, even less calculable. The time, a few years earlier, when Chief O'Rorke found the old-fashioned whorehouse on the "Skidroad" in Seattle. At least he had sworn it was the old-fashioned kind, with plenty of girls waiting in the parlor downstairs and plenty of beds upstairs—all open and above board. Two dollars for a piece and five dollars for all night. Nobody's card or letter of introduction needed. The house was run, he said, by a bawd named Wingfield.

Captain Lindstrom had made light of the discovery and spoke wryly of the place and "Mrs. Wingfield's Old-fashioned Whorehouse." He also joked with the little chief about going to the trouble of finding whorehouses when he was past the time.

Mickey admitted he was past the time—he laid no claims to being a young buck. He had only found the place so he could pass it along to the others because he didn't want the art of carnal copulation to perish from the world. Ole knew why the chief went to such places; he had been with him once when whorehouses were whorehouses. The old fellow went because he liked to have the girls crowd around him. Pinch a nice shaped stern; look at another's leg; get two struggling over him, with their arms around him, each one trying to pull him to her room. "Girls, girls, don't make a *kindly* old man choose between you!" Then he would buy drinks for all of them, give five dollars each to the whores who had scuffled over him and go back to the ship feeling good.

The chief told the crew about Mrs. Wingfield's on a Saturday afternoon when they were waiting for the steamer to take them across to Seattle. The boiler was blown down for scaling and no one needed on board but a watchman. They weren't much interested, except a fireman named Dick who pretended he couldn't wait for the *Bainbridge*. He was going to jump off the pier and swim across, and he was all talk, like his swimming.

Ole didn't think about the whorehouse until that night when he was walking through Pine Street. Then he thought he might have a look. It was spring and he felt the urge—the first in a long time; so long he hadn't known he ever would again. The house was something like Mickey said; nothing special, but good enough, as good as you could expect. Not the usual hush-hush kind of place. He looked the girls over and picked out the one he wanted. There were two pretty ones, but he wasn't interested in them. Pretty women were always spoiled, even if they were only whores. There weren't enough pretty women to go round, so they always thought too much of themselves with the attention they got and didn't give a man much; they only pretended. A pretty woman thought she had given a man something before she ever started. He picked out the one he wanted: one with a plain face and a scar across her forehead. She had a shape, though, and she didn't look jaded like the pretty ones. She didn't look as if she had had a man yet that night. That was as near to a virgin as a sailor could expect. Her name was Jenny.

When they were in the hall upstairs, going to her room, a door opened in their faces and Clark stepped out.

"You won't go with any other girl before you come back?" his woman asked. She stood in the doorway, wearing some light silk thing she had thrown about herself, while Clark held the door for a second and mopped his forehead. He was out of practice, all right. The whore he had been with was tall and slender with brown hair. She might have been pretty once, but there wasn't anything to the tall, slim kind. She was saying, "You won't go with any other girl before you come back and see me, will you?" the way all whores did.

Then Jenny said, "Give us a chance, will you, Big Boy?" wanting to get by. Clark stepped to one side, polite as he always was. Then he saw his shipmate. Ole didn't know why he looked startled and caught. They were both there for the same thing, what everybody has to have. But Clark looked caught just the same, caught and trying to hide something when there wasn't anything to hide. At least, whatever he was trying to hide was in his own mind, and Ole wouldn't have known it was there if he hadn't wanted to hide it. For a second Clark looked as if he wanted to fight, too, like a man who is proud and would rather fight than explain something. Then he flushed dark red and nodded to Ole as he went past. It was the first time Ole had ever heard of a sailor upset over being found in a whorehouse.

Since then Ole had been in the habit of studying Clark's face for an answer to the questions he could never ask. When you have faith that some day your kind will learn everything, it is stupid to share the same stateroom with a man for three years and not know anything of what goes on inside his shell. Tonight, as always, Clark's big, relaxed face told him nothing. Ole dropped his quid in the cuspidor, turned down the lamp and blew it out.

Clark had been undisturbed by the rolling of the ship, the whistle bellowing above, the bell clanking below and the lamp shining on his face. But he stirred in his sleep at the light push of a foot on the edge of his bunk. It was something new. Usually Ole vaulted into his upper berth from the floor.

On deck old Oscar trundled about in the fog, muttering and hissing his displeasure at the inferior quality of the universe as it was revealed to him. In the quiet gloom of the stokehold Mr. Gill sat on the box which Ben had vacated, a benign and monumental figure, taking his ease before the winking fire-doors—the welcoming hearth to which he had turned in his age. Between decks, forward and aft, the crew and officers slept deeply in the rolling ship. Some of them adventured with dreams whose meanings were as obscure to them as the sea creatures that swam under the restless keel of their home.

The thrust of a foot on his bunk had disturbed the surface of Clark's sleep, like a pebble falling into still water, distorting reflections. He was on a torn field at twilight, looking at a little ship propped up on dry land, a long way from any sea. He wanted more than anything else to know if the ship was still sound, but the Trap was waiting for him in the dusk. Fear and desire balanced, and he could neither touch the ship nor go away.

25

II

Backwater Voyage

Henry Clark came into money in Astoria, Oregon.
When the salvage was paid on the barquentine
Cyrus E. Borden, he and his shipmate, Harold Roberts, received five hundred dollars each. That was in addition to
their pay for the voyage. The other members of the *Val-
paraiso's* crew received like amounts, but that was neither here nor there. They drank and squandered and were
fleeced of their inheritance, and it did not affect the
course of their lives. Except, perhaps, "Scar" Butler.
After a knife had been placed in his back, he was thrown
from the window of a house of prostitution, conveniently
built, like the rest of the business district, on piles above
the river. And something like that was certain to have
happened sooner or later.

Clark and Hal were so young that riches sobered them.
They drank beer moderately in a respectable saloon and
considered courses. The salvage was to be spent, but they
wanted their money's worth. Clark had a vague idea
about buying good clothes and taking a first class railroad passage to the Grand Canyon.

Hal disapproved. He was a fresh-faced, curly-haired
man of twenty-four, with ten years' deep water experience
and a manner. "Too risky," he commented. "Things

happen to your health inland; fevers and things. And we might run into Indians. Not that I would mind a scrap with the redskins if I knew the ground I was fighting on." He brushed the ash of his cigar against his glass, thoughtfully. "Fighting natives," he analyzed, "you want a boat you can escape to. A boat doesn't run away, like a horse. And if it stops a few bullets or arrows you know how to make repairs. Now, on a river like this—" His eyes blazed and narrowed. Listening to himself talk, he had overheard something of immediate and unexpected value. His solid young fist crashed down on the table. "By God, Clarkie, I have it!"

So they bought an old sixteen-foot boat with mainsail and jib, a Winchester rifle, a double-barrelled shotgun, fishing tackle, blankets and food. A week after they had come into money, they started their voyage up the great river.

Sometimes they got on each other's nerves, which was only natural. Their chief point of disagreement was the account they should give of themselves. Clark saw no reason against telling the truth. He was two years older than Hal, but with only six years of sea experience, mostly in steam. Therefore, he was anxious to affirm his saltiness. Hal thought he missed the whole spirit of adventure when he resorted to anything as common as the truth. "Sailors? Hell, no! We're gentlemen explorers, back from the Klondike and out to see a little of the world. Don't forget that, Clarkie. And if the time comes, we'll show ourselves as sailors without talking!"

They disagreed on other matters, but without serious rancor. Foc'sle life had taught them to live and let live under trying conditions, and they clashed less than two landsmen would have done. Also, their credulity helped. Any bend of the river, any island on which they landed, might bring some fabulous adventure or an emergency in which they would have to fight and possibly die for one another.

The weather was good to them, and the motherly river. It was early June and there was little rain. At night they camped on a sand bar, or on a nameless island which became their own for a while, where firewood and berries were plentiful. They hunted and caught fish, swam naked in the river and gradually acquired the color and fiber of unspoiled natives. No one bothered them; they passed up the river almost unnoticed. The shores were not all wilderness, but were populated sporadically and unobtrusively: here and there a white pillar of smoke and steam from a busy sawmill; tooting donkey engines and falling trees of a logging camp; a fishing village or cannery; a clearing in the forest or a quietly prospering farm. Passenger steamers and lumber carriers passed up and down the river, but usually at a distance from the boys who found the going best among the islands or near shore. The *Rose City* passed six times; three round trips to San Francisco while they had not covered sixty miles. And they were content.

Around the middle of July, the sailors reached their destination. They did not know they had one or that this was it, but they were a little fed up with the river, which was not salt and buoyant as water should be. At sunset the breeze died. They were close to shore, about a mile below a great sawmill. Hal paddled in the amber-colored water with an oar. Rowing would have been quicker, but there was no hurry. One oar was enough to assist the boat into the mouth of a sluggish creek. When its nose kissed the sand, Clark stepped out and carried the anchor ashore, while Hal collected their cooking gear.

They walked up the creek a little way, exploring, along the kind of beach you sometimes find on fresh water —a narrow strip of sand that looks like a beach, but dead, where the tide does not rise or fall. The sun was setting, but it was already dusk on the creek and the water was a deep color, smooth like brown glass. Fifty yards from the mouth, around a bend, there was light and an opening in the bush. They saw the sunset on a little field of hay and some neglected apple trees. Near them a bird sang with delirious loveliness.

"A boat!" the sailors cried together.

It was a big, bulky craft shored up near the edge of the creek; a sail boat. It looked as if it had been there for years.

"A big sloop," Clark said.

"No, a cutter; look how far aft the mast is stepped."

It was a cutter, deep and substantial, with short ends and a flush deck; the kind that hits with all its weight together—a solid and compact blow—and doesn't give the sea much chance to strike back. You can trust a craft like that, and love her.

"We'll bring our boat up here and then have a look at the cutter," Hal announced. "I bet she didn't begin life on fresh water."

Clark felt that, too. She was from their world; another seafarer who had come up the river on adventure, only years before. Something had happened and she had been trapped up there in a backwater. God knows how many years the cutter had been there, sitting between a hayfield and the creek, with a bend hiding even the river that led to the sea.

Darkness came before they had investigated far; a deeper darkness than they had found on the river. They were surrounded by the land and the bush, with only a narrow creek leading to safety. It wasn't like the Pacific, with a few thousand miles of searoom between you and the nearest land. Clark had a feeling. Ships don't talk, but they tell you things. The cutter was trying to tell him something. He couldn't hear, but he could feel it: a dumb cry of warning. Look out! something had happened to her. The same thing might happen to him.

After supper they took their blankets on board the cutter, up a rickety ladder. There was a padlock on the companion doors, but the fore-hatch was not secured. Sailors ashore defend themselves like that.

They spread their blankets on the berths of the forward stateroom. The boards were hard and they had no donkey breakfasts, but it felt good to lie in a bunk.

"We've got a ship, Clarkie!" Hal said.

"A real little ship," Clark agreed. He put up a brown foot and felt a deck beam with his toes. It was a big honest oak beam and appeared perfectly sound. A square of sky filled the vacancy of the hatch, which they had left open for ventilation. Their lantern, burning on the cabin floor between the berths, was unnecessary. One of them blew it out, and the sky deepened and filled with stars.

"I wish the ship would roll or pitch a little," Clark said, closing his eyes for a moment.

When he opened them, sunlight was pouring down the hatch. Hal was bending over him. "Rise and shine!" he commanded. "Breakfast is ready and there's land in sight on the starboard bow—all round, in fact."

Breakfast tasted good. It always did, but this one was different. The way the branches were moving, Clark knew there was a good breeze blowing up the river, even if it couldn't be felt down by the creek. But Hal didn't say anything about moving on. He didn't want to think of moving on, either.

After washing their dishes in the creek, they examined the cutter. Forty-eight feet overall, Hal decided. Her run was clean and rather fine for a boat with such good beam. There wasn't a sign of paint on the hull, except at the stern where there were some yellowish-gray flakes. Her name was carved there, too: *GALATHEA*. There was no port of registry.

"Soft, I bet." Hal jabbed his clasp knife into a garboard and looked astonished when the blade stuck hard, with only the point buried in the weathered wood. "That's funny; usually the garboards go first." He jabbed other places, then looked knowing. "Sound as a dollar, after all these years!"

They went on board and poked about in the bilges. "Cedar planking on four-inch oak frames," Hal reported. "Look how hard that frame is where it meets the plank! That's where frames go soft first. It just shows you that a boat never rots if it's put together right."

Clark had fallen in love with the *Galathea*, too. And

when he found one frame a little soft where it touched the skin of the vessel, he pretended it was as hard as the others. If you find a little hidden blemish in someone you love, you don't shout it to the world, do you?

In the sunlight again, they had to admit things on deck were rather a mess. The skylight panes were smashed and covered with rotten canvas, battened down with strips of wood. The oak bulwarks were deeply checked and a length of the rail cap was gone. The mast was checked so badly that it was almost in two. A halliard that had been left rove fell from aloft when Clark put his weight on it. Over at the edge of the field the boom and gaff, weathered almost out of recognition, rested on two pieces of timber. The hay was growing up between them.

Hal and Clark didn't talk any more of continuing up the river. They established themselves on board and gathered ferns for the berths in the big cabin. They put up their photographs on the panelled bulkhead, cut each other's hair and kept ship neatly.

Clark was awakened suddenly one night. He thought something had happened, the way Hal shook him. It had, in a way; when Hal got an idea things happened.

"Clarkie, I've been thinking. We could go anywhere in a cutter like this! The South Seas or China coast, or anywhere."

"She isn't in the water." Clark was blinking himself awake.

"She isn't far from it."

"She needs a lot of repairs."

"There isn't anything she needs that we can't do."

"She doesn't belong to us."

Hal seemed to have forgotten that. After a minute, he said, "We could buy her. We have money, haven't we?"

"Do you think we could?" Clark's imagination had taken fire. If they only could!

"I know we can!" Hal maintained. "The man who owns this cutter will never sail her. Likely he knows it by now, and she isn't worth a dollar to him, lying here. You can see it for yourself: the *Galathea* will never get away from this creek alive unless we do the job. Are you with me, Clarkie?"

Clark was with him, passionately. This was adventure, rescuing a gallant little ship from a backwater and returning with her to the good salt sea.

In the morning they rowed up the river to the sawmill, which was rumbling and screeching over its breakfast of logs. The owner of the mill was the owner of the *Galathea*, the mill town and everything else in sight on that side of the river. A foreman raised his voice above the clank of conveyors and the scream of saws, shouting amiable directions.

Mr. Walters was a wiry old boy of seventy, in a black suit with a low celluloid collar, a wiry tie and old derby hat. His eyes were snappy and there was plenty of fun in his face, only you had the feeling that he might get all the fun if you had dealings with him. He was squatting on the unfinished edge of a new dock, with the river beneath him, holding an iron spike which a young laborer was whaling with a sledge hammer.

There was no mistaking the foreman's description, but one doesn't expect a millionaire to work as a laborer's helper. When the spike was driven, the old man took another and the tall youth whaled at that, too, swinging the sledge from the height of his head. After the timber was spiked down, there was a pause.

"I'd rather you were swinging this sledge, Mr. Walters," the young man said.

The old one answered, "Fiddlesticks! I might hit you."

"I might hit you."

"You won't." The old fellow seemed to know. Then he saw Hal and Clark, looking at him and trying to make up their minds when to speak. "You boys looking for work?"

Hal became their spokesman. "I understand you own the *Galathea*."

"Hey, what's that?" Mr. Walters looked puzzled. "You mean that cutter up the creek? What about it?"

"We would like to buy her, Sir."

"How much will you pay?"

"She needs a lot of repairing—"

"She's worth a lot of repairing." Mr. Walters looked at them until they felt naked. "Five hundred, cash." It might have been written on their faces. Coming up to the mill, they had decided that was their top figure. "We'll take her." They had the money with them.

"The sails are at my house," the old man explained on the way to the office. "If you like, you can leave them there till you're ready—at your own risk." He made a note of it on the bill of sale as the boys counted out the amount from their money belts, each contributing half.

In the morning, Hal went up to the sawmill, on a trail that led from their field, and caught a little stern-

35

wheeler for Portland. He was to bring back the supplies they needed for fitting out.

Clark was glad that he was the one to stay; he didn't want to leave the *Galathea*, ever. He cleared her deck of rubbish and admired the improvement from aft, with one hand resting on the weathered wheel. The rest of the day he spent in poking old putty and oakum from the seams with his knife. It was maddeningly slow work, but he wanted to have something to show when Hal returned. He remembered the file and bent the spike end into a hook, after heating it in the fire. It took out the old calking twice as fast. He worked furiously until dark; then he got up, terribly stiff, and lit the lantern. He worked furiously again, passionately, as if he were trying to have the cutter ready for the sea by morning. It was a dark night. Catspaws whispered through the field of hay. He heard the creek gurgling continuously, but could not see it. Outside the circle of the lantern, everything was peaceful, indifferent and cool. He drove himself in a kind of panic, remembering the cutter's mute cry of warning that first night. Look out! If he didn't hurry, some kind of fate would overtake him, too, and it would come so quietly and surely that he wouldn't know it at first, or escape from it afterward.

When Hal returned the next afternoon, things immediately went better. Before dark they had glass in the skylight and the new Charlie Noble set up. They cooked supper on the galley stove, and that night they slept on real mattresses, stuffed with straw. They were living now.

The girls came near the end of July. The deck had been calked and the seams painted for paying. Clark was working on deck, and Hal was clearing the bottom seams for calking. With a tight hull and a tight deck, they told each other, the back of the work would be broken. Their best joke was about that. When one of them had been working in a cramped position too long to be able to straighten up when he stopped, he would hobble about, rubbing his spine, and say: "The back of the work is broken!"

When a sailor says "girls" he usually has one thing in mind. These weren't like that. Clark was paying a seam near the fore-hatch when he heard them. They were coming along the path through the field, singing:

"Down by the old mill stream,
Where I first met you—"

The voices were soft and beautiful. Clark thought the song beautiful, too. It was one he had never heard before, and it was so appropriate that his mind was dazzled. The girls were quite close before they realized anyone was there. The song wavered, then went on resolutely:

"The old mill-wheel is broken—"

When the turn of the path brought them close to *Galathea's* quarter, the girls stopped to look. If the young seamen had been loafing by the creek, they might have turned back or hurried past. There is a security about people at work.

Clark could see the girls plainly now. Two of them, fresh and lovely in their white shirtwaists and lawn skirts. One was short and dark and buxom; the other was fair and rather tall. Clark liked the tall one best. She stood so nicely, with head raised and her big lace hat looking like the petals of a flower.

The short girl spoke first. "What are you doing with the old boat?"

"We are repairing our yacht," Hal's voice answered with dignity from under the turn of the bilge. His answer, framed ahead of time, sounded awkward.

"I thought that was Mr. Walters' boat," the tall girl said. Her voice had a ring you don't often hear, except in the voices of children.

"We bought the cutter from him," Hal explained.

"Don't you work for Mr. Walters?"

"We work for ourselves."

The girls exchanged exclamations of surprise. Things and men that didn't belong to Mr. Walters were a novelty. Clark felt his value increase. He walked aft where the girls were. Two young men and two girls. That was as it should be.

"Good afternoon," he said; "would you like to see our cutter?"

"May we?" the tall girl asked. Suddenly everyone was at ease. Clark scrambled down the ladder and Hal introduced him with a flourish. Henry Clark, son of the Klondike explorer of the same name, who owned the steam yacht *Orion*. That was a good name for Hal to have thought up. He introduced himself, too, with implications. The short dark girl introduced her companion, Miss Virginia Moore, and herself, Miss Grace Jones.

Hal took the lead in showing them the *Galathea*. At first the girls kept together, but Miss Jones took such a lively interest in things that soon she was at Hal's elbow. Miss Moore and Clark found themselves together, a little in the background. Without anyone doing anything about it, they had paired off. Clark was pleased. Miss Moore was a beauty, and although she was tall for a girl, she had to look up a little when she spoke to him. Her hair was golden-brown, more gold than brown, and her eyebrows and long lashes were more brown than gold. After a while he discovered her eyes were a deep blue— so deep that at first he had thought they were brown.

"The fastenings are copper," Hal lectured. "We can put on copper sheeting and forget about leaks and cobra worms. In the South Seas a boat with iron fastenings doesn't last very long—"

"Are you really going to the South Seas in this boat?" Miss Moore looked up at Clark with a new and unmistakable interest.

"As soon as the boat is ready."

"How splendid!" Her eyes said "splendid," too. "It must be wonderful to have money and the will to do things."

"We haven't much money," Clark said honestly. "That's why we're doing everything ourselves."

"But your father—" Her eyes were still upon him, questioning.

"I haven't any father." .

"I thought he owned a big yacht."

Clark had put his foot in it. It didn't matter. He wanted to play fair with the tall girl. He wanted to lay some kind of an offering at her feet. He hadn't anything to give her except the poor truth.

"Hal was only having fun with me," he explained.

"My father is dead, and he never had a yacht. I'm a sailor," he added a little defiantly.

Miss Moore didn't seem to mind. "You are a ship owner, too," she said gravely, indicating the cutter.

Clark didn't feel so defiant. He found himself smiling. "I never thought about being a ship owner. We've been too busy."

"When do you think you will be ready?"

"October," he told her. "We have a lot to do yet, but I think we can sail then."

"I hope you make it, Mr. Clark." Her look seemed part of the hope in his own heart. A few minutes before the girl had been a stranger—a voice singing through the field. Now she was with him in spirit, passionately. "Think of it," she said, "sailing to the Islands!" The way she said "Islands" was wonderful; like some name you say over and over to yourself when you are a child and are half afraid to say because it is magic. "I hope you see them first at sunrise!"

Clark could see the landfall, like a picture. "Tropical places are beautiful when you see them like that," he said, "like a dream." He could see the dream in her eyes.

"I wish I were a man," she said, "so I could go with you."

"I wish you were," he answered quickly. "No, I don't!"

They got self-conscious, because they were blushing.

"What are you two talking about?" Grace had come back to them, sparkling with information. "You ought to be looking at the cutter instead of each other. It's a wonderful boat, Virginia. You ought to see the construc-

40

tion: four inch oak planks nine inches apart on two and a half inch cedar frames—"

"Two and a half inch cedar planking on four inch oak frames," Hal corrected, standing beside her.

"And sound as a dollar," Grace wound up. She got that right anyway.

After a few minutes the girls decided it was time to leave.

"We were going somewhere when we stopped to look at the cutter," Grace explained significantly.

"We were going swimming," Virginia elaborated to Clark.

Grace nudged her, too late. "Now you've told," she said, blushing.

Clark didn't understand at first. Then he realized the girls weren't carrying any packages. Grace was so modest she kept reminding a man of things he mightn't have thought of without her assistance.

"I hope you will come back and see how we're getting along," Hal said when they were leaving.

"We will."

"Thank you, that would be nice."

"You will come back, won't you, Miss Moore?" Clark demanded.

"We will," she answered. "And I'm going to try to think of something we can do to help." There was such a sweet, serious ring in her voice. Clark wished that he, the cutter, everything could be much finer than they were.

"Nice girls," Hal observed after their guests had left.

"Very nice," Clark answered. They didn't admit to

each other that anything much had happened. They turned to and worked furiously.

When it got too dark to work on deck they unshipped the steering wheel, with infinite difficulty, and carried it below to scrape by lantern light.

The next time the girls came the deck seams had all been paid and the deck had two coats of buff paint. It looked wonderful. The wheel had come out fine. There was no dust in the air by the creek and the varnish dried smooth and bright and hard.

After admiring the improvements they all sat on the grass near the creek, tossing pebbles into the water and talking about the Marquesas Islands; also about themselves. Grace kept house for her father, who was a foreman at the mill. Although she didn't say so, you got the impression that he was a lively card; a fine fellow any time and a prince when he had a few drinks. Grace seemed a little scandalized and very proud of him. Virginia was her cousin from Portland, and she came to visit every summer. They had plenty of freedom and knew how to use it; they were fine, sensible girls.

Hal and Grace sat together, and Clark and Virginia. Virginia didn't let them get far from the subject of the *Galathea* and the Islands. "We shouldn't come here at all—we only take you away from your work," she told Clark. "That's wrong, because we want to help you."

"But we work so much harder when you are gone."

She wasn't convinced. "Probably you work too hard, making up for the time we waste. There must be something Grace and I can do to help."

"It helps a lot just to see you."

"But something real. We're not helpless, even if we are women. I do want to help." Her eyes were serious. "I want to see the *Galathea* sail for the Islands, even—" She didn't say it, but Clark knew. Even if she never saw him again, even though she couldn't go herself. And he knew that she liked him.

"You do help," he said.

"But something real," she repeated. "Aren't there sails to mend? I can sew very nicely, Mr. Clark."

"I don't know," he told her. "We haven't had time to look at the sails yet."

"When you're done with the *Galathea* you don't want to have to wait for weeks, maybe, mending sails," she reminded him. "They should be ready." She was on her feet, and Clark got up.

"Where are you two going?" Grace asked. They didn't answer. Grace didn't really want to know. She was only calling attention to the fact that Clark and Virginia were two, and that Hal and she were two.

When they had gone a little way Clark explained: "The sails aren't on board; they're still at Mr. Walters'."

They walked along the edge of the meadow, talking about sail mending, then turned back. No, thought Clark, that was only what they appeared to do. Really they went much farther and they hadn't just talked about sail mending, even if that's what their words were about.

Next morning Clark and Hal went up the river to the mill. Hal thought it a fine idea to put the girls to work on the sails. He was sure they would learn quickly.

It was only eight o'clock, but the mill was screeching and grumbling, and Mr. Walters was helping spike

43

down timbers on the new section of the dock. He gave the seamen a sharp, humorous look. "You boys after your sails?" He appeared surprised when they said they were. But he wrote an order and directed them to his house. "Go ahead, Frank!" He held another spike with his blue old hands and the sledge came crashing down.

Mr. Walters' place was so big the seamen could make nothing of it. An immense green-painted house, all dormer windows and porches and bay windows and chimneys, surrounded by acres of shrubbery and gardens, dotted with summer houses and fancy little buildings. Clark felt like a poor intruder. Even Hal was over-awed. He took out Mr. Walters' order and held it conspicuously to show that he had a right to be there, and he and Clark talked in lowered voices as they made a wide arc through the grounds in search of the carriage house.

Clark was afraid to think what a suit of sails might look like after years in a carriage house, but he felt more hopeful when the uniformed footman led the way upstairs. The place was as well-built as any house, dry and airy. From the window he could see the grounds and the rear of the great house. Two gardners were working in the distance and a tall, lonely woman walked up and down a path with an immense dog. A black bear cub on a chain walked round and round a stake. It made Clark feel uncomfortable.

The bags were heavy, particularly the one with the mainsail. They had to make three trips, and it was near noon when they started down the river. Clark felt better afloat and he and Hal talked in their natural voices again. They decided the solitary old woman walking in the garden with the Great Dane was Mrs. Walters.

44

Maybe it wasn't much fun belonging to a man whose idea of a good time was holding spikes while a laborer whaled them with a sledge hammer.

"Did you see the bear cub?" Clark asked.

"No. Where was it?"

"In the garden back of the house, on a chain. It went round and round."

"I didn't see it."

"It went round and round." Clark didn't want to talk about the bear; thinking about it made him uneasy. But he had to say something. You had to look out when you were so far from the sea. The bear had been caught in some kind of a trap.

"Was it very big?" Hal wanted to know.

"Just a young one. It went round and round."

"They soon get tame," Hal said.

"There! Am I not a good sail-maker?" Clark had left the seam he was calking to come over and see how Virginia was getting along. She was sitting in the grass with the leach of the forestays'l across her lap. Her hat was flung behind her and her golden brown hair was disordered and lovely. A buttercup looked over the edge of the sail where it fell from her lap and rested on the grass.

The patch on the sail was done the way he had taught her: the edges turned under and sewed down to the sail, then the sail turned over and the frayed edges cut away and turned under and sewed down to the patch. The stitches were short and even.

"That's good," he said. "Even an old sail-maker would have used more homeward-bound stitches."

Her eyes were very dear and proud. "I wouldn't use

45

homeward-bound stitches on the sails that are going to take the *Galathea* to the Islands!" Again that magic in the way she said Islands. Then she became thoughtful and pushed the sail from her knees. "I want to ask you something, Clarkie."

He dropped on the grass beside her.

"I—why can't Grace and I go with you to the Islands?"

Clark caught his breath and stared at her.

"You need a sail-maker at sea, don't you?"

"Yes." His lips were dry.

"And there'll be plenty for you and Hal to do. We'll be a great help, really." She nodded wisely.

Clark came out of his daze. "Would you go, Virginia?" he cried, jumping up and slapping her on the shoulder. It was the first caress he had ever given her, and she winced at the blow.

"Isn't that just what I was offering? Please sit down and talk sensibly. Now it's settled that we're going, isn't it?"

Clark's daze returned. He had never let himself think of it; he hadn't thought of it, except in dreams: Virginia standing beside him on deck, the cutter rising and falling gently with the sea, and the enchanted island of Nuku-heva rising out of the sea at dawn.

"Grace," Clark objected feebly, "would she go? Have you asked her?"

Virginia didn't seem worried on that score. "Let's ask her, Clarkie. We'll ask Hal, too. He's one of the owners."

Grace was scandalized. "Why, Virginia Moore," she said, blushing, "the idea of going across the Pacific in a boat with two men! You're daffy!'' After a minute she said, "So am I!" And she bounced around, shaking hands with her fellow lunatics. "It's settled then, isn't it?"

"What do you think, Hal?" Virginia asked. "Is it a perfectly mad idea?"

"Of course it's mad!" Grace proclaimed, holding onto Hal's arm and jumping up and down. "I'm going, aren't I, Hal?"

When Hal had decided that, altogether, it would be a very good idea, everyone shook hands. Virginia's hand lingered in Clark's hard paw and he felt her fingers tighten on his. Her fingers seemed to say: "Now I've started something bigger than myself; I'll do my best, but please help me."

On Saturday afternoon they quit work and had a picnic by the creek. Hal angled for trout a little upstream, with Grace to help him. Probably she was more help to the fish. Clark and Virginia could hear her, exclaiming and giggling, as they spread things out on the grass in the shade of some alders.

The picnic was really a celebration. It was a holiday, too. Grace's father was going to a lodge supper and the girls wouldn't have to hurry home. The sunset light touched the *Galathea* and the hayfield, then slipped away and left them in the dusk. It grew dark and stars came out, but it was still warm. Grace had got over being shocked at Hal's lying with his head in her lap. Clark moved closer to Virginia, but didn't touch her. He could have put his arm round her and she wouldn't have minded; she would have gone on talking about the

47

Islands and the Valley of Typee in her sweet, ringing voice. Maybe he didn't want to do it that way, when she was talking about something sacred.

"I wish we could go swimming," Grace spoke up suddenly.

"We can." Hal didn't sound too interested.

"We can't."

"Why not?"

"You know."

"I don't. Why can't we?"

Clark just heard the whispered: "No bathing dresses," and a giggle.

Hal didn't think much of that. "Clarkie and I don't wear anything."

"Why, you shocking boys!" After a minute, Grace asked, "What is it like, swimming without—swimming at night? I never did it."

"It's different," Hal assured her. "It's the best time to swim."

"Is it? I wish we had our bathing dresses."

"We won't wear bathing clothes at the Islands," Hal said.

"We won't? Why not?"

"Too warm. Anyway it would be silly. You aren't taking a bathing suit, are you, Clarkie?"

"I haven't one," Clark confessed. Hal was right, in a way. Girls in bathing dresses and long stockings was not his idea of the Islands.

"But, if we didn't wear bathing clothes we'd be—"

"Sunburned," Hal suggested. Clark had to laugh.

Maybe it was his laugh that set Virginia off. "I wish

48

you would settle it," she cried impatiently. "Are we going swimming, or aren't we?"

"It sounds nice, swimming at night," Grace told her, "but you know we haven't got our—"

"Stop!" Virginia ordered, jumping up. "Let's have it over with. Come along Grace!" She stepped to the other side of the alders, with Grace following. It was quite dark.

"A swim would go good." Clark could just make out the white band of Hal's singlet. His shirt was coming off over his head. Then he started to undress. It was almost as if they had reached the Islands already.

In the water it seemed so natural. Even Grace forgot to be shocked. Opposite the cutter the deepest part of the creek was up to Clark's armpits. He could feel the steady current, like a sea-tide. Only the flavor of salt was missing. The forest on the far side of the creek shut out half the sky. There were a few stars in the other half. They played about in the water, keeping fairly close lest they lose track of each other. Clark could just make out the faces and shoulders above the dark water. Hal was so tanned he seemed to be in a separate shadow. At a distance of a few feet he became invisible. Clark must have been nearly invisible, too, for once Grace turned suddenly and bumped into him without knowing he was there. Her body felt large and cool and very smooth, but not exciting; it seemed quite natural.

Hal swam down the creek with the current, using long, slow strokes that sounded almost a minute apart.

"Don't go too far," Grace called after him.

"Are there any deep places?" Virginia asked. Her face

49

and shoulders caught the light of stars, millions of miles away, in a faint, white gleam.

"This is the deepest I've found," Clark said, "up to my armpits."

"I wonder if I could float?" She lay back and floated, a dim white shadow in the black water.

"Virginia, we can see you." Grace was shocked, but only mildly.

The current carried Virginia down toward Clark. She was very lovely, like something floating in a dream—a dream of the Islands.

"Shall I catch you?" Clark asked.

Virginia tried to stand and her head went under. He caught her arm and drew her up.

She blew out water and gasped a little. "Thank you. My foot hit a rock."

"Did you hurt yourself?" He was still holding her.

"No. It was very smooth." She was looking up at him, one arm raised to push back her wet hair. She seemed far away, as if her body were still floating. "It was deeper than I expected."

They could just hear Hal swimming back against the current. Grace was working down the creek to meet him. She was a little worried about his having gone so far in the dark.

"This is the deepest part," Clark told Virginia. "It gets shallower above here."

They could hear Hal distinctly now—the slow, powerful thrust of his strokes. Grace was feeling her way down stream with her feet, more slowly than Hal was coming up. She was only in the water up to her knees now. Clark could see her fine, healthy woman's body by its own light, it seemed.

"Shall we try where the water's not so deep?" Virginia asked.

They turned and pushed slowly against the current, keeping close by the sound of their voices, but not touching each other.

"I don't suppose we should be doing this," Virginia said. "But I was angry a while ago. I can't bear to see something fine spoiled by silly talk."

"I know. Lots of fine things are spoiled that way. And everybody was so natural as soon as we were in the water."

"I'm glad you understand, Clarkie. It was wonderful floating. Strange, too; it didn't seem real. Like floating on the darkness, with nothing else in the world but a star I saw a long way off. Did you ever notice, no matter how many stars there are, you never can find one exactly above you?"

"I never thought of that." He stopped, looking up. "I see what you mean—they're always a little somewhere else. I think you could find one above you in the Southern Hemisphere. There are so many, and they're so bright."

"We'll try when we get there," she said. "It's going to be very wonderful."

"Better take my hand," Clark said; "there are stones here."

"Thank you." Her hand was firm and trusting in his.

They went on, not thinking about being naked and not remembering how they had happened to start up the creek. The water shoaled to their knees. They were opposite the upper end of the meadow. Ahead the creek disappeared altogether. The forest closed in on both sides and there was nothing but darkness.

"I think we should start back," Virginia decided. "The water feels cold now. But it's been lovely." She was shivering.

"Let's leave the creek then. We don't have to go back over all those stones. We can walk along the meadow."

The girl hesitated.

"It would be easier," he urged.

"All right," she said. "The creek doesn't seem friendly any more; just cold and dark."

They stepped out of the water, feeling the gravel under their feet, then the fine sand, and after that the grass. The white gleam of Virginia's body was very sweet in the starlight. But she shivered.

"Are you still cold?"

"A little."

"Virginia," Clark said, "Virginia, don't shiver so! I'll warm you." He drew her to him and wrapped his arms about her. Her body was cool and fresh against his. New and beautifully strange. Then she seemed to remember something she had forgotten and tried to draw away.

"No, no! Not that!"

"Virginia!" He held her closer and kissed her shoulder and face and hair. Her hair was soft and wet, but the flavor of salt was missing. After a while he felt her body growing warm against his. She wasn't struggling any more, only looking up at him, dear and lost.

"Clarkie," she said in a small, ringing voice, "you will be very good to me, won't you?"

52

Afterward they were quite a while finding Grace and Hal.

Next day Clark didn't know what to think. How did Virginia feel about it now? She wasn't that kind, but she had let him. He had seduced her. He had hurt her, too, though he tried to be gentle. No, he hadn't done it, really. She had been seduced by the Islands. What baffled him most was the recollection that their being naked together had seemed so simple and natural. Unexciting. He had done what he had done because that was supposed to be inevitable under the circumstances. What would she do now—go back to Portland? What if she went away without coming back to the *Galathea*? He didn't know. He loved her. He would try to follow her, probably.

When the girls didn't show up at the usual time, Clark took an axe and went up the creek, looking for a straight young pine for a new mast. If he couldn't be with Virginia, he wanted to be alone. He walked in the woods without being able to decide on anything, and finally went back down the creek.

From the meadow he saw Hal and Grace standing close together under the cutter's stern. Hal had his arms round Grace. Then they kissed each other—a long kiss. Virginia was sitting on the grass, her hat beside her, sewing on the storm trys'l. She looked up and saw him, and he knew she had been watching for him. She waved her hand with the palm on it. Then she went on sewing. When he stopped beside her and she looked up, her face was shy and proud and tender. They kissed each other without caring if the others were looking. He asked her if she would go for a walk and she held his hand tightly and said "yes." He was all on fire.

They were living now.

Early in September Clark and Hal came to the end of their salvage money. They didn't want to admit it to themselves at first. But even a thousand dollars can't last forever. They had to make a stake somehow before sailing for the Islands. There seemed to be nothing for it but to work in the sawmill.

After they talked it over, the change didn't sound so bad. They could still live on board the *Galathea*. It wasn't far to the mill. With two of them working they should have a good stake by spring. Sundays and holidays they could work on the cutter.

"It may work out just right, the way I analyze it," Hal said. "Spring will be the best time to start for the Islands. We'll have all winter to catch up on little things. We'll get a book and study up on navigation."

"We'll have the hull finished before bad weather sets in," Clark said. "Then in the spring we can step the new mast and reeve the running rigging."

They didn't talk about how the girls would take it. That part made them feel uneasy.

The girls took it well, considering. Grace cried a little, but Hal managed the situation handsomely. Virginia didn't make any comments, but she asked Clark to take her for a walk. He wondered if she was going to tell him that she was to have a baby. Things like that happened even to people who weren't married. He loved her, desperately; nothing would make much difference.

That wasn't what Virginia had to tell him. She had four hundred dollars in a Portland bank and she wanted him to take that and go on with the *Galathea*. They walked along the meadow by the creek, arguing.

"It will be better to start for the Islands in the spring," he told her. "It won't seem long, and we'll be getting ready. We're going through with it, all right. You trust me, don't you?"

"Clarkie," she said, "look at me! Haven't I trusted you?"

He drew her to him, kissing her passionately. But that didn't settle the argument.

"We belong to each other, don't we?"

"Yes, Virginia, we belong."

"We've shared everything else, haven't we?" Her eyes were shy and proud.

He answered her with his eyes.

"There's no reason why I shouldn't share what money I have."

She had given so much already: her weeks of patient sewing on the heavy sails, and her delicate, intoxicating love. He couldn't take her money, too. Never!

"There's Grace," she said, "and Hal. Suppose something happened between them?"

Clark had thought of that. But he couldn't take a girl's money. "Hal's a fine fellow," he said.

"And Grace is a fine girl. But she's hot-blooded, Clarkie, and a little reckless. I'm responsible for all this and I don't want anything to happen."

"Nothing will happen, Sweetheart," he said. "We're all together. We can be here all day on Sundays. And you will manage to meet me evenings, won't you?"

"I shouldn't," she answered, caressing his hand, "but you know I will!"

"And everything will be just as it was before," he said.

Virginia let him make love to her and she was very dear. But she wasn't sure that everything would be the same.

The rains began the middle of September. There was only one rain, really. It began and never stopped. The world was green under steady gray rain. The path across the field turned to mud. It wasn't so muddy through the woods, but the ground was full of water, like a wet sponge. Squishy. Morning and evening.

A man was killed on the docks near Clark and Hal. He was a slow, clumsy Pole and his partner on the loading car was always driving and cursing him. He tried to hurry and fell from the car onto the dock below, exactly on top of his head. His partner said it was very neat for such a clumsy ox. The man lying dead in the rain had a wife and new twin boys at home.

One night Clark came back from a walk with Virginia in the rain. Hal was packing his duffle bag. "I'm through, Clarkie," he said. "Making a pier-head jump when the *Palmyra* goes out tonight. I've had all I can stand."

Clark had seen it coming. Hal wasn't very big and loading lumber was heavy work. And the day before Mr. Jones had a long talk with him. Clark knew Hal had trouble being with Grace, and was taking chances.

"Have you talked to the girl?"

"Sure." Hal drew the cord of his bag. "She's willing." He sat on the edge of the bunk he was leaving and filled his short pipe. "I don't know but it will work out best that way. I'll save as much as I would here, almost, and keep my hand in at sailing. I'll be back in the early spring to help fit out."

"Why not stay and work on the cutter?" Clark suggested. "I'll earn enough. And Virginia is keen about putting some money into the boat." He was willing to sacrifice her money in this kind of emergency.

"How much has she got?"

"Around five hundred."

Hal considered. Then he got up briskly, shaking his curly head. "No good, Clarkie. I couldn't do anything in this blasted rain. They say it won't stop before next May. I'll be back by then. Remember me to Virginia, and don't give up the ship."

Clark stayed on at the mill; maybe he wasn't a sailor after all. He and Virginia were married early in October. She had been having trouble with her parents over not coming home at the end of summer. Clark decided it, though he had never before thought of marrying. But they were madly in love and it seemed the only way they could be certain of being together.

They rented one of the mill cottages and Virginia spent her four hundred dollars on furniture. That was a surprise for Clark. She made the place look lovely. Clark saved his money, and for Virginia's twenty-second birthday he bought her a fine piano. That was a surprise, too. At first he thought she was disappointed, but then she said it was beautiful. She was everything to him that a woman can be to a man. They were living now.

At the mill, Clark was moved from one job to another.

Sometimes Mr. Walters had him work on the docks. He would hold spikes while Clark swung a sledge hammer. He was afraid that some time he would miss and break the old man's hands, but he never did. He found that Mr. Walters only worked as a laborer when business was bad; then he turned economical. If business had been good that first time, he probably would not have sold the *Galathea*. He liked to collect people and things and keep them.

Clark and Virginia were very happy, only they worried about Grace. They felt responsible for her. Her father was drinking a good deal, too. When Hal didn't come back in the spring, Grace ran away with the purser of a river steamer. Afterward, she ran away with a cigar drummer. Virginia and Clark did everything they could. Billy Jones finally drank himself to death. But after a while Grace married a young farmer who lived near the Dalles. She settled down and made him a good wife, and she could talk for hours about the manufacture of butter.

Clark kept in good health and never missed any time at the mill. Every morning, except Sunday, he left at 7:30; every evening, he came home at 6:30. Sometimes he reminded himself of the little black bear that used to be chained behind the Walters' mansion; the one that went round and round. They didn't have it any more. Once the Great Danes broke out and killed it before anyone could interfere.

Clark and Virginia didn't have any children, though after a while they wished it would happen. In time, Virginia wanted one very much. Sometimes, in bed at night, she would snuggle against Clark and say in her dear, ringing voice: "A baby or two would be nice—a boy, specially."

He would hold her close in his great arms and say, "a girl, specially!" He wanted it to be like her.

Virginia stopped saying that when she found she wasn't going to have either. But they had each other. Only, after a while, Clark saw his wife so much that he began to forget exactly what she looked like. Sometimes he was restless and dimly dissatisfied. He didn't know with what, though he knew it wasn't Virginia. Maybe it was the river, which wasn't buoyant as water should be. And the flavor of salt was missing.

Clark became foreman at the mill and saved money without really trying to. After a while he bought timber land across the river. The company that owned the surrounding land offered him a tenth of what his timber was worth. When he declined to sell, the company logged off its land and set fire to the slashing in very dry weather. It was the way big companies did. From the mill Clark could see his timber going up in smoke and flame.

Clark came home one rainy September evening and found Virginia in bed. She thought it was a touch of influenza; there had been a good deal of it that fall. Somehow, he seemed to see her clearly for the first time in years. She was a little away from the other parts of life she had been mixed up with and he saw that she was lovely. Her body was languid, but her cheeks were flushed and there was a bright, secret look in her eyes. He kissed her on the mouth, though she told him he must not. When he wanted to call the doctor, she held his hand and wouldn't let him go at once.

"Talk to me a little while first, Clarkie," she coaxed. "I never see enough of you." Her voice had a childish, caressing ring which he had forgotten to notice for a long time.

He sat on the edge of the bed, a little awkwardly because he didn't know what to talk about. He remembered he hadn't been much of a success. But she did most of the talking.

"Clarkie, do you remember how the four of us were going to the Islands in the *Galathea*?"

"Yes, I remember." He was embarrassed and faintly apologetic.

"We were all a little mad." She looked at him tenderly. "Sometimes, I wish we could recall some of that madness. I've been lying here thinking about those days. Do you know what I think?"

He caressed her warm hand. "What, Virginia?"

"We should have gone, dearest. I know it was mad. Maybe that's why we should have done it. There are always so many people to stay and do what's sensible. We would have gone, somehow, if we had refused to give up. Maybe we wouldn't have found what we expected. I don't suppose people ever do. But we would have seen the Islands at dawn, from the deck of our own ship. That would have been an adventure. We've never had any adventure, Clarkie, except each other. We've been too sensible. Sometimes, like now, I'm afraid we do live only once."

Once, at most, Clark thought sadly.

"If this is all there is," she said, "maybe everyone should do something mad, to remember."

He kissed her without being able to answer. How could he have known that his wife—a married woman—had the same dreams as a girl? Why had he thought she didn't? What was wrong with marriage that it made such a difference? It took the edge off life and made people forget the things they wanted to do. There had never been anything to hold them, yet they had stayed eighteen years in one dull place. Even now, there was nothing to prevent their going to the Islands.

Clark saw the *Galathea* once before he left. It was by accident. The day that Mr. Walters died at the age of ninety, the Perrys' little girl disappeared and Clark joined the search. It led him to the creek, which he had avoided for years. The section had been logged off during the summer. Above the meadow and on the far side of the creek, the forests had been cut down. The new sky they had uncovered looked crude and glaring. A donkey engine still stood in the torn field; the banks of the stream were raw and ugly. Only the *Galathea* remained untouched, sitting patiently between the field and creek. He had gone to her rescue once, only to be caught in the same backwater. Since then, the very forests had gone down to the sea while he and the cutter remained. He had betrayed her, or else she was part of the trap. He did not know.

At first he saw no change in the cutter. Then he remembered all the work that he and Hal had done: calking and painting and paying. The seams stood open and there was hardly a trace of paint on the hull. Only on the stern there were a few yellowish gray flakes. Her name was carved there, too: *GALATHEA*. One strange word, with no port of registry. There seemed to be a meaning in that.

Without wanting to, he jabbed one of the planks with his knife. The blade stuck hard in the weathered wood. Still sound after all these years! There was something frightening about that; it was taking her such a long time to die. Her heart must be very strong. The doctor had said something like that about Virginia.

Clark went on up the creek. Near where the water shoaled, he turned for a moment and saw the *Galathea* looming out of her hideous surroundings like a landmark in hell. He did not look back again.

Afterward, Clark saw the Islands from the *Ventura*, on the way to Australia. They were as beautiful as he had imagined them, but something was missing. He wasn't seeing them right. The way to see the Islands is to sail your own boat across the Pacific. That way, you discover them. You and she are on deck; her hand is firm and trusting in yours. The cutter lifts and falls with the sea. It seems to lift more than it falls. Flying fish are bright silver; white pilot birds circle the truck of the mast. The land breeze flows over the two of you like a sudden tide of perfume. And then you see the Island of Nukuheva rising out of the sea at dawn. That is the only way you ever see it.

The *Ventura* stopped at the Marquesas and Samoa. Clark didn't go ashore at either place; he felt tired and a little unworthy. The *Ventura* sailed without his having set foot on the Islands.

Later, Clark was on the East India run, in the *Santa*

Cruz. Once in San Francisco, when they had been taking fuel, he stopped at the chain rail forward and looked at one of the men on the oil barge. The man was standing at the rail of the barge, not six feet away, looking at him. He was a short man, bald in front and on top, with light-colored curly hair on the sides of his head. It seemed to Clark that at some time they must have been in the same ship. He tried to remember which one—there had been so many.

The man stared at him and took a pipe from between his yellow teeth. "Say, is that you, Clarkie?"

Then Clark remembered. "Hal!" Hal was shorter than he remembered him and he didn't have an air any more. He looked just every-day.

"Remember the salvage money from the *Borden,* and how we went up the Columbia in a skiff?"

Clark remembered.

"And the old cutter we found there, up a creek. We had a crazy idea of fitting her out and going to the South Seas. What boys won't do! It was fun though, for a summer. What was her name?"

"*Galathea.*"

"*Galathea,* that was it. I suppose she's there yet."

"I suppose."

"And the girls! I'd almost forgotten them. By God, that was something. And we tried working in a sawmill. That was hell. You wanted me to stick with you." Hal spat into the dirty bay. "I see you cut and ran, too."

"Yes, I left, too," Clark said.

"So you're still in deep-water packets. I was in that one a few years ago. You can have the East India run.

Stinking holes: Singapore, Saigon, Calcutta. Nothing in it, being carted round to foreign ports. Th' barge here suits me fine. They feed good and there isn't much work, and we don't go anywhere."

The barge had cast off from the steamship.

"See you again some time, Clarkie. I used to wonder what happened to you. Say, that was the life, up the river! You had a swell girl. What was her name? Virginia?" He called the name doubtfully across a widening strip of water." I'll always remember what a sweet voice she had. Don't suppose you ever hear from her?"

"No," Clark answered. "I don't hear from her."

Hal shouted something about "all these years," and "if you ever want a job on th' barge . . . " He and the barge passed astern and were gone.

Clark, too, was tired of being carted round to foreign ports, but he couldn't rot on a barge. Not yet, anyway. And he hadn't been a success ashore. He would have to keep on being carted about the world because he didn't have anywhere to go.

He got down on his luck in Seattle, and when he came out of the marine hospital he joined the lightship. There was nothing else he could get at the time. The lightship was hell at first. Then he saw that hell has its points. On a lightship you didn't sail and you didn't rot. He stayed on.

III

God and the Lightship

"I<small>N THE</small> hour of his extremity, every man turns to God,"
Mickey O'Rorke observed dogmatically.

"And what does he get?" Allen asked.

The men about the carpenter's bench laughed. Yet the
very fact of the discussion showed there was something
in what the chief said. In the extremity of a rainy day
the crew had turned to God as a subject for argument.

Chief O'Rorke was over seventy, upright in carriage
and full of malice. He could hardly have afforded to
stoop, being under five feet in height. Yet he had the
shoulders and bones of a strong man. He was born in
Ireland in the year of the Potato Famine and had thereby
lost nearly a foot of his potential height. All his life he
had remembered that invisible foot and carried himself
accordingly.

"Look at Bob Ingersoll," the chief said. "He was a
great atheist and a brave noise, but when he lay dying
he cried aloud to God."

"He sent for a priest, too, didn't he?" Clark asked
slyly.

"That is a lie," Allen told the chief. "They always
make up that stuff when a man is dead and can't defend
himself."

Mickey looked at the fireman speculatively and opened a valve that allowed water to run from the scuppers above into a 'tweendeck tank for the boiler. He caught a sample of the water in one paw, held it up to his grizzled cat's face and lapped critically. There was not a trace of salt; the deck had been washed clean and the heavy rain was unmixed with spray. He opened the valve full, then turned it back slightly. "Blaspheme away," he said cheerfully. "Say what you like against God. Right now the sweet water is falling from Heaven for our boilers!" He ambled out of sight around the fidley to open the starboard valve, hitching up his disgraceful old pants as he went.

Allen Ross looked after the chief affectionately. "You would know Mickey was Irish," he observed. "He always gets religious in the rain. Just the same, that is a lie about Ingersoll."

The bell machine on the bulkhead filled the silence with its hum and clicking, the bell clanked away under the sea and the Heaven-sent water gushed into the tank.

Soft, thumping footsteps sounded on the companionway. Oscar came below, like a dripping haystack in his yellow sou'wester and slicker. Water ran from his drooping yellow moustache and he looked immensely disgusted.

"Start the whistle!" he said to Mr. Gill. The rain was becoming heavy.

Mr. Gill eased his noble weight down from the carpenter's bench. "Right, Oscar, all right." He began opening the drains of the red monster beside the fidley.

"Is it wet on deck?" Allen inquired.

The fat seaman gave him a contemptuous look. "What you tink?"

"If it is wet, don't mind," the fireman advised him. "The chief says God sent the rain."

Oscar made a vulgar noise which he always seemed to have at his command and stamped above, softly, in his big rubber boots.

"Have you ever read Ingersoll's Lectures," Ross asked the others.

The whistle engine rumbled a discourteous answer. The lever bucked on the eccentric and the lightship shuddered with the screeching cry of the whistle.

"I have read Ingersoll," a new voice observed quietly, "and I don't think much of him."

Captain Lindstrom had stopped at the carpenter's bench to see if he could be of any service in the argument. He found during his eight years in the lightship that arguments on abstract subjects preserved the sanity of his crew, and he did what he could to promote them. The carpenter's bench was in a strategic location for such bouts; it was neither forward nor aft, a kind of public square where officers and crew met and disputed on a basis of perfect equality. Captain Lindstrom had even observed that a carpenter's bench should be approached in a spirit of humility.

The captain was a man of average height, with remarkably wide shoulders under his square-cut coat. With his black beard and mild, intelligent eyes and longish hair swept back from his white, high forehead he might have passed for a Russian Christus.

"Ingersoll is too sure of himself," he observed good-naturedly. "He was too much like what he fought. Another evangelist, only he had his engines going astern."

Allen grinned and Clark asked quietly, "Are you sure he was going the wrong way?"

The captain had not made himself clear. "Only in relation to the evangelist. Say they were two ferry boats going in opposite directions, each one sure the other was going backwards."

"Ferry boats have no sterns," Ben commented dreamily; "they look both ways at once."

"A ferry boat has two sterns," Mr. Gill thought.

"A ferry boat has two bows and two sterns," Clark maintained.

"A boat with only two ends can't have two of each."

"Count them," Clark suggested. He moved Mr. Gill's box of safety matches on the bench. "There's a bow and there's a stern." He moved it the other way. "There's a bow and there's a stern. How many's that?"

"Two!"

"Four!"

"Six!" Ben had a new idea. "Four bows and two sterns!"

"What?" Clark had been gone one better. "How do you count, Ben?"

The boy showed him. "Starboard bow and port bow—"

"That doesn't count," Mr. Gill said with mild finality.

"Why not?"

The captain intervened. "Starboard or port or weather

or lee bow only means that side of the bow. It would take too long to say 'starboard side of the bow.' ''

Since it was a point of seamanship, his decision was accepted.

"Now we are back to two bows and two sterns," Clark observed.

"Two bows and no stern."

"Two sterns and no—"

The profane shout of the whistle intervened.

Allen was amused and irritated at the endless possibilities for argument in the captain's too-happy simile. Unless it were headed off, it might sink the religious issue and reel along for days, and even weeks. "Captain," he said quickly as the whistle blast died away, "the chief says when Bob Ingersoll was dying he cried out to God. Do you believe that?"

Mickey had returned and was standing by the bench.

The captain answered with a slow, amused smile. "I've heard that." He smiled more broadly. "You must admit that Ingersoll had given God a lot of his attention!"

The little chief looked about brightly, feeling vindicated.

Allen remembered the original argument. "Do you think most men turn to God when they're dying?"

The captain looked out of the portlight of the half-door at the gray, rain-tormented sea.

Ole came by, freshly shaven, in a clean shirt and dungarees. He paused at the carpenter's bench long enough to hear the question. "God!" he said impatiently, half under his breath, and walked on, disappearing around the fidley.

"I haven't seen many men die," the captain said quietly.

The whistle bellowed, vibrating the bench under his listeners. After a minute it died away and there was the comparative quiet of the thump and whine of machinery and the clank of the submarine bell.

"Death is a primeval thing," the captain said at last. "Older than religion. As old as life, almost. The first living thing may have died after a minute. Probably it wasn't much of a success. The first life started in the sea, out there. The sea is older than life or death. That's why it is an unmoral kind of power. There aren't any moral questions without life and death, and the sea was too old to learn when those came along." He was in danger of launching on one of his favorite themes, but this time he remembered himself. "Turning to God is a comparatively new idea. I don't suppose a dying man does it without prompting. A dying man is like an animal crawling away by itself. It's the animal in man that dies."

"And the soul lives on!" Mickey proclaimed gleefully. He was more pleased at having got the better of Allen Ross than at having been assured of immortality.

The captain looked at the old chief in honest surprise.

Allen saw the look. "Does it?" he wanted to know.

"If you broke up a violin and burned it," the captain illustrated, "you would only destroy material things—wood and the intestines of cats. The notes of music can't be chopped up or burned."

"They would be gone just the same when the violin was done for," Clark protested.

70

Captain Lindstrom seemed pleased. "Just that," he said.

"Where would the music go?" Ben demanded with a flash of interest.

The whistle raised its iron roar in derision of all music. Mr. Gill eased down from the bench and went aft, disappearing toward the fire room with ponderous agility.

"Would the music have to go anywhere, Ben?" the captain asked gently.

"If it was gone and hadn't been destroyed—"

"It couldn't be destroyed, not being material. But it wouldn't have to go anywhere, would it? Couldn't it just not be there any more?"

Ben looked his disbelief, but said nothing.

"There will always be music," the little chief maintained.

"There will always be men," Allen reminded him. "But the same man will happen only once."

"Once is enough." Clark stirred and sat up on the carpenter's bench with a kind of sigh. "I can't see what I've done to deserve to live forever. I'm willing to let the next man have his turn."

"Me, too," Allen agreed. "I'm going to have some fun first, and call it a day."

Ben turned restlessly and looked out of the portlight at the gray, rain-vexed sea that was older than life or death.

"We're all here for a good time," the captain said indulgently.

"On the lightship?" Mickey asked quickly. "It's like going to jail for a good time!"

71

"You've been in jail here twenty years because you like it."

Allen laughed and Ben smiled dutifully. The discussion was beginning to weary him.

"There are different kinds of a good time," the captain went on. "You may think it's one thing or another, but when you have a chance to find out, it is doing the work you like. I'm not the first one to say that," he added modestly.

Ben slid from the carpenter's bench and walked away. He had heard enough for the day. However lively a discussion was, it always made him restless after a while. On the way forward he looked into the galley. Harry was peeling potatoes, and the big cook sat near the range in a kind of stupor, his shaggy head sunk in his hands. He made the boy think of a great, sick dog.

The messman looked up hopefully from his work. "Hello, Ben. Are they still talking religion?"

Ben nodded. "Still at it."

"I'll be out there myself when I get the things for supper." He picked up another potato and peeled rapidly. There was something childlike about the little man, sitting on a low bench and hurrying through his stint with hopeful eagerness. His thin, white arms looked as breakable as china, and his drooping moustache seemed to be spun out of the same fragile stuff. Ben felt sorry for the messman; he had not complained, but everyone knew he did all the galley work while the powerful cook moped in a corner and pitied himself.

"Don't let the cook work too hard," the boy said, raising his voice a little as he passed on. It was none of his business, but when he saw an injustice he felt obliged to strike out.

In the stateroom he shared with Allen Ross, the boy sat on his grimy bunk and contemplated his books: Shakespeare, Loti's *Iceland Fishermen*, Hardy's *Tess of the D'urbervilles*, Tennyson, Robinson's *Principles of Steam Engineering*, the *Oxford Book of English Verse*, *The Rubyiat*, and Ibsen's *A Doll's House*. It was hard to decide what to read when he didn't really want to read anything. He picked up the *Oxford Book of English Verse*, without much conviction, and went to the door. Reading at the mess room table was sometimes a good change from reading in his own bunk.

Across the mess-room, through another open door, he saw Ole sitting on a bench unravelling a strand of rope. The seaman looked up with a beckoning nod, and Ben went over to his door, the blue and gold volume in his hand.

"Come in," Ole said, still working. It was the first time he had invited the young fireman into his room.

Ben sat on Clark's bunk and watched. The seaman had made one end of the rope fast to a hook near the door and was combing out the unraveled yellow fibers into something like a hank of hair.

"Crossing the Line, we used to make hair like this for Neptune," he observed.

"What are you making now?"

"Nothing. I was just cleaning my comb." He held it up for the boy's inspection. "See how bright and clean it is."

Ben was disappointed. He had expected something

more. The strange, grave seaman had the air of being able to conjure Neptune out of the depths of the sea by merely putting his hat on backwards.

"Are they still talking about God?" Ole asked abruptly.

"They were when I left."

"It is stupid to talk about God, and you are wasting your time listening to them," Ole reproved. "There is no God."

The boy fidgeted. "How do you know?" He saw himself drawn from one religious argument to another.

Ole was not going to argue with him; he was going to tell him. "How do I know? I am not a child; I am a grown man. It is all right for children to talk about God, the way they talk about trolls in the woods." He turned on the bench and fixed the boy with his grave, reproving little eyes. "Grown men should not believe things like that; they should not waste their time talking about such things. You think you know, but you only know what you have been told. I am not telling you the superstition others told me. I am going to tell you what I learned.

"When I was a boy, a little younger than you, I believed in God. I believed the way you do, because I had been told. I come of a good family, too. My father was a paper manufacturer in Halmstad, a man who read many books and thought deeply, but always in the way he had been taught to think. My mother was a Dahl, and that is how I came to go to sea."

Ben had heard Ole speak of his mother. "She is still alive, isn't she?"

74

"Yes," Ole said, "I had a letter from her in the summer, though I have not seen her for over thirty years. The Dahls live a long time. My grand uncle Olaf was ninety-one when he died. He believed in God, but except for that he was a man. He was a great captain, too. He ran the cotton blockade in the Civil War, with a sailing ship, and was never caught.

"You can see why I believed in God. I went to church every Sunday and listened to all the pastor said. I thought a lot about God, too. Above the altar in the Halmstad church they had a sign in gold letters: 'Praise be Unto God in Heaven.' I thought that was fine. I used to look at it and think what a big boy I was. It seemed to make everything all right. 'Praise be Unto God in Heaven!' "

The fat seaman gave him a contemptuous look. "What you tink?"

"If it is wet, don't mind," the fireman advised him. "The chief says God sent the rain."

Oscar made a vulgar noise which he always seemed to have at his command and stamped above, softly, in his big rubber boots.

"Have you ever read Ingersoll's Lectures," Ross asked the others.

The whistle engine rumbled a discourteous answer. The lever bucked on the eccentric and the lightship shuddered with the screeching cry of the whistle.

"I have read Ingersoll," a new voice observed quietly, "and I don't think much of him."

Captain Lindstrom had stopped at the carpenter's bench to see if he could be of any service in the argument. He found during his eight years in the lightship that arguments on abstract subjects preserved the sanity of his crew, and he did what he could to promote them. The carpenter's bench was in a strategic location for such bouts; it was neither forward nor aft, a kind of public square where officers and crew met and disputed on a basis of perfect equality. Captain Lindstrom had even observed that a carpenter's bench should be approached in a spirit of humility.

The captain was a man of average height, with remarkably wide shoulders under his square-cut coat. With his black beard and mild, intelligent eyes and longish hair swept back from his white, high forehead he might have passed for a Russian Christus.

"Ingersoll is too sure of himself," he observed good-

IV

The "Stadsholmen"

"PRAISE be unto God in Heaven." Ole Hanson had become a sailor and a man. The church service gave him a new feeling of strength and grave importance. In his prayer, Pastor Bergson spoke of "those who go down to the sea in ships." That was for the officers and crew of the new bark *Stadsholmen*, and it included Ole. He opened his eyes to better enjoy the solemn moment. Uncle Olaf, "Captain Dahl," as he must call him now, was sitting beside him in the pew, great-shouldered, with his beard resting on his deep chest, completely hiding Ole's slender, studious father. John Hedburg, Ole's classmate from the high elementary school, was on the other side. The boys had dreams of the voyage which they only confided to each other. They were both sixteen.

Ole's eyes roved across the aisle, to where the women and girls sat. Little Kristina Hedburg had her eyes open and her head turned toward Ole and her brother. "Those who go down to the sea in ships." She too had opened her eyes for the grand and solemn moment. Widow Hedburg, bent in prayer beside her daughter, was from Swedish Finland and both her children had delicately rounded faces and great blue eyes and their gold hair was so thick it appeared darker than it was. Across a sea of bowed heads, Ole and the girl exchanged a grave, buoyant look. His gaze roved on, but her eyes fixed in his mind the pious scene and the smell of varnished pews, hymn books and Sabbath clothes. As the pastor's prayer ended, Ole's eyes came to rest on the shining words above the pulpit: "Praise be Unto God in Heaven." There was a lift of bowed heads being raised, like a field of grain after a wind passes. He and John looked at each other. Their eyes agreed the prayer had been splendid.

John was as beautiful as his sister and of much more importance because he was a man and a member of the *Stadsholmen's* crew. He and Ole practiced the English language with the aid of a dictionary when they were alone. They would need that when the ship reached Galveston, in the United States of America. They had rather decided to run away and hunt buffaloes. After that, they might go to the gold fields in California. In a few years they would return to Sweden, rich men.

Herr Hanson had wished his son to learn his business, but from the beginning of his friendship with John Hedburg, Ole felt the need of something more adventurous than making paper on the quiet bank of the Nissa. Then Grand Uncle Olaf quit the sea and settled himself in a villa looking out on Cattegat. He was seventy and for a generation he had been a Halmstad legend, but even to Ole, who had never seen him before, he did not seem an old man. The captain made himself at home in Halmstad and lived easily, but his talk of other lands and far seas fell on his nephew like restless seed.

After two years of quiet life, Olaf Dahl suddenly became bored. He collected timber and workmen and before anyone quite knew what had come over him, he was building a ship beside his villa. He was not a ship-builder and there were no plans so far as Ole knew, but in two years he had produced a vessel that was the admiration of Halmstad and the surrounding country. It was a beautiful three-masted barque of twelve hundred tons burden. Visiting sea captains were unsparing of their approval, and even rival builders declared she would be fast and handy.

Uncle Olaf was pleased and a little surprised at what he had done, like an old man who finds himself with a beautiful new bride. He tried to explain to Ole how it happened. "When I let go both my anchors here, I thought I had done with the sea. Another man could have ended his days quietly; I had it in my heart to do that. I have lived a long time but old age has not come to me. So I had to put what I saved and learned from the sea into a new ship. Pray God it turns out well. The sea brings many chances."

Ole and John Hedburg talked things over at school and pledged themselves to sail in the new bark. But Herr Hanson was against his son becoming a seaman. "Don't be carried away by what your uncle Olaf has done," he cautioned. "He does not belong to our age. Remember, he made his fortune through running the cotton blockade in the American war against slavery. It was no better than piracy. You will do well to learn the manufacture of paper. As the world becomes more civilized, people will read more and the demand for paper will increase, while there will be less demand for physical strength and daring."

The mother, who was a Dahl, saw otherwise. "The boy has set his heart on seeing the world," she said. "Sooner or later he will go away. It might as well be the sea. At least a ship will bring him back sometimes. The boys who go to the lumber camps in America do not come back. And they soon become forgetful and do not write to their people any more."

But Herr Hanson could only see Ole's future and the future of the world in terms of paper. He did not relent until the bark was launched. There was a great crowd at the ceremony, and many gentlemen in tall hats and frock coats. The Governor of the *Lan* of Halland was there, and his daughter broke the bottle of champagne over the vessel's bow and named her after the island in Stockholm where Captain Dahl was born. Perhaps it was because the Governor and his family had a hand in it that Herr Hanson yielded.

Later, there was a grand dinner at the villa. When the guests were standing about the long *smorgasbrod*, the boy's father poured him a glass of *branvin*. "Drink and sadness are the curse of our people," he said," "but you are a man, now. You must look out for yourself."

Ole emptied the little glass and wrestled with a need to cough. It was his first taste of spirits and he found it a fiery drink. After it he bore himself with dignity and did not eat as much as he wanted of the smoked goose breast and thin-sliced raw salmon. But the glow of his first *branvin* had been slight compared with the solemn intoxication of the church service. Had he not been included in the Pastor's prayer for "those who go down to the sea in ships?" He was now a sailor and a man, having been called to the attention of God who holds the Atlantic Ocean, and even the United States of America, in His hand.

On Monday afternoon there was a good slant of freshening wind for the *Stadsholmen* weighing anchor in the roads. Captain Dahl was doubly pleased, having no taste for tugs. Ole and John tramped round the capstan with their watch mates, singing and heaving at the same new bar. The boys had already learned their insignificance among a picked crew, where even their fellow "ordinarys" held able seamen's certificates, but that only put them on their mettle. They were even pleased that their entrancing new profession was something to be won and learned. And they never thought to question the overbearing attitude of the men who stood so easily on the footropes, high aloft, loosening the new white sails.

To each other, they did not appear insignificant. Whether they washed paint work or cleaned the chicken coop or filled the galley coal box, the work took on dignity because it was part of a great adventure. On their watches below they practiced knots and splices, when the most superior and scornful seaman would go to some pains to correct their mistakes. Or they would settle themselves in some snug corner on deck and talk of what the voyage might bring.

"*Many buffaloes roam the plains of America,*" John would sometimes say in English. The sentence enchanted him.

"*Allow us yump on our rapid horses and give them a pursuit,*" Ole would answer solemnly.

"*Where is the way to California? There is much gold in America.*"

"Allow us try and get some."

"The day is fine on the sea, is it not?"

"Yes, is it not?"

"The sails make shadows on the deck and the winds blow freely."

In a little while they would be talking Swedish again. English was fun, but they never found the words to say what they felt and the language sounded stilted.

The weather remained moderate through Cattegat and Skager Rack. Although the boys had not got their sea legs yet, on the second day they ventured aloft as high as the main upper topsail yard. At that height the ship appeared uncomfortably far away and too narrow to support her masts and sails. John went out on the footrope a little way, quite fearlessly, and gave his chum an impish look. "Come on, Spider," he said, "we might as well get used to walking on a web." Ole followed his example, but could not keep back unpleasant thoughts of what would happen if the rope carried away. The rolling of the ship was much more noticeable aloft and the orderly deck was far below. Above, the royal yard seemed an unattainable height.

When they reached the deck, Captain Dahl left the poop and came forward. The boys thought he would tell them they had no business on the yard. But he only stroked his beard thoughtfully and said, "When you are aloft at first you should not look down. Even in a cart, you might get dizzy looking at the ground. Look at what is around you and keep a good hold with one hand. Then you will be safe enough." He did not show the boys any special consideration, but he treated his crew well and did not wish to have anyone killed on board.

Ole and John were seasick while cleaning the chicken coop off the Bay of Biscay. They took turns at cleaning and being sick. The chicken is a filthy bird. No one paid any attention to them, but they were ashamed and miserable.

Then the *Stadsholmen* picked up the Northeast Trades. The boys came to life at once in the fine weather. They had vomited away the hold the land had on them and were ready for the sea. They discovered it was pleasant to sit on the royal yard, a hundred and fifty feet above the sea, and argue points of seamanship. They learned the speed with which one can slide down a backstay and not be burned, and they passed to the leeward of the chicken coop with fine indifference. Sometimes at night they went out on the end of the flying jibboom and watched the stately bark coming after them, with her new white sails rising like gleaming turrets in the starlight, and her sharp cutwater whispering through the warm, phosphorescent sea. At mealtime they ate like wolves and looked forward with glee to cakes at coffee time. Captain Dahl allowed them tricks at the wheel, under his watchful eye, and they went aloft with the others. There was little loosening or taking in of sails, but sometimes they spent a whole watch aloft, renewing chafing gear.

John got a plug of tobacco from somewhere and startled Ole by appearing with a bulge in one cheek and his delicate, girlish mouth stained with tobacco juice. He was still a good deal of a child, in spite of his courage and growing skill as a seaman. Much he and Ole did and said to each other was the sheer nonsense of boys away from their mothers, but they discovered how good it is to be young and alive in the sunshine. The old shellbacks came to watch their antics with toleration, and even a kind of shy pride.

Ole was the more serious of the two, perhaps because he was homely. Sometimes in his bunk before he fell asleep, he thought gratefully of the inscription above the pulpit in the old church at home, "Praise be Unto God in Heaven." God must be something like Uncle Olaf, he fancied, immense and bearded and ageless, but ever so much more powerful. Uncle Olaf was all-powerful on board his ship and more than a match for anything the sea might do. But God held the sea and the ship and all her people in His hand. It was because of Him that all these things had their being. And it was because of God that Ole was Ole, sailing toward a new land in the splendid *Stadsholmen*. It was through His loving kindness that he and John were the same age, with the same dreams, able to read the thoughts in each other's eyes. Both of them knew what they would never have confided to anyone else, and what they only told each other with their eyes: the *Stadsholmen* and her voyage were not things of necessity or profit. They were a splendid adventure and part of the beautiful and mysterious purpose behind this life.

They were a day through the Windward Passage, in squally weather when it happened. Near the end of the first dog watch, Captain Dahl ordered a reef taken in the main course. He was standing beside Ole, who was at the wheel, conning the helm in a tricky quartering sea. When the sail was clewed up, six of the men sprang into the rigging and ran aloft to reef. The seas were running higher than the amount of wind justified, and the bark had a jerky motion. John Hedburg was the second aloft. Johansen's broad, bare back was bending over, ready to haul out the earing at the end of the weather yardarm. John took a position a little farther inboard, turned on the footrope and waved to his chum. His hair, which had grown long on the voyage, rippled like a clear flame in the wind as he tossed his head. Ole caught the lovely, impish expression on his face. It said: this is something like, you steering and me aloft. How about a real storm?

Ole was too busy with the kicking wheel to make any response, but he knew John understood. He heard a great thunder on the loosened sail. His glance had left the yardarm when it happened. Afterward, he thought he had glimpsed something falling, but it might have been Lundquist, who burned his hands on a backstay. Johansen's bull voice roared out from aloft and Captain Dahl started forward. Almost at the same instant, there was a thud on deck. When Ole turned his eyes to the weather yardarm, his chum was gone. Everyone was coming down from the yard, but he felt suddenly hollow and sick. They were working over someone on deck. The men who had been forward were running aft. They were running swiftly, but it seemed to take them a long time to reach the foot of the mainmast. A wave raced away toward the setting sun with an evil glitter.

The crowd near the mainmast divided and Captain Dahl emerged, carrying a limp blue figure. It was John Hedburg, and he looked as if he might be dead. But that was impossible. The captain's face was grave and John lay very still in his arms. He showed no positive sign of injury. A dark stain on his mouth might have been blood, or only tobacco juice.

After a sickening interval, Johansen came to the wheel.

Ole was surprised to hear his own voice giving the course before his hands relinquished the spokes. When he stole below, they had John on the high berth in the captain's stateroom. He had vomited and the steward was cleaning up the mess. Captain Dahl cut the boy's clothes away so as to disturb him as little as possible. There was no mark of injury on his white skin. No broken bones. Just knocked unconscious. His breathing was quick and light, but steady. They turned him over, and there was a dark bruise on his back, below the shoulders. The captain touched that dull red mark. "I know nothing about spines," he observed regretfully. "If it were an arm or leg—"

"Has he broken his back, sir?" the steward demanded hoarsely.

Ole had not dared to ask the question.

His uncle straightened up and looked at the steward heavily. "I don't think so. Injured, perhaps, or it may be nothing. Boys are sometimes very tough." He stroked back John's yellow hair, disclosing a bruised lump on the back of his head. It, too, might be a serious injury, or nothing. Four bells sounded above. The bark staggered as she ran before a lumpy sea. Ole sensed that someone was standing partly down the companionway, waiting for news.

"Bring one of my nightshirts," Captain Dahl ordered.

John looked like a child in the immense, white starched garment. A child in his father's nightshirt. The hem came below his feet. They rolled up the sleeves far enough to free his limp hands, with a row of callouses across each palm. Then they tucked him under the covers. His breathing was still quick and light, but showed no sign of failing.

"That is all we can do now," the captain decided. "Let me know if he becomes conscious, or if there is any change. You can watch him, Ole; the steward has his work." He went above with a firm, heavy step.

"Do you think he is badly hurt?" Ole asked the steward.

"Yes. Very likely he will die." The steward was a slight, red-faced Stockholm man with rusty orange-colored hair and a hoarse voice. He always gave the impression of being angry. Now, Ole decided, he really was angry. "You boys think you're doing something big going to sea," he croaked. "Oh, yes! This will teach you. You ought to be home with your mothers. In my last ship we had an apprentice who thought he was a sailor man. He was fifteen and got the syphilis in Melbourne. Off Staten Island, a sea washed him overboard. You should have heard him call, 'Mama!' The Old Man thought it was too rough to heave to and lower a boat. He could swim, too, but that's all the good it did him, swimming off Cape Horn. '*Mama!*'"

Ole felt ill, but he managed to say with dignity, "Get out of here, will you? You're making too much noise."

"You think so," the steward answered hoarsely. "I'm not making enough noise to wake *him*." He waved his elbow toward the unconscious boy.

"Will you get out of here before I throw you out?" Ole was full of tears and rage.

"Who's making a noise now, my sailor man?" The steward drew the curtain so the light no longer shone on John's face and took a bath towel from one of the drawers under the berth. "We'll find out who's noisy and who's quiet," he continued darkly, folding the towel and spreading it carefully beside John's head. "We don't want him puking over any more sheets. You don't think we have a laundry on board, do you?" As he was leaving he said, "Maybe this will be a lesson to you about going to sea. Don't call me unless you need help. I'm late with the Old Man's supper as it is."

In a little while Ole became lonesome. It was even reassuring to hear the ugly steward working about in the captain's pantry. John slept without any sign of pain or waking. His long, curved lashes rested on his cheeks and his disordered hair gleamed in the shadow like gold. He looked less like John and more like a sleeping girl. Ole wanted to be with his chum, but he wasn't. He was alone with himself, near where John was alone with himself. There was no crossing the distance between them. He took John's hand, small and slim under the big, rolled-up sleeve, but it lay limp and nerveless in his. He called his friend by name, shaken by the sound of his own voice. John's silence was like a reproof.

Captain Dahl and Olsen, the mate, looked in later. The mate stood by awkwardly, with a look of honest distress while his captain leaned over and listened to the boy's breathing. After he had done that and felt his pulse, he said, "There isn't much change, except that he seems feverish. We might get him to drink something."

"Can I help, sir?" Olsen asked.

"Raise his head, easily now, with the pillow underneath."

Olsen raised the boy's head with immense tenderness and Captain Dahl tilted a glass. Some of the water ran from between the indifferent lips and made a wet spot on the nightshirt, but the captain caught most of it with the towel. Some must have gone down. John strangled a little and then was quiet.

"Lay him down," Captain Dahl said. "That is all we can do. Ole, you may eat with us if you wish. We can see in here from the saloon."

"Thank you, Uncle, I couldn't eat."

"Very well. The steward will relieve you when he is through."

Ole had sometimes imagined himself seated in one of the arm chairs at the massive saloon table, under the skylight and telltale compass. He had not expected the opportunity to come so suddenly, or under circumstances that made the thought of food nauseating. Things like that happened. Special privileges for children in a house where someone was very ill or dead—when the most coveted liberties turned to choking dust.

Uncle Olaf and the mate were eating. He could hear the click of knives and forks and the occasional sound of a cup set down on its saucer. They were eating heartily and talking as if nothing terrible had happened. A smell of meat and vegetables and coffee invaded the stateroom. It was disgusting and unnatural. Seas overtook the staggering bark and swept by. Bells were struck and feet resounded on deck. All that, too, as if nothing had happened. It seemed to Ole that he alone bore the weight of disaster. John slept as if he had become a machine with that one function. In his loneliness, the boy strained his ears to catch the comforting sound of voices. Between seas, he was able to make out some of what was being said. Uncle Olaf, who usually kept his own council, was explaining some plan to the mate. "Continue to Galveston—" A sea carried the rest away. Then another lull, and the careful, grave voice. "New Orleans would mean leaving him alone in a hospital. . . . The wind never veers when it is like this. We should have it dead aft for Galveston tomorrow . . . ." Olsen put in something, then another sea. "Plenty," the captain affirmed, "too much, perhaps."

After the captain and mate had looked at John again and gone on deck, the young second mate came below, humming to himself. "And how is the patient?" he asked cheerfully, putting his head in the door.

"About the same," Ole reported, "he doesn't show any signs of coming to."

"Well, now, you mustn't feel so bad about it. I've seen a man out for twelve hours and then come to as good as ever. Don't take it so hard. You'll see young Hedburg up and about tomorrow, as bright as if nothing had happened."

The pink-faced mate seemed confident that everything would turn out well. Too confident, perhaps. John breathed, and that was his only sign of life. If only they had a doctor on board! A doctor would know just what to do to fix him up as good as ever. But a hospital was better yet, when it was something serious. Uncle Olaf hadn't wanted to put in at New Orleans, where John would have been left alone. Ole wouldn't have wanted that, either. They would put him in a fine hospital at Galveston and the crew would be able to visit him. The

American people would be touched by the sight of a beautiful foreign boy brought in from a ship. They would respect Uncle Olaf's great shoulders and immense beard; they would know he was a famous captain. Probably, some fine lady would notice the golden-haired boy in the captain's arms, as beautiful as a sleeping girl. She would insist on taking them to the hospital in her carriage. "Quickly, to the hospital!" she would tell her black coachman. The coachman would crack his whip and they would whirl away through the bright sunshine, along an avenue bordered with wonderful tropical flowers and waving palms.

When the second mate had finished eating, the steward came in with an oilskin coat on his arm. "The sick watch is changing," he announced hoarsely, "but first help me put this under your friend. We don't want him to muss the captain's berth, do we?" The steward showed unexpected skill and consideration in getting the oilskin under the sheet. Then he said, "Go on, now, Get something to eat. Your supper is on the saloon table."

Ole wavered.

"Get out of here. Your friend won't run away. And be sure to eat; even nurses need strength."

The boy ate alone, or tried to eat. He was immediately discouraged by the heaping plate which the steward had set for him. Ordinarily he never got quite enough, but now he was surfeited at the start. There was a big plate of cakes, too. He and John had always been so gleeful when they managed to snitch an extra cake, which they divided afterward in some snug corner on deck. Now, a whole plateful had been put before him, with no one watching. That was a bad sign. The steward must really think John was going to die. People try to console you for the loss of someone you love with a plate of cakes. The sight of the cakes was oppressive, like flowers for the dead. He pushed them further away.

On deck there were sounds of activity. They were getting on more sail. Ordinarily that wouldn't have been done at night, with the wind hardening. They were thinking of John. The *Stadsholmen* would make a splendid dash to Galveston to save his life. God was good; there was plenty of wind. And had not Uncle Olaf predicted it would haul dead aft? The thought comforted him and he was able to eat. He even managed a cake with his coffee. On an impulse, he slipped two more of the cakes into his pocket. The second mate had predicted that John would be up and about in the morning, as fine as ever.

The steward forced Ole to go forward when he had eaten. "You have no business hanging around when you aren't on sick watch," he proclaimed hoarsely from the door of the stateroom. "Do you want to spoil the ship's discipline? You threw me out when you were on watch, now I throw you out. You'll have plenty of nursing tomorrow. I'll call you if anything happens. Get forward, now."

Ole slunk forward. His watchmates were arguing, but they suddenly fell silent as he entered the foc'sle. There were several cakes grouped timidly on the mess table, although the men got only one apiece. That and the sight of John Hedburg's empty bunk was answered by a lost feeling about his heart.

Johansen asked from his bunk, "How is the boy, Ole?"

"About the same; he hasn't come to yet," Ole answered. He was close to tears. The others murmured sympathetically but did not speak directly to him. He took off his jacket and lay in his bunk, with his face turned toward the side of the ship.

Eight bells were striking when he woke. It was broad daylight and no one had called him to go on watch. The deserted foc'sle gave him a feeling of foreboding. Then he remembered and tumbled out. The port watch was just coming up to the foc'sle when he opened the door. The men drew aside to let him pass.

"The boy is no worse, Ole," little Lundquist called encouragingly.

The wind had freshened and the seas were running higher than the evening before, but the bark was storming along under full sail, making splendid weather of it. Ole's watch mates, gathered in the waist, gave him encouraging looks and called, "He is no worse, Ole!"

He brushed by the steward, clearing away the breakfast in the saloon, and went into the stateroom. It was true John did not appear any worse, but neither did he appear any better. He lay in exactly the same position, breathing quickly and lightly, with his long, golden-brown eyelashes resting on his cheeks. There was something mysterious in the sleep which had taken him so completely. The steward looked in, with a coffee pot in his hand.

"He looks just the same doesn't he?" Ole observed.

The steward gave a snort of distaste. "Just the same after I cleaned him, you mean! He must be changed and cared for like a baby. You overslept, I suppose, and want breakfast. There may be something left. God knows I have enough to do without nursing and feeding boys."

Captain Dahl came in from the wet deck, immense in his oilskins and boots. "There is little we can do for the boy," he told Ole, "except watch and pray. Every hour or so you might give him some water, but disturb him as little as posssble. We may be in Galveston tomorrow evening. I am only a seaman and this is a case for doctors." He squinted at the barometer above the writing desk and went on deck. It was the first time his nephew had ever seen him worried.

Ole, on the contrary, felt easier. John had not become worse during the night, and he was certain he would not die. Tomorrow night he would be in a hospital, where the doctors would know just what should be done. Meanwhile, Ole would watch and pray. He had been doing so already.

John remained unconscious all day, sleeping as if he were beyond the reach of death or waking. Sometimes Ole was filled with anger that his chum who had been so quick and self-reliant had become helpless as a sick baby. Sometimes he was overawed by the depth of his sleep. It was like a secret he had discovered and would share with no one, not even his dearest friend.

The next morning he was still sleeping, but his face was flushed and he appeared more feverish. Some change was taking place within him, but there was no saying what that change might be. Ole stayed with him almost constantly, now and then wetting his delicate, girlish mouth and sponging his face and hands.

He went on deck only once during the afternoon. The wind had risen and the sea appeared dangerously high, but the bark was running off under full topsails, topgallants and foresail. She drove on furiously under a low sky, taking scarcely any water on deck. In the heavier gusts, she seemed to partly lift out of the sea, half sailing and half flying through a roaring storm of spray. It did not seem necessary to ask if they were nearing port. Ahead, Ole made out two in-bound steamers, racing almost abreast of each other, pitching like rocking horses and spouting black smoke over the sea before them. The *Stadsholmen* rushed past a heavily-laden black ship, hove to under dark stormsails. A sea swept the stranger's decks, leaving nothing but a foc'sle and four yellow masts and a poop rising out of boiling whiteness. A third steamer was hanging on astern, but losing ground. One moment she showed nothing but a red forefoot and sharp black bow, and the next, the full length of her deck, surrounded by white water. For an instant there was a faint, acid smell of coal smoke—the smell he associated with a harbor.

Below, John slept, indifferent to the rush and increased motion of the ship, but his fever was running higher. Ole poured a little water between his lips, smoothed back his damp hair and bathed his face. "Don't die, John," he said, "please. We're so near port; we'll be in Galveston this evening." He felt better when he spoke to his friend, even though there was no response.

It came to him later that John might have heard. He might be paralyzed, as the steward said. Perhaps he heard everything, without being able to move or speak. He took the boy's hot, moist hand in his and spoke again.

"John, I'm here beside you; it's Ole. You had a bad fall from the yard, but you're going to get well. We'll be in America in a few hours! You're going to a hospital and I'm going with you; I won't leave you alone, John. You ought to see the wonderful race the *Stadsholmen* is making. She has passed everything in sight, big sailing ship and steamers; we must be doing twenty knots. And the watch below is staying on deck, ready to help with anything that will get us there faster. It's been like a dog watch all afternoon. They're doing it because of you, John, and you must get well for us!"

He was positive that John's hand exerted a faint pressure on his. It was an answer through the walls of his enforced silence that he heard and understood.

Ole was still murmuring to him in the dark when the steward came to light the lamps and put the fiddles on the saloon table. Not that it was much use, he said. The weather had gone thick and dirty, and the *Stadsholmen* was closing with the land like something fired from a cannon. Probably no one would come below until they were anchored in Galveston Bay—if they found the entrance, he added darkly. No pilot could board them in weather like this. He departed, grieving over the unclean night.

The sharp detonation of an order set off an explosion of activity on deck. Ole conveyed the news to his chum. "The helm has been shifted. Now they're bracing the yards. We must be heading in between the islands. You'll be safe now, John!"

John lay without answering, as Ole bent over him and smoothed back his damp golden hair, but his flushed face was proud and beautiful.

A hail for all hands on deck drifted past with the sound of the wind and rain.

"We must be in," Ole said, touching his lips to John's forehead.

"ALL HANDS ON DECK!" Blows thundered on the companionway.

It came to Ole that "all hands" included himself. He stepped into the saloon doubtfully, and a great lurch of the ship hurled him against the table. The steward burst out of the pantry. "On deck, you fool!" he croaked as he dashed by, wiping his hands in his apron.

Ole followed him to the poop, where he was instantly soaked. The darkness was full of activity but he understood nothing. And he saw nothing until a watery light appeared somewhere to starboard. It was gone instantly in a black deluge of rain. A sea thundered and broke over the stern, carrying him away. As he brought up hard against the skids of a lifeboat, he felt the ship's speed decrease exactly as if a powerful hand had been laid upon her. Then she stopped altogether and her sails were blown away.

"She's struck," someone observed as if he expected to be contradicted. Seas swept the deck.

Captain Dahl's voice roared out: "Lay aloft, all hands! Ole!"

Ole groped his way to the mizzen shrouds and ran aloft. The wind was strong and solid with rain. A sea rose from nowhere and its crest lashed against his feet on the ratlines with the viciousness of a personal attack. There were other men in the rigging. "Go higher!" a voice called. He climbed higher. Bigger seas burst roaring out of the darkness. The ship lifted and settled with

97

a dull shock. The seas were more on the beam now, crashing on board constantly. Ole watched, wet and bewildered, expecting them to stop presently. The spray whipped his face and uncovered head. He put up his hand, to climb higher, and touched a booted foot on the rat-lines above him. Then he moved over and pulled himself up beside a shadow in the rigging. "What happened?" he demanded.

"Sandbar." It was Lundquist's voice. "Wind shifted all at once and piled us up."

"Are we in Galveston Bay?"

"We're outside, gone to hell somewhere off the island."

Then Ole understood that they were shipwrecked at night on a foreign shore. It was a romantic possibility that he and John had discussed at length. Now he was less certain about the romance, wet and cold, clinging in the rigging, with seas thundering on board and the splendid *Stadsholmen* pounding her heart out on the sand What did John think about it? John had been hurt and was lying below in Uncle Olaf's berth.

He shouted to Lundquist: "John's below! Won't the sea get in?"

"Must take his chances! Anyone would be swept away before he got to the deck. Wait till the wind and sea go down."

The wind and sea were rising. Ole began to whimper.

Uncle Olaf was shouting from the mizzen top: "Ole! Is the boy there?"

"Here!" He answered.

"Climb up. Keep a good hold!"

The wind tore at him as he climbed. Then he felt a

powerful hand helping him into the mizzen top. "Uncle," he cried, "John is below!"

The answer was a rope passed under his arms, around the mast and under his arms again.

"Uncle, John is below and the sea will get in! Uncle!"

"Have you a knife?" Uncle Olaf puffed as he tied a knot and did not seem to understand.

Ole found his clasp knife, the one his mother had given him for his fourteenth birthday, and handed it over. He thought his uncle dropped it into the sea. "Uncle!" he screamed above the wind, "John is below; he will drown!"

The rope was passed around him again in the darkness. "We must try to save ourselves. It is all we can do."

A deep humming sound travelled over the sea from windward, like the drone of swarming bees. The bees turned into a great railway train that bore down on the ship. Then it struck. Ole was surprised beyond thought, bewildered and outraged. He was convinced there had been some ghastly mistake. His arms and legs encircled the mast of their own accord, like sagacious animals bent on saving themselves. He could not breathe because of the solidified air and water that pressed upon him. He was convinced that if his hold relaxed the rope about him would break and he would go flying away to leeward.

An explosion of thunder and a dazzling burst of light surprised his eyes into opening. Against a low, scudding cloud he saw the slanting mainmast, with the figures of men clinging in the rigging and shreds of sails and rope streaming out from the threshing yards.

John Hedburg was a boy he had chummed with when

99

the world was still in its right mind. He could not think clearly, but he was under the impression that it was a long time ago. His own name was Ole Hanson, and he was sixteen in April. His home was in Halmstad, in the *Lan* of Halland. The darkness about him caught fire and burned with a flickering blue light under the low scud. He looked down and had a clear, brief view of the poop, with the skylight and companionway gone, and square black holes, like open graves, where they had been. Then the sea rose and buried the deck.

John was down there, drowning or drowned already! All the quarters aft had been filled by the sea.

He began screaming, "John! John!" but could not hear the sound of his own voice. He knew as certainly as if he had been there that John had regained consciousness at the last moment, when the sea broke in. He felt the boy's terror when he found himself alone in the state-room, deserted by his shipmates, unable to move, with the sea pouring in. Left to drown like a rat!

He began to pray out of habit. Then he stopped. What use was there in talking to God, with John lying dead below him? If there was any God, or if he was worth anything, this would never have happened. John, too, had put his faith in God, and what had it brought him? A rat's death at the age of sixteen. "There is no God," he told himself, "there is no God!"

Ole tried to shout his discovery aloud, but the hurricane tore the words from his lips as they were formed. It would have done the same with a prayer. When he had exhausted himself with soundless shouting, he pressed his face against the mast and sobbed in heartbroken misery, with the blown spray burning him continuously, like a shower of sparks.

In the smoky dawn, the hurricane was still blowing. He was numb inside his soaked clothes and permanently cramped about the mast. His lips burned with salt and thirst, and the chattering of his teeth shook him so that all that he saw was blurred. The masts of the *Stadsholmen* still stood, canted to leeward, with men hanging in the rigging. Sometimes the water slid below like a crushed and frenzied river, and sometimes it leapt into tremendous, foaming seas that reached up for the men in the rigging. A mile or two to leeward, across a hell of water, there was some kind of a city, with the sea spouting white and high against a breakwater and blowing over the city like clouds of smoke. There was wreckage on the sea, and once the yellow mast of a ship was swept past the *Stadsholmen*. Ole thought of the black ship he had seen hove to the day before. As the mast rolled, he glimpsed something shapeless lashed to the top.

After some time, he perceived that Captain Dahl and the mate and Lundquist were in the rigging near him. Probably they had been there all the time. They looked exhausted and their faces were scarlet from the whipping spray. The four in the top were near each other, but they were not together. Each one was alone with himself. Ole tried to shout from the walls of his solitary misery that there is no God, but the wind drove his voice back upon him like the cracked chirruping of a bird. Uncle Olaf seemed to think he had asked for something, and hitched himself nearer, chafing his arms and legs with his great red hands. The boy shook, with chattering teeth, and could not stop. He only knew with his eyes that his uncle was touching him.

It was night again. The wind had died but mountainous white seas swept through the darkness and leapt up the mast. The mast shook with each sea. It might go any time, and he would go. The sooner the better. John was dead and there was no God. He was freezing outside, raging with thirst inside and vile with his own filth. John had died alone in the dark, deserted by his shipmates. The sea had rushed into the stateroom and found him sleeping like a beautiful girl. When he woke and cried out, alone in the dark with the monster, there was no one to help him.

Ole, too, would die like that in a little while, alone with the sea. Uncle Olaf would die, and Olsen and little Lundquist and great Johansen and all the others who had sailed out of Halmstad in the new ship. Perhaps some of them still wanted to live. He wanted to die. That would be much better than living through torment and going back to tell Fru Hedburg and Kristina how he had laid aloft to save himself and let John drown. He tried to locate his knife with a numbed hand. He could cut his lashings and be done with it. Then he remembered his uncle had tricked him and thrown the knife away. "There is no God," he said, and was able to hear his own voice at last. That gave him courage. He moistened his split lips and shouted into the darkness, across the frenzied sea, above the grave of his shipmate, "There is no God! There is no God!" It hurt his throat and cracked his lips still more, but he had the satisfaction of performing a duty and afterward felt much more composed.

They were rescued the following afternoon. Ole remembered indistinctly being lowered toward a white lifeboat. The boat was a great distance below him one instant and received him with a bump the next. He had no recollection of landing on the American shore.

In the hospital they tormented him by speaking English and giving him little sips of water. But he took some comfort in hearing Johansen's good Swedish voice roaring for water and plenty of it. One morning he woke in a white bed and was brought a tray of breakfast. It was surprising to find himself hungry and very much alive. Captain Dahl came in a little later, dressed in an extraordinary suit of gray clothes. He shook hands with Ole and asked him how he felt.

Ole considered and suddenly found there was nothing the matter with him. He was all for getting up at once.

Captain Dahl stroked his great beard and hesitated before speaking again. "They have found John Hedburg's body, Ole. I arranged to give him burial this afternoon. If you feel strong enough to attend, I shall bring you some clothes."

The service was in English. Ole listened intently but understood little other than "John Hedburg," and now and then "God," at which he ground his teeth. Once, he made out the solemn words, "Those who go down to the sea in ships." The young pastor intoned slowly, with great sadness. His voice was like the tolling of a bell. "Those who go down to the sea in ships."

Ole might have been back in the old Halmstad church.

Uncle Olaf was there beside him, with his beard resting on his deep chest. And the other members of the crew were there, as they had been at that farewell service. His gaze roved across the aisle to where the women and girls would be sitting. He half expected to find Kristina Hedburg turned toward him with her grave buoyant look. Instead, he saw only the rusty-haired steward weeping into a remarkable red and white handkerchief. Then he knew this service was a mockery of the other, and that the other had been a lie. Uncle Olaf's shoulders had a new droop under the coat that did not meet across his chest, and there was more gray in his beard. The *Stadsholmen's* crew were mocked by their outlandish, cast-off clothing. Kristina was far away, dreaming of her brother in the luminous Swedish night. And her brother lay before the altar in a closed coffin. (Captain Dahl had not let Ole see the body. He was shocked at the thought.)

The crew stood in a group at the cemetery during another prayer. Two grave diggers leaned on their shovels and some Negro children looked on from a little distance, like black trolls, wondering at all the fair Swedish heads bowed in the sunshine. The coffin was lowered into a hole partly filled with water. The grave was near a young palm tree, uprooted in the gale.

When they were driving to their hotel in a livery hack, Uncle Olaf talked to Ole as if they were men of the same age. He had arranged to send the crew back to Sweden, he explained—those who wished to go. Johansen and Peterson and Lundquist and Williams and some of the others had already found berths on ships in the port.

Olsen was going second mate in a steamer to South America. The *Stadsholmen* was a total loss. That sudden shift in the wind. Ten minutes more would have saved them. But there was no use talking about that. "It was God's will," Uncle Olaf said.

At the hotel Ole thought he would suffocate, indoors on a hot day in the company of a man who believed in God's will. "I think I'll take a walk," he said.

"Very well," his uncle agreed. "Try and be back for supper. About six, say. The Southern cooking is excellent. I remember a splendid restaurant where I ate when I was here in '66. If it is still in existence, I think we can find it."

"That would be fine, Uncle Olaf," the boy answered, picking up the floppy straw hat which had been provided for him.

The captain fumbled shyly in his unfamiliar pocket and handed Ole a huge silver coin. "It is a dollar," he said. "You might want to buy something."

Ole pocketed the dollar and went out, with a backward look over his shoulder. Uncle Olaf was walking quietly up and down, with his head bent in thought and his great beard resting on his folded arms. His dignified and alien figure overawed its badly fitting suit and the cheap hotel room. Ole never saw his uncle again.

On the water front an affable little man recognized him as a sailor and conversed with him in wretched Swedish. Out of the goodness of his heart, the little man advanced money for an outfit of clothes and shipped him off to Pisco, Peru, in a full-rigged ship that carried sky-sails and a remarkably brutal lot of officers. Ole had become an American seaman. The only comfort he got from his new berth was the circumstance that no one on board mentioned the name of God except in blasphemy.

When they were towing out to sea, they passed the wreck of the *Stadsholmen*, with the sea washing about her on the bar and gulls sitting white on her canted masts. Ole had shed no tears at the cemetery, but now he felt them choking him as he thought of his bright shipmate who had died there at the gateway of the new world. As he lingered by the bulwarks, a voice growled out behind him and a tremendous kick from the mate sent him about his business. His tears never fell.

V

Defeat of the Vikings

Ben was impressed with the incident of Ole's youth, but only up to a point. It must have been uncomfortable, having to cling in the *Stadsholmen's* rigging during that hurricane, but in the relationship between man and God it proved nothing. He told Ole so. Everything considered, the barque's crew had come out of it rather well. They might all have been lost.

Yes, Ole agreed, they might have been lost for all God cared. It was an accident they lived; it was another accident that John died. There was no God.

Captain Lindstrom darkened the doorway and listened, gravely pleased with the healthy sound of wrangling. Once he threw oil on the flame of Ole's indignation by quoting: "Not a sparrow falls to the ground without God noticing."

The stumpy seaman looked at him with infinite disgust.

"How can you believe rubbish?"

Even Ben did not take Christ's assurance in a literal sense. Naturally, whatever proved incongruous with the facts of existence was not to be taken literally.

"It is not a question of belief." The captain smiled over the nice point he was about to make. "It is a scientific fact. The earth's gravity attracts lesser bodies, but they also attract the earth to a lesser extent. The earth rises an infinite fraction of an inch to meet a falling sparrow. You spoke of someone who fell from the rigging of a ship. He weighed much more than a sparrow and would have moved the earth much more out of its course. A god of any sensitiveness could not have failed to notice."

Ole opened a little tin of snuff and measured a pinch. "And what does it prove?" He put the snuff in his cheek without waiting for a reply.

"It proves Christ knew what he was talking about."

The seaman pursed his long lips and thought. Then he asked: "Does a man hit any easier when the earth comes up to meet him?"

The captain answered truthfully, "Harder."

Ben fidgeted on the bench. The discussion wearied him. He dropped out of it altogether and lost himself in a dull reverie, comparing his childhood with Ole's. They were very different, Ole's in an old, substantial world that hardly changed in centuries; his own in a world hardly older than himself and growing up as he grew up. The two worlds didn't seem to have any relation to each other—except that both had led to the lightship and the bitter sea. Then it came to him that in both there was the same material, only he hadn't recognized it at first. He raised his drooping shoulders and head, looking in a kind of consternation, as if something remarkable had just happened in the rolling little cabin.

"You spoke about the young men who went to the lumber camps in America—" His voice cut through the argument between the seaman and captain, who looked at him expectantly. "You said they forgot Sweden."

"That is so," Ole agreed. "At least, in a little while they quit writing home."

"I know," the boy said with clairvoyant confidence. "They stopped writing home because they were dead." He clinched the matter by adding, "I went to their funerals."

Captain Lindstrom asked gravely, "Was it as bad as all that, Ben?"

Ben assured him it was, and plunged into a description of logging methods in which there was no thought of a morrow, either for forests or loggers.

"I know nothing about logging," the captain reminded him. "The general picture will do." Seating himself on Clark's bunk, he asked: "How do you come to know so much about it?"

The fireman looked at him stolidly. After a while he answered, "Because my father was sorry for sea captains."

The captain looked delighted. "I hope you are his son. You must tell us about it."

Ben's father, then a young medical student, had come to the Northwest for his health and taken a laborer's job with the largest sawmill in the world. They turned out a million feet of lumber a day; Ben showed a certain American pride in the fact. His father happened to take the fancy of the owner and his rise was like a magazine story of success. Until he became general manager and the double invoice system was explained to him: one invoice with what the ship called for, another with what was on hand or easiest to load on the ship. The consignee had the privilege of returning the lumber, at his own expense, from Buenos Aires or Hong Kong—or he could take it out on the man nearest him.

The former medical student sickened of watching captains sail away to trouble at far corners of the earth. "It hurt Father," Ben explained, "Captains are an innocent, trusting lot."

"I know," Captain Lindstrom agreed.

Ben's father stepped out quietly. He had grown up against the horizon, driving steers from Texas to fatten in Kansas. In the lumber industry he had his chance at wealth. After giving up his job, he never saw the horizon or money again. He bought some land on the Olympic Peninsula, near one of the southern fingers of Puget Sound, and started clearing it for a farm.

The captain looked startled. "It must have been a wild country," he suggested.

Ben, who had grown up there, had never thought of it in that light. "The Indians weren't hostile," he assured his listeners.

One judged that the hostility of Indians would have been superfluous. The land, which had to be taken on faith, was covered twenty feet deep with fallen trees and a hundred and fifty feet deep with standing ones. When the earth was finally uncovered, it was sour and poisoned by the hostile evergreens. Nothing that grew there could be sold for cash; the stores in town were owned by the logging company and they only paid in trade goods.

The boy's first recollection of the farm was seeing his

delicately brought up mother make bread by the light of a lamp which burned with a sickly yellow flame. It was not quite noon, she explained, but the cow had come home and the chickens gone to bed.

Ben knew these things were wont to happen with the coming of darkness and he was not experienced enough to see the fallacy of darkness at high noon. He centered his attention on the only remarkable feature of what was occurring: the fish-tailed flame of the lamp which finally burned in the stinging, pitchy gloom without illuminating anything. Later, when his mother paused in telling stories to remark that it was evening, there was a kind of sunrise in the west—where the big trees at the edge of the clearing began to blaze like torches. The saving rain chose that moment to begin.

That was known as the Dark Day. Ben thought the others, who hadn't seen it, would never believe a summer noon could be blacker than midnight.

"It is easy to believe," Ole said, spitting elegantly into the cuspidor. "I saw it."

"You did? Where were you?" Ben's eyes leaped with astonishment.

Ole was surprised at the question. "Why," he said, "I was here, of course. The coast from Vancouver Island to as far south as we could see was buried under smoke. When it blew out to sea it was like a fog, only nastier, and it made us cough. We had the whistle and bell going all one day. Mickey thought there was no sense in our wasting coal here because they were wasting wood ashore."

Ben considered it a fabulous coincidence that he and

Ole had once looked on from opposite sides of a thousand-mile forest fire. He plied the seaman for details until Captain Lindstrom reminded him he was off the course. . . .

The boy's father tried to escape the lumber industry, but he didn't escape its sight or sound or smell. All he had escaped was a share of the profits. In summer, the haze of burning slashings hung perpetually over the fifteen-acre clearing in its hollow square of fir trees. During the six months of rain—when sounds carried well—the tooting of donkey engines, the hollow roar of trains over trestles and the booming of logs going into the bay intruded on the stillness of the fields.

When a donkey whistle tooted rapidly for a long time, Ben said, you knew the man who had been hit was still alive. They were calling for a locomotive to take him to one of the two doctors in town. If he survived first aid, he was sent on the steamer the following morning to Olympia, where there was a hospital and where amputating was done.

The town belonged to the logging company. Railroad tracks ran on one side of the hideous main street. Long trains of flat-cars, pyramided with logs, went thundering through the town, with blond brakemen balancing on the topmost logs. (The logs would be white with snow from the foothills long before and long after there was any in the valley.)

Ben's family drove to town in the spring wagon every Sunday for Sunday school and church. The logging works had a habit of intruding funerals on the church service. They also intruded on the funerals. The minister's well-practiced words about "Death in the midst of life" were often punctuated out of all meaning by the compelling, slow "Boom, Boom, Boom," of logs being unloaded into the bay. Even the Methodist choir, singing "Nearer My God to Thee," would falter and look discouraged when a trainload of logs thundered by a short block away, vibrating the flimsy church and rattling the ghastly windows.

The child never questioned the necessity for a procession of young men going out of life, but he could not accept those windows. They were of rippled glass, stained to virulent red and purple and orange. He fancied that if he touched one of those windows with his tongue he would die a horrible death, and he never looked at them without feeling mortally ill.

No, Ben said, the Methodist church wasn't specially favored. There was a Baptist church a block away from the other side of the railroad tracks, and the Baptists got their share. Frequently, there was a funeral in each church. Sometimes, there was one service for several men. Like the time the snow brought down a tree across a railroad cut. A train with a pusher engine rushed through in a blinding snowstorm, early in the morning. The fallen tree just cleared the loaded cars; the brakemen, stationed at intervals on the topmost logs, saw nothing through the swirling snow and were mowed down one after another.

Captain Lindstrom thought figures would be interesting. Ben didn't have them, naturally. He only knew that casualties were high in those early days—what with a dangerous business run by rugged American individualism and employing men who drank insanely. He did remember one Memorial Day, in the cemetery which was on a dry prairie above the town. The children were picking wild strawberries among the graves and Ben wandered away and was lost. While he was lost, he came across a large, barren plot of ground with ordered rows of white-painted boards, as if a little army had fallen there. There was a fascinating monotony in the inscriptions:

JOHN LARSON

Killed June 2, 1909

IVAR SWANSON

Killed December 24, 1908

KARL STROMBERG

1889–1909

Killed May 6, 1909

LOUIS CARLSON

Killed October 5, 1909

CHRISTIAN NIELSON

1885–1908

Killed January 2, 1908

The inscriptions did not date back far; the black lettering was effaced in a year or two. One of the inscriptions particularly impressed Ben with its completeness:

OLAF BERGSON

Killed instantly by a falling tree

September 7, 1909

That plot may have been one of the reasons why Scandinavian women thought their sons became forgetful when they went to the lumber camps of the New World.

VI

The Box

THE three-days' argument on religion ended inconclu-
sively about two o'clock, when Captain Lindstrom
observed that the *Governor* was due. Harry had just come
from the galley, with a dish towel over his shoulder,
and scored a momentary victory for the forces of atheism.

"I just figured out why ministers dress in black," he
announced. "Black is the color of death, and wherever
holy people go their clothes remind others they have to
die. That means they should give to the church to help
them through the mess. It is a way of scaring money out
of people."

"There must be another reason," Mickey O'Rorke
said, and walked away.

"I believe you've got it, Harry," Clark declared.

"It's the old story of keeping people in ignorance and
superstition," Allen said.

Ben had listened to the argument for two days without putting in more than a question or two. To him the
value of religion was an established fact which could not
be argued away. Ole had kept clear of the dispute altogether, believing religion too cheap a fraud for serious
argument.

Captain Lindstrom put the argument back to where it

had started by remarking mildly, "Harry may be right about the reason for the clergy wearing black. But that doesn't prove anything, does it? It is true we must die And if religion assures us of a hereafter, clergymen and nuns do people a service by reminding them of the fact."

"But there isn't any." Clark said quietly.

"How do you know?" Ben asked doggedly.

That was the trouble. No proof could be offered for either of the positive, opposing opinions.

Oscar drifted by, following his sleek paunch and muttering to himself.

Allen called after him, "Oscar, come here a minute and help us out!"

Oscar stopped and half turned, looking at the group about the carpenter's bench out of one suspicious little eye. In silhouette he was rather like a penguin in overalls. "Heh?" he grunted.

Allen winked at Harry. "Oscar, how's your theology?"

Oscar wheeled in his original direction and stamped away, muttering savagely and lifting his fat legs high to deliver a series of thunderous, classical comments.

It was then that Captain Lindstrom made his remark about the *Governor* being due from San Francisco.

Ben slid from the bench and went forward to the companionway. He was sick of the diet of bread and soup and raisins to which the crew had been reduced. The *Governor* usually dropped a box of fresh meat and vegetables and oranges in passing. It was something to look forward to.

The little old Chief was standing on the steps, looking

up at the last of a flurry of snow. He moved over and Ben stopped beside him. Great white flakes drifted over the companionway like a vast flock of white butterflies. The air was filled with them, fresh and beautiful after the staleness of the 'tweendecks.

Mickey turned his old, cat-like face to the fireman and threw up one arm in a gesture of surrender. "Ben, Ben!" he cried. "Sometimes I don't know if there is any heaven or any God, or if Christ ever walked the earth, or if Mary was his mother. But I do know this: every snowflake is saying a prayer as it falls into the sea!"

Ben did not answer. Under the torture of beauty, the Chief's cry suggested something so much nobler than his unbathed and stunted self. It was like an Easter promise of resurrection.

The snow ceased all at once, as if the supply had run out, and Ben went on deck. A passenger steamer was coming up from the south, the *Governor*, he judged, but the weather did not look suitable for lowering a boat. The seas ran by sullenly, with a threat of becoming heavy with the least goading from the wind. The steamer was about eight miles off, standing close in toward the lightship. Ole, walking up and down the rolling deck with his arms folded over his chest, gave Ben an unsmiling nod. "There's the *Governor*," he said, but did not appear much interested.

Clark came on deck and stopped beside the boy at the rail. "She'll pass close," he observed. He had pulled on a blue sweater that reminded one of the breadth of his shoulders and the comparative narrowness of his hips. He looked almost youthful, except for his face and eyes.

"She'll pass close, holding that course." Ben liked the sound of Clark's voice; it was a deep voice, with an echo of something fine defeated.

The cook came up and sat on the skylight, with a greenish overcoat wrapped around his shoulders and his thick mop of hair standing up straight. Sometimes he looked at the approaching ship with greedy, wolfish eyes, and sometimes he bowed his unkempt head and rocked back and forth, moaning as if in pain.

The others were appearing on deck. Captain Lindstrom rested his arms on the rail and looked at the weather, undecided. Oscar sulked in a corner by the companionway. Old Mickey prowled about the steam winch until he found a grease cup that needed filling.

"Ben," he called, "bring the grease and give this a *dahsh*!" When the boy brought the grease he insisted on filling the cup himself, scolding under his breath, "Ben, Ben, you break me heart with your carelessness! Only yesterday I told you to fill these cups. See how long you would last with another chief!"

Mr. Gill boosted himself up on the companion slide, like the rising of the full moon, and looked with uncritical and benign eyes at the scene of scolding and indecision and insanity.

The *Governor* was coming up rapidly, growing in size as she came, developing a white bridge, passenger decks and lifeboats out of what had been a bulky blur of superstructure.

"Chief," the captain said, "get steam on the winch."

"Allen," Mickey called down the companionway, "steam on the winch!"

Presently the steam began to crack and thump through the cold pipes on deck. Oscar waddled up to the captain. "Going to lower the boat?" he asked suspiciously.

The captain looked at him mildly. "If they drop a box, and you and Clark want to go."

Oscar said nothing, but began overhauling the falls, which led through deck blocks to the winch which the chief was warming up.

When the *Governor* was about a quarter of a mile up wind, heading to pass the lightship at about the same distance, a ball of steam blossomed from her stack. Simultaneously, a white-coated figure on the lower deck poised a box over its head and then dropped it into the sea. Manna had fallen from heaven. Nothing remained but for two men in a fourteen-foot boat to row out and secure it. The rich note of the whistle boomed out pleasantly.

The wind had freshened a little and the seas ran gray and sullen, but the weather must have appeared calm enough from the bridge of the big steamship, where a good man was endangering the lives of others with an act of kindness.

Captain Lindstrom studied the sea to windward. "I don't like the looks of the weather," he observed. "Don't go unless you want some ugly work."

Clark and Oscar looked at each other.

"It doesn't look too good," Clark said.

"Yah, rotten!" Oscar muttered.

The ship loomed big as she passed, with passengers walking her deck and a few of them waving from the rail. A man and woman, walking from aft forward with the wind behind them, passed with startling speed. The beat of engines echoed about the lightship, giving her the illusion of being under way.

"O, Christ!" The cook threw off his overcoat and ran to the rail, with one arm raised. "The ship!" he cried. "There they have lights and music and women and dancing! In the morning they will be on the land. There will be houses and stores and cars. Here we have nothing and go nowhere!" He bowed his shaggy head on the rail, between his arms, and moaned.

Ole, the watchful, had followed the cook to the rail. Now he studied him with cool curiosity. "Like a wild animal," he observed. "Some day he will jump overboard when a ship passes."

Clark and Oscar were still standing inactive. The box which the steamship had dropped was nearly abreast, a yellowish box riding low in the gray sea a quarter of a mile off.

"It isn't worth the chance," Captain Lindstrom said.

Clark shook his head and Oscar observed, "Rotten!"

Ben watched the box disconsolately.

Then, when it had been settled that the risk was too great and everything against the attempt, Clark and Oscar moved by a common impulse, obscure and contrary, and climbed into the little boat. Clark put in the plug and the oars were got ready. "Lower away when you like," Clark said.

Mickey sprang gleefully to the winch lever and Captain Lindstrom studied the seas. After a minute he made a downward gesture with one hand. "Lower away!"

The boat descended smoothly. Then the lightship

rolled down her starboard side and a long sea picked up the boat. Clark and Oscar cast off the hooks as the tackles fell slack and got out their oars almost instantly. They rowed strongly and evenly on a diagonal course to windward and seaward, heading up a little when a sea was steeper than the others.

Ole spat over the side. "They won't make it now," he said quietly. "If they were going, they should have started before the box drifted down."

It did not seem so certain, however, that the two seamen would not make it. They were drawing away rapidly and the box was not far off, just abreast of the lightship. They headed up into a sea that threatened to break and then stood out again, rowing strongly. The box was not much more than a hundred yards from them. Clark's powerful blue figure and Oscar's dumpy yellow one diminished and became impersonal objects in an impersonal struggle. The tossing red boat was like a toy.

Everyone was lined up at the rail, except the cook. He had gone back to huddle on the skylight, moaning after his vision of electric lights and music and dancing.

"I hope they make it," little Harry said vehemently. "They had their nerve going out in this!"

They're the boys to do it," Mr. Gill declared placidly, filling his pipe.

"They can't do it," Ole insisted woodenly. "See how far the box has drifted."

It became plain to everyone that the thing was not working out. Clark and Oscar were heading in the direction where the box had been, but it was not there now. It was some distance off and abreast of them. The boat itself had actually fallen astern and was being carried off in the powerful current that set north toward Vancouver Island.

"They've had enough of that," the captain observed suddenly, and walked forward to where the whistle cord entered the pilot house.

The men had already seen their predicament and were heading back toward the lightship. At first it appeared that they would have no trouble making it. Each time they rose with a sea, they seemed nearer. Yet, as minutes passed, everyone had to look a little farther aft to see them. They were working in toward the ship but gaining nothing to windward. If anything, they were falling astern. Clark, nearest the bow, was rowing with savage strength, but Oscar's nicely-handled oars seemed to have no power in them.

When the little boat came in line with the ship, it was a hundred yards astern. In the straight row against wind and current, the boat rose and fell without changing its distance. Clark's fine back and shoulders heaved with a steady flow of power that held the current at bay without being able to overcome it. The crew had gathered aft to watch the struggle. The box which the men had gone to retrieve drifted into the distance, quite forgotten. It had become a question if they could save themselves.

After a while it became plain that the boat was farther away. Clark's arms and back kept up their rhythm, but they had become diminished, spidery members, struggling forlornly in the gray immensity of the ocean.

"A squall is coming up." Ole's even voice broke the silence.

The men looked at the gathering grayness to windward, then at each other.

"We ought to do something about Oscar and Clark!" Harry declared passionately.

"What shall we do for them?" Mickey asked pointedly.

"Go after them!"

"In what?"

Harry was not novice enough to suggest moving the lightship from her station, which would have been comparable to taking away an important lighthouse to look for someone lost in the woods. "We could take the other boat," he said. "I can row."

Ole pursed his long lips and shook his head. "Four of us in the twenty-foot boat wouldn't make out as well as two in the little one. We'd all land up on The Graveyard, and leave the ship with no crew."

"But we can't let them go!" Harry blinked away angry tears. The toy boat was dwindling astern, like something unimportant and already past, but the great-hearted little man was fired with the same spark that kept the toy figures at their losing fight. "We must do something! Where's the captain?"

The captain had already sized up the situation and gone below.

"In the morning they will go ashore and walk on streets where there are stores and theatres and cars!" the cook proclaimed, breaking into the group and glaring about savagely. "Stores and crowds of people. Here we have nothing!" No one paid any attention to him except Ole, who measured the distance between the man and the rail with calculating eyes.

Captain Lindstrom passed through the group quietly, with a big reel of cotton rope and a white wooden float in his arms. Ole took the reel without comment and let the tough little rope run out as the captain dropped the float over the taffrail. At first it merely bobbed astern, then a sea carried it away and it began to drift rapidly with the current and wind. Ole unwound the line smoothly, never letting it out too fast and never checking the drift of the float. The captain guided it over the rail, now and then looking over his shoulder toward the gathering squall.

The white float dwindled on the gray seas, but ate up the distance bravely. Now it was half way to the tossing boat where Clark and Oscar carried on their losing fight. It was three quarters of the distance, almost in line with the stern of the lightship and the boat. The squall still held off, though it might come down any minute. The white float rose in clear sight, two seas away from the boat. Ole unwound more line, smoothly, with wooden gravity. There was not much more on the reel. "About fifteen fathoms left," he reported.

Captain Lindstrom glanced over his shoulder. "Ben, there is a new heaving line in the pilot house. Have it ready."

The boy ran forward, but the little messman was there ahead of him, holding the door open as his contribution to the rescue.

It did not seem that the extra line would be necessary. The boat and the white block rose on the same wave, ten fathoms or so apart. Ole continued to unwind. The float disappeared for a few unpleasant seconds. Then it rose triumphantly one sea astern, where it would be in plain sight of the rowers.

"Belay," the captain said quietly.

Nothing remained but for Clark and Oscar to head over a little and pick up the line. A minute passed and they were still heading for the lightship, rowing with forlorn desperation and losing ground.

"They don't see it," Harry lamented.

That seemed highly improbable.

"Chief," Harry suggested, "can't you get your gun and fire it to attract their attention?"

"Yes, they ought to be shot if they can't see that," Ole commented.

Captain Lindstrom scratched his head. His worried face was faintly amused. "Blow a long blast on the whistle," he said.

Harry sped limping forward and hung on the whistle cord until Mr. Gill went after him and pulled him off. 'You'll take all the steam out of the boiler," he remonstrated gently.

In answer to the minute-long whistle blast, Clark's back and arms labored with the fury of desperation and Oscar's oars seemed to gain a little power. Still they did not head over toward the line.

The thing became ludicrous: two men fighting for their lives with salvation staring them in the face and getting bored waiting. The gray squall that was blotting out the sea to windward was not so funny.

"Ben," the captain ordered, "four *short* blasts on the whistle!"

Then, while the boy was still running forward, the

boat headed over. A few great strokes, and Clark pulled in his oars and reached over the side. Oscar's weary oars were folded away and Clark waved one arm to signify the line was fast.

"Bear a hand, gently, now, and steady!"

The crew strung out along the deck and pulled in the line, with Ole coiling it away neatly. There were willing hands enough, but there was also a quarter of a mile of line to come in. Harry was soon panting and Ben's face was tense with effort as he heaved. The others were taking it a little more easily.

"Byes, byes, you're killing yourselves!" the chief declared, jumping about and hitching up his old pants. "Captain, if you lead the line to the winch, I'll give it a dahsh of steam."

It was not a bad idea. Ole cleared the drum of the boat falls and took a turn with the line. Mickey braced himself at the lever, gleefully, like a child playing engineer with a real engine.

"Heave away, gently."

The winch chattered steadily, with Ole taking in the slack and Captain Lindstrom watching the boat astern. Wind and rain swept over the ship as the squall broke. Everyone was immediately wet through without noticing it. The little boat dropped out of sight in the trough, then rose buoyantly, with rain and spray flying over the two men. They were crouching to offer less resistance to the wind. They vanished completely in every trough, only to reappear closer. It became possible to make out Clark's features; he was facing forward, with his shoulders hunched, looking grimly amused. Oscar kept his back to his rescuers, slumped down on the after thwart like a discouraged yellow haystack in the rain.

"Easy, now." The boat danced up one sea away from the pointed stern of the lightship. "Avast heaving."

The line was cleared and handed forward, with Clark and Oscar sliding out their oars to keep clear of the rolling ship. They were looking up at the faces along the rail, Clark faintly apologetic and amused and Oscar disgusted.

Mickey crowed down triumphantly, "The byes can row away, but it takes the steam to bring them back!"

Oscar glared hatred at the little man, and when he had got the hook in the stern ring-bolt he shook his fist. But Mickey was back at the winch, still beaming with triumph as he carried out the order to heave away.

The dripping red boat was hoisted level with the deck. A few gallons of water poured out when Clark removed the plug. The fourteen-foot craft had done very well. Oscar went directly to the chief at the winch and shook a fat fist under his nose.

"You laughed at us!" he choked. "You laughed!" His little eyes were blazing. "You try it out there! Laugh! Rotten, by God! People are rotten!"

Mickey did not understand what it was all about. He saw no harm in having expressed elation when his department scored in the rescue. So he merely blinked up with his faded old eyes and the face of a puzzled cat until the seaman stamped below, muttering to himself.

Clark was explaining to the captain. "I saw the float directly it drifted by," he said, breathing heavily. "But I supposed it was just something adrift. I didn't pay any more attention to it. When you blew the whistle, I thought you were recalling us to the ship. And we were already doing our best to get back. It wasn't until later I noticed the thing wasn't drifting any more. Just then Oscar said, 'There's a line on that.' Then I saw it, too. A good thing; I was getting played out."

The crew settled back to routine, and the incident of the box became a subject for academic discussion to everyone but Harry and Oscar. The little messman treated Clark with a new interest and respect, and listened patiently to Oscar's angry railing against the chief.

Oscar's struggle with the sea and Mickey's gleeful outburst had started a ferment in the sleek old seaman's mind. He became almost articulate and showed everyone the three stubs of his missing fingers. They had handicapped his rowing, he explained. If he had put all his strength into his good hand, Clark would not have been able to pull evenly. After his maimed hand gave out, he had had to row as if both of them were crippled. It was rotten, he said. And it was rotten that the chief had laughed. By the third day he had become almost voluble. He even told a curious story about himself, resentfully, but in some detail.

VII

Little Oscar

BEN lay awake in his bunk, thinking about the thing that had happened to Oscar when he was a boy on the training ship. The story held him with a morbid fascination. Or perhaps it was natural. He didn't know, Ben was eighteen and mature for his age, and he had never been with a woman. He was in about the same situation as little Oscar.

Not quite. Ben at least had an idea of what it was all about. He had grown up on a farm and been around with boys and heard a lot of talk. Oscar hadn't even those advantages. Ben imagined what he was like at fifteen: a plump, pretty boy with a soft mouth, blue eyes and yellow hair. Quite a baby, no doubt. Brought up in the mountains by two maiden aunts. They must have been fanatics: so holy and never saying anything about sex. Not like the Swedes Ben had known, who sometimes made him blush with their natural frankness. When Oscar asked questions they hushed him up; it was something too sacred to talk about. When he got to be a man he would find out. Until then he must keep his mind pure. How would he have dirtied his mind thinking about something sacred? That was always the hitch with religious people who were ashamed to tell.

Oscar saw there was something behind it. A real religious mystery one didn't have to take on faith when he got to be a man. Grown people did something children didn't do. It took a man and a woman, he thought. There was a difference between them, more than showed with their clothes on, but he didn't know what it was. While he was still younger, he thought women didn't have to go to the out-house; something about his aunt's purity may have suggested that. Afterward he discovered that they went, although they tried to conceal the fact, and they seemed less perfect in his eyes. Oscar had put the matter more bluntly.

Sometime after he had decided the sacred mystery was between men and women, the boy made up his mind that his aunts didn't take part in it, which was strange when they strove for holiness in all other directions. The only man who came to the house was the pastor, and Oscar was always there to see what happened. The two women and the man did nothing but eat cakes and drink tea and talk, talk, about purity and sanctification and religious experiences. Only, when the aunts were tidying up the perfect house and getting the tea things ready, they fluttered a great deal. And after the man was gone, they talked and talked about what he had said, with a kind of urgent excitement, so their words said one thing and their voices another. Oscar could feel the excitement, but didn't know what it was.

Once he thought something would happen. The time the pastor told of another pastor who became perfect in holiness and succeeded in raising a woman from the dead. They were all greatly excited. In her excitement,

Aunt Minnie got up and came close to the pastor; so close she almost touched him. She became different, too. Her cheeks got pink and her eyes were bright, and Oscar could see her breast rise and fall when she breathed. She looked so young and different the boy wasn't sure who she was. Her face made him think she was the woman who had been raised from the dead. Then he looked at her dress and knew she was Aunt Minnie. Only she was so changed and excited. She didn't seem to be sure who she was, either, and Oscar thought she wanted the pastor to raise *her* from the dead. But that didn't seem to mean anything because she was alive already.

Afterward, the boy determined to become a pastor; he was sure the call would come to him. He was going to live a life of perfect holiness and go around raising women from the dead. That would be exciting.

Ben didn't think Oscar had managed better than any other boy who had been told to keep his thoughts pure. He went right on wondering about what men and women did together. And he decided his aunts and the pastor didn't do it because the pastor didn't stay long enough. Maybe his being there had something to do with it, too. He tried going outside and watching through the window, but it didn't make any difference. He wanted to give them every opportunity.

He thought the opportunity had come the time the pastor was detained at the house overnight during the great snowstorm. His aunts were excited, too, and made themselves ridiculous doing all kinds of things for the man's comfort. When they started to make up a bed in the parlor for their guest, little Oscar was disappointed.

He asked why the pastor couldn't sleep with Aunt Selma in her big bed upstairs. Aunt Selma pretended not to hear, but the pastor blushed very red and Aunt Minnie gave the boy a furious slap and sent him to bed.

That must have puzzled the young innocent a good deal, Ben decided. Getting slapped and hustled away for trying to give a pastor and a sanctified woman the opportunity to do something sacred.

Oscar hadn't said how he came to join the training ship at the age of fifteen. The Swedes seemed to take it for granted that the sea was a proper career for a boy. It might have been his aunts' idea. Anyway, they didn't seem to have been concerned. They took him on the railroad train to Gottenborg and saw him installed in the big sailing ship. After Aunt Minnie had reminded him to say his prayers every night, and Aunt Selma warned him against bad words and impure thoughts, they jolted out of his life: two good ladies sitting thin and upright in a cart. No doubt they were comforted by the thought of having done everything humanly possible to prepare their nephew for the sinful world.

The boys in the training ship must have been precocious; some of them, anyway. Oscar said he wasn't the youngest. None of them was over eighteen, but more than a few had been on foreign voyages and had experiences. There was the kind of talk a boy hears when he gets with boys of his own age and a little older. Plump, pretty little Oscar listened with ears like ventilators. There was no one to tell him it wasn't the kind of talk for a boy of fifteen; and there wasn't anyone to slap him when he asked questions. Though the older boys laughed immoderately at some of them.

They cleared up a good deal of the surrounding mystery. One didn't have to wait until he was married—that was a joke. And as for waiting until he got to be a man—that was the way to become a man. There was nothing to it. You just picked up a woman and went to her room and did it. Afterward, you paid her a *kroner* or two.

Oscar wanted to know what it was like.

That brought quite a laugh. It was wonderful, but the boys couldn't tell him much about it. They weren't too sure of themselves, and beyond a certain point they were as prudish as Aunt Minnie. He would have to find out for himself.

So it was a real mystery, something that couldn't be communicated. Oscar was eager to find out for himself, only he didn't know how to go about it.

There was really nothing to it, the older boys said. In all the cities there were beautiful big houses for the purpose, and wherever you went ashore there were women on the street who let you do it for a few coins. They laughed again when Oscar asked if the women didn't mind. That was the way they made their living; some of them were rich ladies. They stopped you on the street and asked you, and you went with the one you liked. It was best in a foreign port, though. In Sweden someone might recognize you, or a policeman might see your uniform and ask questions.

So Oscar found out everything without really finding out anything, except that the sacred mystery of his aunts was an exchange of love between a man and a woman; the act that had generated him and everyone else in the world. It was odd that it should be sold, but he fancied that part of it was something like putting money in the collection box in church. The boys had omitted details. They gave Oscar credit for knowing something, whereas he knew nothing.

It was near midnight, but Ben could not sleep. The thing kept working in his mind. He, too, knew everything, much more than Oscar had known, without really knowing anything. The weather must have cleared. The whistle and then the bell had stopped and the ship was silent except for a thump from the forepeak as she settled back on the mooring chain with each sea. The little stateroom was dark, but some light came as far as the door from the lamp that burned low in the messroom.

Sometime Ben would find out everything. He had heard much more at home than Oscar, but it did not seem to help. There had been so much about disgrace and disease and death and the startling ease with which girls can be ruined. It seemed to him that life without love would be a dead, meaningless affair. But the things he confidently expected, the excitement and peace and beauty, were so tangled in his mind with ugliness and danger that he was repelled as strongly as he was attracted. If he had the opportunity now, tonight, he wouldn't have the nerve. His whole training, home, school and church, would shout out against it. He would be deafened and paralyzed by those warning shouts. Everything in his life was against it—except the impulse those things hadn't been able to kill. And he knew that in the end the impulse would win.

Sooner or later he would cross the threshold, and the

din of warning would be shut out as if he had closed a door. If he only knew what he would find on the other side of the door! Little Oscar had found what others discovered to be beautiful or thrilling or necessary, and to him it had only been ugly and terrifying.

Ben could visualize the scene up to a certain point, but after that he was in darkness. At night in London, somewhere across the Thames from the Isle of Dogs. Soft, pink-faced little Oscar in his neat schoolship uniform, in a murky upstairs room with a big, coarse-voiced woman. Frightened at the strange dark nook in a foreign city, and at the red-faced woman who spoke to him harshly in a foreign language full of hard "k" sounds. Six weeks before, the boy had been saying his prayers and climbing into his pure little bed opposite the window that looked out on saintly mountains, crowned with snow.

Little Oscar hiding his face in the corner when the woman began taking off her clothes. He hadn't understood that part of it. Even then, he only thought she was changing her dress.

Presently, the woman called to him, impatiently. She was ready he thought, and became more panicky because he didn't know what was expected of him. When he turned, the whole thing became a terror. The room was full of dancing shadows and the flickering gaslight played fitfully over the obscene mysteries of the woman on the bed. That finished him. He didn't want to do anything but get away. Oscar became a very little boy again, much younger than fifteen. A child full of unreasonable terrors.

He ran quaking to the door and found it locked. But he didn't go to pieces completely until he looked back. It wasn't even the woman coming after him that did it. It was the sight of a child's foot sticking out from under the bed.

Ben couldn't quite visualize the rest. It was veiled in the mysterious gloom of a long-ago London night, and his own ignorance. He didn't believe that part about the child's bare foot. Oscar had thought he was in the den of a monster who fed on children, and he imagined the details. After all, he got out alive, with nothing more happening than what he came for. The woman only took two shillings from him, and he didn't get a disease. It could have been much worse, Ben thought. Yet it seemed that for Oscar it couldn't have been worse. At the time he felt nothing but terror and disgust. And afterward he hated his dead parents and nearly everyone else but his aunts for having been soiled by the thing. And he hated his aunts for lying to him about sacredness and love. It was rotten, he said. That may have been when he began saying everything was rotten.

Oscar had other women afterward, but it was always rotten, he said. People were animals. He was an animal. It was a rotten business. Ben didn't believe that, but it was his faith against Oscar's experience. Supposing Oscar were right? What if love proved to be a rotten lie? He had plenty of confidence it wouldn't happen that way. Even Oscar's brutal experience had its fascination. It excited the boy and would not let him sleep.

He was still pondering it when Allen Ross entered the room with considerate quietness.

"Hello."

"Not asleep yet?"

"What time is it?"

"Seven bells." The shadowy figure moved the bench over and stood on it. "I was after a cigarette." The figure descended and sat astride of the bench. The boy blinked at the flaring match.

"I didn't expect to find you awake."

"I was thinking about Oscar. That time in London."

"Yes?" The cigarette glow lit up Allen's bright, homely face and a span of his bald young head. "The big jade gave him his fifty cents' worth, didn't she?"

"I expect she did. But I don't see why he should have been scared," Ben lied in the hope of information.

"Well, he's not the first one to have been scared. He wasn't ready; he wasn't prepared for it."

"Not old enough?"

"That was part of it. But mostly his mind wasn't prepared."

"Oh." Ben saw, but not clearly.

"It was the fault of Aunt Selma, and the other one. All the Aunt Selmas aren't dead yet, either. The boy got fed too much religion and not enough facts." Ross's face appeared and disappeared in the darkness with the pulsing of his cigarette. "And it's not all clear sailing the first time with a woman. It takes confidence, and usually you don't have it without experience."

Ben had been afraid of something of the kind. "I suppose not," he said.

"And Oscar was worse off than the average, not knowing anything. I bet he was scared plenty."

"You don't believe that about his seeing a child's foot under the bed, do you?"

"Sure. Only it wasn't the way he thought. The English have to have their home-life—even the whores, I suppose. This one had a child, and they lived in one room. He was taught to hide under the bed when his mother was waiting on a customer. I've heard of that sort of thing in Limehouse. Oscar wouldn't have seen even a foot except that he bolted for the door."

Ben felt vastly relieved that there hadn't been a child's corpse under the bed. His shipmate had cleared that murky London room of its nameless terror. It became the pathetic and understandable story of two children, and a woman who took from one to feed the other. Only what the woman had done was not entirely understandable.

"Would any woman have done what that one did to Oscar?" he asked anxiously. All the implications of his home teaching and the tone of the religious-medical book in his father's library suggested that a woman never did more than submit in passive martyrdom.

"Not every one," Allen thought. "Some would have been more gentle. This one may have been the kind that goes wild when they know it's the first time for a boy. Or maybe she needed the two shillings and was afraid to take it without giving him something for his money, whether he liked it or not. She gave him plenty, anyway."

Ben was still troubled a little. "Even if Oscar didn't know what it was all about when he started, he found out, didn't he? He got what others have liked. You've said it was beautiful. And he found it beastly." He was querulous and impatient, mostly with himself for knowing so little and thinking so much on the subject. He felt at a disadvantage with Ross, who was widely experienced with women. He didn't envy his roommate, who had had the gonorrhea and was therefore not quite clean physically. But it irked him that he was the cleaner mentally. He talked about everything naturally, with a kind of rough good taste. And he never harped on physical details, as Ben did in his mind. There ought to be some state between being clean physically and a little dirty mentally, and clean mentally and damaged physically. But how were you to manage it?

Another match flared and the homely, reassuring face came out in the darkness again. "I didn't say it was beautiful; I said it could be. Lots of men never find it that way. Most of them feel something the way Oscar does. I've talked a lot to whores, and learned a lot from them. When they're through, most men feel disgusted. They're ashamed and haven't any respect for themselves or the whores. And some of them have no respect for their wives, either, because they do the same thing as whores. A man like that tries to get back his respect by blaming the whore—gets virtuous after he's had what he wants and abuses her for being in that kind of business." Allen's sarcastic smile came out in the cigarette glow like the grin of a Cheshire cat. "No, I guess it isn't beautiful very often."

"Wouldn't it have made a lot of difference if Oscar hadn't been with that big, coarse prostitute?" Ben asked hopefully. The word "whore" grated on his ears and he couldn't bring himself to say it with any naturalness.

Allen was silent a little, considering, with his eyebrows wrinkling together in the cigarette glow. "There are all kinds of women, in a way, but they're all women and a lot alike. And they're pretty good and square if you treat them decently. It's something like your Joseph Conrad said about ships: 'It's not the ships, it's the men.'"

"But a boy with a big, coarse woman like that—" Ben harped on the subject, perversely fascinated by the Amazon of Oscar's adventure.

"You mean it would have all been different if it had been a trim, beautiful young thing. Not a whore at all, but a refined girl from a good family. Maybe her first time, too?"

"Something like that." It was the ideal situation Ben had pictured.

"I knew a boy who had his first time with a girl like that," Allen observed. "She was a little beauty, too."

"And didn't it make a difference to the boy?" Ben wanted to know.

"It was different from Oscar's case, all right. After it was over, the boy killed her."

"Killed her?" Ben was horrified. He had been thinking of the boy as himself.

"Strangled her to death," Allen explained.

"But why?"

"He felt dirtied, I suppose, and he blamed her. Probably she was to blame, if you want to call it that. She had a lot of fire in her, and she loved him. I suppose she started it."

"But why should he have felt dirtied when she was

young and clean and beautiful?" Ben was at as much of a loss as ever. A boy choking a girl to death in return for the perfect gift of herself!

Allen's face came out in the darkness again with the pulse of his cigarette. "At first, after it's over, a man feels something like disgust, not that it's always as strong as that. Maybe I have the wrong word. But there's a sort of rebound. He's had enough and a little too much. The things about the woman that seemed so attractive before get to be too much. A woman doesn't feel that way. Usually, she's harder to start, but after she's started she doesn't turn back, like a man. And she's more loving than ever. When this girl was like that, all affectionate after it was over, it probably disgusted the boy to where he couldn't stand it. He was very religious, too. Everything he'd heard about sin and the flesh and the wickedness of women all fitted in with his feeling of disgust. The girl's beauty didn't help a bit, and her loving him made it worse. Probably she seemed like a kind of monster to him: too hot and too much for him and wanting more. The only way to get rid of her was to kill her. It was his religious nature and training that did it. I suppose it was what they call a religious murder. The boy said afterward he thought he was struggling with the devil when he killed her. The poor kid looked like the devil, all right, when he had finished choking her."

Ben lay back in his bunk, feeling ill. Supposing he had been the boy? But he would never have done that; it wouldn't have ended that way. He believed in God, but he also believed in love and would have suffered a good deal for it. In his mind he was already committed to the flesh, and once he started he wouldn't turn back.

Footsteps coming forward. Clark's tall figure, heavy-shouldered and slightly stooped, passed through the mess room and disappeared in the darkened doorway of the room he shared with Ole. There was something encouraging in the glimpse of the big seaman. Ben had never heard him talk about women, but when others said this or that about them there was a look in his face as if he was remembering something fine.

The boy half sat up, propping one elbow against his pillow. "It doesn't happen that way very often, does it?" he asked, "that a man should want to kill the girl?"

Allen's reassuring smile came out in the darkness. "It's the only case I know of where he actually did, anyway."

Clark's figure retreated through the mess room, into the alleyway. The watch had been called. Ben felt better; his mind was more at ease than it had been before that horrible story. One point still troubled him, however, "About the disgust," he said, "I didn't know it would be like that."

"It's nothing much," the fireman assured him. "It would hardly matter at all if you were prepared for it And afterward it goes away altogether—unless you've made up your mind that it's a dirty business. If you're that kind, I suppose you never get over it, and you try every time to make yourself clean by giving a woman hell for doing what you wanted. It's all in the way a man thinks about it." Allen located the cuspidor by the glow of his cigarette stub, which he dropped to a wet death. "I'll give the fires a 'dahsh' of coal," he said, rising. "I cleaned them just before I came up."

"Turn in and don't bother with them." Ben swung his feet to the floor and began feeling for his shoes.

"You'll want a cup of coffee," his roommate said, going out.

Ben found his left shoe and began putting it on—to make sure he wouldn't lose it while searching for the other. There was a lamp on the bulkhead, but the darkness was more friendly. A ship that exists to give light should have its haven of darkness inside.

Ole entered the mess room from another dark cubicle and passed through, hitching up his breeches with a two-handed gesture that seemed a part of his rolling walk. Ben found his other shoe and started lacing it. He could have slept peacefully, now that it was time to begin his watch. Not really tired, but a little sleepy, and his mind which had kept him awake was now at rest. It made him feel strong to know that an embrace with a woman was not something to which a man abandoned himself, but a responsibility and an art to be learned. And a man found there whatever was in his own mind: beauty, or shame and ugliness.

As he passed through the mess room, on his way to the galley for coffee, he heard old Oscar turn over in his sleep and say "Blah!" less with his voice than with his stomach—as if he wished to vomit up life, whose taste he found revolting.

The galley lamp was lit and Harry was poking about when he should have been asleep. "I found a jar of marmalade, Ben. I thought you might like some." He looked at the boy with hope and apology. "Do you suppose the others think I'm lying down on the job? I know there should be a midnight lunch every night, but there isn't anything to set out. I tell you, it's no fun!"

"Why worry?" Ben asked. "It's the cook who lies down on the job, while you do his work and your own." He helped himself from the jar, which Harry steadied lest it be knocked onto the floor by a roll of the ship and its precious contents lost. When the marmalade used to appear on the table the crew referred to it as celluloid shavings in vaseline; it was poor stuff, but spread on pilot bread it was better than rancid butter.

Harry had more than the midnight lunch on his mind. Some kind of excitement was passing through his frail body like a powerful current of electricity. After a while he cried out abruptly, "I would like to put all the religion in the world in a bag and drop it into the sea!"

Ben never felt like arguing with Harry. He was sorry for him and puzzled. Harry was so small and gentle that the violent things he sometimes said were unsuited to his body; they seemed to tear him to pieces without having any effect on others. The boy murmured his sympathy, not with the sentiment but with the man.

"I've been thinking of the story Oscar told us this afternoon," the messman explained. "It wouldn't let me sleep."

So Ben wasn't the only one.

"Those two religious old ladies ruined his life." Harry nodded mournfully. "Such a waste; the waste of a life! Oscar has fine qualities, but he's still just a little boy ashamed of knowing something that should be as natural as eating and drinking. That's why he can't look anyone in the face. Religious people are worse than murderers when they have any say about sex.''

The boy murmured again and gulped his coffee.

"It reminds me of a book Mrs. Bell had," Harry went on. "According to the title, it was scientific. But it was a mixture of sermons about Jesus and lies about men and women. Probably it's made more misery in the world than the plague, but Mrs. Bell thought it was the gospel.''

"Who was Mrs. Bell?" the boy inquired.

"My wife, of course.''

It had never occurred to Ben that Harry might have a last name, and as for a wife— Yet he should have known it. Harry looked for all the world like a henpecked little husband. His wife had no doubt weighed two hundred pounds and ruled with a hand of iron. "I didn't know you had been married," he commented politely.

Harry sighed. "Maybe I still am.''

"You don't know?"

"No. I was back once for three days, and then I went away. It was too much, oh, it was too much!''

Ben was embarrassed and he felt too inexperienced to make any comment. He rinsed his cup at the sink and guessed he'd better have a look at the fires. He hadn't supposed all the wives in the world could generate the current of agony he had seen tear through the little messman when he said, "It was too much!''

Harry's thoughts went on when he was alone. He was glad the fireman hadn't asked any questions. It would be impossible to tell anyone about those three nights—those three days and nights—before he slipped down to West Street and gave himself up to the crimps again. He'd had a hard life, but sometimes he thought Mrs. Bell got the worst of it.

VIII

Daughter of Crazy Horse

THEY traveled west toward the river through the hottest night of summer. The man was burdened with the tepee which was too heavy for him. The girl was not yet four and she had already walked a long way when she should have been asleep. She was a small child, even for her age, and she appeared still smaller pushing her way through the palpable sticky web of the dusk. The father shifted the tepee from under his arm to his tired shoulder and looked down at the lagging little figure, self-reproachful for having brought her on such a journey. She stopped altogether, looking ahead steadfastly. He stopped to wait for her, but her feet began moving again after a moment. A wagon went by, with the horses' feet clucking in the melted asphalt and the wheels making a sound like falling rain.

The child took a few quicker steps until she was ahead of her father, then turned, blocking his way and holding up her arms.

"Carry me, Daddy. I'm so tired."

He stooped and picked her up with his free arm. Her arms settled about his neck and her damp cheek pressed against his. The folded tepee ground his shoulder. The wagon was drawing away ahead of them, with its wheels on the hot asphalt still making the tormenting sound of rain, like a shower passing without drops or coolness.

"Didn't I walk a long way without asking you to carry me?"

"You were very good," he said. "We'll be home soon, now."

She took one arm from round his neck and pushed the damp hair from her face.

"Daddy."

"What is it, Martha?"

"My hair ribbon came off."

"Never mind."

She leaned over perilously and stuffed the ribbon into the breast pocket of his coat.

At Sixth Avenue and Clinton Place he put her down. It was as far as he had strength to carry her, and they had to wait for the traffic. Carriages sped, wagons clattered and drays rumbled over the cobble stones. An automobile grunted past, guided by a beautiful young lady who chatted casually with the gentleman beside her. Harry felt sure she was one of the Astors or Vanderbilts. "Get a horse!" a boy called rudely. The young lady tossed her head and said something to her companion. He flicked the ash from his cigar with one hand while he twirled one of his moustaches with the other. He was probably a young rake, but a perfect gentleman. Sticky fingers and a warm mouth pressed against Harry's hand. He hardly noticed at first. When he looked down, Martha was holding his hand in both hers, kissing it.

"For carrying me," she explained between kisses.

The traffic changed. Harry balanced the tepee on his shoulder and took Martha firmly by the wrist for the crossing. "Come on," he said. His shirt sticking to his back and arms, irritated him.

Martha squirmed her wrist out of the grip of his fingers and looked up belligerently without moving.

"Hold my hand." From babyhood she had rebelled against being treated like a piece of baggage. He gave her his hand because he was too tired to argue and she was in the right.

They crossed and started up Greenwich Avenue, in the shadow of Jefferson Market. The ugly walls and towers of the prison exhaled heat, as if their red, dull glow had been produced in a furnace. Martha drooped and lagged behind. The awkward tepee gnawed at the man's shoulder and the dismal heat of the pavement stung through the soles of his shoes. A barrel organ blared out close by—so suddenly that Harry's heat-dulled brain could not tell him at once what it was. Darkness going up in spontaneous combustion. Or maybe the seed of some tropical vine dropped in the hot and fertile gutter. Bang! The seed exploding into growth, going up a foot a second. Every crashing note a gaudy flower, the plaintive ones twisting vine and leaves. Imagine something like that happening in New York! Would they call out the police reserves? The fire department, probably, with ladders and axes. Not that they could cut it down. Growing sixty feet a minute and spreading in all directions over Greenwich Avenue. All of them together couldn't do anything about it. Only when the Ginney got to the end of the barrel organ piece the great vine and leaves and flowers would disappear. They wouldn't go away exactly, but they wouldn't be there any more. Then the firemen and all would go home and know they had been crazy with the heat, trying to cut down a music tree.

Harry stopped at the cross street and set the end of the tepee on the pavement, waiting for Martha. She walked steadily, but so slowly and deliberately it was a question if she would ever reach the corner. She pushed the damp hair away from her face, looking ahead gravely without seeing anything—without seeing what he saw, anyway; walking slowly with her own little world inside the world that is much too large for anyone. A small tired child plodding through a hot night on a journey that was endless so far as she was concerned.

Bringing home the tepee hadn't been the easy triumph he had expected. It had gone wrong from the first, weather and everything. He should never have started out with Martha on such an expedition on such a night when it was her bed time. But Dorcas was at one of her temperance meetings. He was as well pleased that she was. If she were home when he brought the tepee into the flat, she would point out that it was a big, clumsy thing for which they had no room. And she would be sure it had cost a lot of money and that he had taken food out of his family's mouth to indulge his insane hobby. It would not help a great deal when he explained that the beautiful tepee had cost him almost nothing. It had been part of a Red Wing sheet and pillow case display at Wanamaker's and Harry had made a bargain with the window dresser. The tepee had cost only two dollars. He would not mention the third dollar that went to the watchman. But even the most artful handling of the truth would not help much. Dorcas would point out bitterly that he showed no end of enterprise and ingenuity in amusing himself and none at all when it came to supporting his family. He had friends in the Indian Rights Association in Philadelphia and the Metropolitan Museum and the Department of Anthropology of the American Museum of Natural History. When he saw a snake-oil seller on Broadway with a really fine agate knife among his rubbish, Harry attracted the medicine man's attention and the knife with an ease which amounted to genius. But when it came to making a living, he was just a pants presser who was afraid to ask for a raise. He had heard that more than once.

A pants presser had no business making a hobby of the American Indian. Harry felt that sharply the time he sent ten dollars to the Indian Rights Association. The rent had fallen due immediately afterward and there was a ten dollar deficit which he stubbornly refused to explain. Dorcas had seared him with her blazing eyes and her voice that went up like mounting flames. Probably he had spent the money on prostitutes. He never went near them. Or on drink. He had not even drunk beer until his wife joined the W.C.T.U. Even then he only drank a little on rare occasions to save his self respect. Then Dorcas decided the ten dollars had gone in some way to the Indians. He denied it unsuccessfully; he could not deceive her. She was too keen for him. The Indians, the Indians! Why didn't he go and live with them? Why hadn't he married a dirty squaw? What was it going to lead to? Would they be allowed to go and live on a reservation when they were put out of the tenement?

He had sat, unmoved, in the kitchen during the tirade. He was very nearly comfortable while Dorcas lashed herself into a frenzy. There was something comfortable about being in the wrong and not having to strike back or do anything but correct his wife when she exaggerated. The truth was enough. He was like two people: a man being whipped for having done wrong and a referee seeing that the man wasn't struck any foul blows for what he hadn't done.

It lasted two hours, at least. Dorcas exhausted herself beating him the way you beat a feather pillow which yields at every blow without yielding anything. When she went to the bedroom to cry, or maybe start packing to go to her cousin's, Martha took up the cudgels. She had heard the whole miserable fight when she should have been in bed. That was the worst part of such things. Dorcas got a kind of relief from them and Harry took his punishment comfortably. But as a result Martha was always neglected in some way. She knew her father had done something very wrong because her mother had said so and he had not denied it. She came over to him, very tiny and righteously angry, and began to scold.

"Why did you do it?" she demanded. "Why did you do it? Do you want us put out on the street?"

When he said nothing she did what her mother should have done and used physical violence. She beat him with both fists while she went on asking, "Why did you do it? Do you want us put out on the street?"

Harry was only dully aware of the small blows raining against his forearm and thigh. He looked stupidly at the blur of Martha's face, with loose hair shifting across her forehead, and her flying fists. It made him sick to have the child mixed up in the business. Women are dirty fighters, he thought, even when they are in the right—as they often are. They have no delicacy about whom they bring in on their side, strangers and even babies. They don't care what they fight with or how much mischief they make.

Martha had picked up a pie tin and was beating him with that. She wasn't wasting her breath on scolding any more, but setting out in a business-like way to punish him. He felt the tin plate even less than her fists; he would hardly have noticed it at all except for the wretched little thunder it made against his leg. He wanted to tell her she was being silly and tiring herself for nothing, but he did not feel sufficiently wise or superior to give advice just then.

The child stopped beating all at once. Maybe she suddently realized she was doing her best to annihilate her own father, after having forgotten what started the attack. Her eyes darkened with grief at what she had been trying to do. She looked altogether terrified and lost. The pie tin clattered on the floor and her arms reached up swiftly and blindly for her father's neck while her loud, heartbroken wail burst on his ears.

That time it had come to him clearly that a pants presser with a family had no business making a hobby of the American Indian and for some time he was more guarded in his enthusiasm. But here he was, caught again. He had known from the beginning he could not afford an express wagon to bring the tepee home. But what he had not known was that it was bigger than it looked in the store window—too high to be allowed even on the rear platform of the horse car. And after a few blocks he realized it was too heavy and clumsy for him to carry with any comfort; and when he had to carry Martha, too, it became an agony.

Probably there was something wrong with him, as Dorcas often suggested. No reason why he wasn't at home, with his shirt and shoes off, sitting on the fire escape if there was any breeze, and Martha fast asleep with her bed pulled up near the window. Nothing to prevent it except a silly spark of enthusiasm that sent him wandering through hell with his burden while Martha plugged along behind him like a little lost soul, never questioning the wisdom or the necessity of their wretched journey.

She came up to him at last. He balanced the tepee under his arm and gave her his hand while they crossed the street. If only he could breathe, with his lungs or his skin. Too much steam in the air for either. A glass of steam beer would be a godsend. He couldn't take Martha into a saloon, though. Three-and-a-half-year-old daughter of W.C.T.U. worker found in Kelley's saloon. He wouldn't, anyway. The heat had come up through his shoes worse while he was standing still. Three more blocks, then all the flights of stairs. He could make it somehow, if only Martha didn't ask him to carry her. He couldn't refuse her, and he couldn't carry her any more. If only she didn't ask him! He felt it coming. She would hurry ahead a little, then stop directly in front of him with her arms up. "Carry me, Daddy; I'm so tired." And he didn't have enough strength left to pick her up, let alone carry her. She was drawing ahead now, determinedly. It was a bad moment. She stopped squarely in front of him and he winced as her arms started up with the familiar gesture.

Then her mouth that was already shaped to say "Carry me," changed to a mysterious smile. Her half-raised arms sank to her sides and she let him pass. A moment later he felt the balance of his burden disturbed and looked back over his shoulder. Martha had put up her arms again, about the end of the tepee poles, and she answered his look with a smile of mysterious and important triumph as she staggered along under her share of the burden.

The tepee was a gray-white cone in the September dusk. It had gathered some soot from the tenement roof where it was pitched, but the smoke of a campfire would have produced the same effect.

Pitching the tepee on the roof had been Dorcas's suggestion. The first time Harry had started to set it up he was conscious of her look, which was like hot flint. The tepee was even larger than he had thought; it threatened to crowd the table out of the dining room.

"If you want to set that thing up," she observed harshly, "you'll have to take it on the roof. We need room to live."

She was right, at least about his having to put it up somewhere else. He was not so sure about the roof; it was an unknown country a few feet above his head. He opened a door in the hall, climbed the narrow dusty steps and pushed up a hatch that opened on daylight. The roof was discovered, with its possibilities. He washed the steps and lugged up the precious tepee. Martha came toiling after him saying, "Don't help me, don't help me!" when he reached down his hand.

Martha had never had so much open space to herself before.

"Oh, Daddy, where are we?" she asked, looking with large, admiring eyes across the expanse of tar and gravel. "Is this the West?"

She helped him set up the tepee and spread sheets of the *Sunday American* inside. After they had brought up Harry's Indian clay pipe and tobacco and Martha's footstool and doll the place had something the feeling of an encampment. By the time the sun set in gold and grime beyond the New Jersey shore, Harry was wondering how they had ever lived without a tepee.

In midsummer it had been too hot to stay in the tepee for long. Now, in late September, it was pleasant in the tepee and still pleasant outside. Martha was sitting on the footstool beside the door flap, undressing her doll for bed. Harry was sitting on a piece of carpet near her, smoking his pipe and wondering what to do with the quarter he had found in the pocket of a pair of pants he had pressed that day. Whether to return it to its owner or give it to Martha. Ever since he had told her it would take a lot of money for them to go out West she had been saving coins in her china pig bank with a great singleness of purpose.

Martha undressed the doll slowly, frequently scolding it for some pretended resistance and then hugging it tightly against her breast.

"You're spoiling that baby," Harry protested.

She laughed wickedly. "I don't care." After a while she tucked the doll under a square of cloth inside the tepee. Then she came back and squatted beside her father. It was quiet on the roof at sunset. Only a faint sound of street traffic and a woman's voice from a window calling, "John-e-e, John-e-e!" to a boy who never answered. Whistles began to hoot and bellow on the river. A fog must be coming up. It seemed to bring the river nearer. After a while the river seemed nearer than the street. The fog would bring some of the chill of the river.

Martha hitched her footstool nearer and nestled against her father. "Tell me about the West, Daddy," she ordered. It was only since they had brought home the tepee that he had told her of his secret ambition to move out West. He had hardly thought she would understand. When he told her she understood perfectly; the spirit of it, anyway. Now he had to tell her about the West nearly every evening.

"The West is out that way," Harry began, pointing with his red clay pipe toward the smoky afterglow over Jersey City.

"Across the river?" Martha asked.

"A lot farther than that. It would take days and days for us to get there on a fast train."

"A train with chewing gum?"

"No," he told her. "A train that runs on the ground out in the sunshine and under the stars."

"A train with beds and a little restaurant?" she suggested.

"Yes, a train with beds and a restaurant, where we would sleep at night and get up in the morning and eat breakfast while we looked out of the window at the prairies and mountains and hills—"

"Could we climb the mountain hills?"

"Not till we got out West. The train would be going fast all the time we were eating and sleeping and looking out of the windows."

Martha snuggled her head contentedly against her father and patted his arm.

"We wouldn't want the train to go without us."

He took the pipe from his mouth and bent over to kiss her touseled hair. It smelled like the feathers of a little bird.

"What is the West like, Daddy?"

"It's a big place—"

"Bigger than this roof?"

"Much bigger."

"Bigger than a whole street?"

"A lot bigger than that; bigger than everything you ever saw."

"Bigger than a whole world?"

"Not quite," he admitted, "but it's very big, with mountains and plains and rivers and trees and grass—"

"And no policeman?"

"No policeman," he assured her.

She became excited as she always did and jumped to her feet. "Oh, I will run and run and run!" She waved her arms and ran in a little circle, coming back to him like a homing bird. "And the flowers!" she prompted, sitting on the footstool again.

"Yes," he said, "there will be flowers everywhere, as far as you can see, all kinds of flowers: buttercups and loupine and poppies and wild roses and columbine—"

"All colors?"

"All colors: blue and purple and red and orange and yellow—"

"And pink, too—that's baby red."

"Yes pink, and white, too. Every color of flower growing everywhere."

"And I can pick some, Daddy?"

"All you want."

"The man who owns them won't care?"

"No one owns them; they are just there for children to pick."

She jumped up and embraced him, gritting her teeth in her ardor. "You are a good daddy," she said, raining kisses on him. "You are the best man in the world!"

He always winced when she said that; his intentions were the best in the world, but beyond that he deserved no praise.

"And there will be Indians, won't there?"

"Yes, Martha, there will be Indians." He felt troubled in anticipation that the Indians of the reservations would not match the unspoiled Indians of his dreams.

"Tell me about the Indians," she ordered.

"They live in tepees, like ours," he told her, "only made of skins. All day they are out of doors in the sunshine, hunting and fishing and picking berries. And they ride ponies—"

"O-o-h! Will they let me ride a pony?"

"I think they will," he decided. "The Indians are mostly tall with black hair and brown skin from being so much in the sun, and they wear feathers and blankets—" Then he remembered, as he was supposed to. "Why, Martha, you've seen Indians! The time we went to Buffalo Bill's show—"

"I remember, and I saw the lady in the sky and I thought it was one of the Indians because she had a bow. Oh, that was so silly of me!" She put on a pitying expression. "I was only three and a half years old." Now she was almost four.

It was a favorite experience, one that one or the other of them would recall when they were feeling particularly affectionate. They had talked a great deal in advance about the Wild West show. Harry had taken occasion to tell her about the Indians they would see and he demonstrated how they shot with bows and arrows. Nearing Madison Square, he had pointed out the Garden, where the show was being held. Almost at once Martha became excited. "Daddy, an Indian, an Indian!" she cried.

He had turned everywhere without seeing anything that looked like an Indian, and all the while Martha kept up her clamor. Finally he picked her up in his arms and asked her to show him the Indian. And she promptly pointed to the statue of Diana. The mistake had amused him, and it also amused her.

The cyclonic show of cowboys and bronchos, Indians and wild animals had been too much for the child's attention, but she had carried away one clear impression —the lovely statue of Diana poised, bow in hand, against a lovely April sky. It was her favorite part of the Wild West show. In time it became Harry's favorite, too.

Harry talked on about the Indians, about the hardy virtues of the great Sioux chieftains, until Martha's attention began to wander and she excused herself to go into the tepee to find out if her doll needed anything. She could listen as well as anyone and ask sensible questions and remember things afterward. But she could not listen for long; she was a very little girl.

Martha gave her doll a drink of water and put her to the bathroom before tucking her under the square of blanket again. Then she started playing with a bright tobacco tin which Harry had left in the tepee, and forgot to come out. Now and then she called to her father, more to hear his voice and know that he was near than anything else. He sat with his face toward the West, with his mind still going on from where he had left off talking.

After a while he was half roused by clanging bells and the galloping hoofs of fire horses passing in the street below. He felt dimly that Martha hadn't called to him for quite a while, and when he looked she was asleep among the newspapers in the dusk of the tepee. The tobacco tin had slipped from her relaxed hands and she was breathing with quiet, untroubled rhythm. Her eyelashes were dark crescents on her cheeks. Around her the black newspaper headings stood out obstinately in the deep twilight: MURDER AXE FIEND UNMENTIONABLE DIVORCE SCANDAL, SECRET SIN PASTOR UNWEDDED MOTHER YELLOW PERIL FOREIGNERS WAR.

Harry was still hesitating about taking Martha downstairs when he heard Dorcas coming up on the roof. He hadn't expected her back so early. She had been out helping the Cause by selling a new kind of flavoring extract made without alcohol. He could see no sense in it, selling such stuff to a few people who were already too holy, in the midst of a well-liquored city. But he didn't want to tell her so. When he let her go her way altogether she made fewer rows about him going his way.

"Why isn't Martha in bed?" Dorcas asked, coming across the roof toward him. She looked very tall in the dusk, in her long white skirt and shirtwaist, with a flat-brimmed black hat high and severe on her head. Harry was nearly always a little afraid of her, and sometimes he was very much afraid.

He got up from the carpet, holding his Indian pipe in his hand. "She fell asleep in the tepee," he said guiltily. "I wanted to be sure she was sound asleep so she wouldn't wake when I carried her down." Then he realized it was a confession that he had intended to put her to bed without brushing her teeth, and he braced himself for the attack.

Dorcas didn't answer. She sat on Martha's footstool and drew out her long hatpins. There was something different about her this evening, languid. Perhaps that was why she had come home early. She pushed the pins back into her hat, slowly, and put it aside on the piece of carpet. Then she got up and looked into the tepee, with one hand resting on the door flap. There was not enough light for her to see that way and she knelt down, regardless of her white skirt, with her head and shoulders inside the tepee. Harry knelt beside her and put his head in, too, looking at the child asleep among the newspapers in the deep twilight of the wigwam. The ugly headlines of the paper had sunk into darkness, but Martha's face was still visible, faintly; tender determined little face with dark crescent lashes. He could just catch the sound of her breathing, so even and profound that it was like the wash of the ocean on a quiet shore, a long way off.

Dorcas bent over her, kissing her swiftly and lightly. "Lovely," she murmured, "she is so lovely!" She was shaken with the realization. She drew back to look. "We have a lovely little girl!" Her hand found Harry's and squeezed it. Gropingly it came to Harry that she wanted him, that this was what she had come home for. She was sick of going about from house to house in the evening, trying to sell vanilla flavoring with no preservative, when she could be at home with her own child; in bed with her own husband. He put his arm about her waist and she did not resist when he drew her close to him. Her mouth was not hard, as it usually was; it yielded with a kind of promising languor. Warm and inviting.

He terminated the kiss because she usually hated long kisses and ended them if he did not. This time he sensed that she was disappointed because he had quit too soon. She did want him, then! The knowledge gave him strength and confidence. He put one hand against her starched shirtwaist, over one of her small, firm breasts. Usually she hated that, too, and pushed away his hand. Now she only trembled a little closer.

"Dorcas," he said gently and authoritatively, "you're going to be—" He was about to say, "You're going to be my squaw in my tepee," only he remembered the biting things she had said about squaws and tepees. She caressed his hand with her finger tips, waiting for him to finish. He realized he should have said it anyway; there was no bitterness in her now and it would have pleased her. But now he couldn't say it with the right confidence. So he kissed her again, still too briefly, partly from the grip of habit and partly because he was eager and no longer quite sure of himself.

"I'll put Martha to bed," he remarked, letting her go. "It won't take a minute."

But for all his eagerness he carried the child down with infinite care, washed her face and hands gently and carefully and undressed her for bed. When it came to putting her in her nightgown she sat up for him, with her eyes still fast shut, and her arms thrust above her touseled head. Then he laid her down tenderly and drew her nightgown over her perfect little legs and tucked her in.

He was kissing her good night when she opened her eyes and reached up her arms, with a delicious dreamy smile, and encircled his neck, drawing his head down against her little breast with a gesture of unconscious womanly tenderness. He marveled, as he often did, how he and Dorcas had ever made such a child. She was so much more complete than either of them and she found it so natural to love the two of them, who found it so difficult to love each other. She had never really been a baby, it seemed to him; from the beginning she had been a person with a will of her own and a capacity for love.

166

And since she was not much more than a year old she had been trying, unconsciously and then consciously, to fill the gap between her parents.

Harry waited until the small arms relaxed and released him and Martha turned on her side. He kissed her again, lightly on her fresh cheek, but she only turned farther away, a little impatiently, as if she had already done all she could for the time being and wished to be alone with sleep.

He was in the hall, on the way to the roof, when he heard Dorcas coming down. He remembered how warm and yielding she had been, and his heart sank. It might already be too late; on the rare occasions when she was like that he had to act quickly and surely before she changed. If he had hurried the least bit she would have been still on the roof, beside the tepee, and he would have taken her there, thrillingly. But he was never able to hurry with Martha; he loved her so much and she loved him so that hurrying would have been like breaking faith.

Dorcas came down the steep, narrow steps with her hat in one hand. It was too late now, as far as the roof was concerned. If he had finished saying, "You are going to be my squaw in my tepee," or if he had told her to stay, it might have been all right. But he had only said that he was going to put Martha to bed. He was disappointed, but he couldn't blame her because he had managed things badly. She came down slowly, with still a trace of promising languor. When he helped her down the last step she reached out and smoothed his forehead and hair with an unaccustomed, timid caress. Timid, when he was nearly always afraid of her! He started, a little too late, to put his arm around her, but she had already passed, on her way to the bedroom.

She stood before the cloudy mirror, in which one saw darkly, brushing her hair by the light of the squealing little gas jet above the bureau. Harry sat on the edge of the bed, where he had often been told not to sit, unlacing his shoes and watching her; she was usually annoyed to have him see her when she was not fully dressed. Dorcas seemed to feel that people are not complete except when they have all their clothes on and their hair fixed. When she was not completely dressed and her hair wasn't rolled on top of her head she was annoyed or apologetic because of her incompleteness.

He unlaced the other shoe and put it under the edge of the bed beside its wrinkled mate. When he straightened up he saw Dorcas, still brushing her hair, through the rough white iron bars of the bedstead. One of the flimsy, hollow brass balls had come off the foot of the bed, leaving the brutal iron screw which it had been supposed to conceal. Harry was in the habit of looking at the erect, threaded plug of iron when he was dressing or undressing; it hypnotized him. It seemed to have a meaning, too. Sometimes he didn't mind looking at it. Other times, when he thought of the missing brass ball, it made him feel suffocated and a little ill. The ugly snag of iron seemed to say: this is what the religious, goody-goody world is like when the tinsel comes off. It was so hateful and unnecessary, he thought; life didn't need to be like that. The brutal spike of iron was only there to support the brass ball; the poisonous, dishonest ball had been there to conceal the spike. Both were mean and unnecessary.

The light sank to a kind of twilight; Dorcas had turned down the gas. That meant she was going to finish undressing. The knowledge excited him and he pulled his shirt off over his head hastily, popping a button across the room. Usually Dorcas finished undressing under her nightgown, but he had once come in unexpectedly and found her stark naked, with her dark hair all down. He hadn't thought her incomplete. She was lovely and it was as if he hadn't really seen her before. Maybe she was a little angular, but smooth and straight with a kind of grace he never suspected her of having. He thought she wouldn't be angular at all if she let him caress her enough. Once she had sent fifty cents for a prescription she had seen advertised in the paper. It was guaranteed to develop perfect busts. When it came, in a plain envelope, it was nothing but a printed picture of a man's hand, with the words: *Massage daily with this.* She was very angry at having been cheated, and when he thought they ought to try it, she said it was disgusting.

When Dorcas turned down the gas she came over to the bed to get her nightdress from under the pillow. Her wrapper was open a little in front and she didn't have anything on under it except a corset cover and corset and black cotton stockings. It was quite exciting. She smiled at Harry, almost shyly, as she reached for the nightdress. The smile decided him. He reached under the pillow before her and took out the folded garment, without offering to give it to her.

169

"You wait until you're ready for it," he said with authority, smiling back to her.

It worked. She pouted a little without looking at all severe, and he was no longer afraid of her. She took off the ugly wrapper and glanced back at the gas jet, maybe to see if it could be turned a little lower. Then she unfastened the hooks and eyes of her tight corset cover and slipped it off, standing before him in her corset and stockings.

"Now," she said pleasantly, "may I have my nightgown?" There was a nice gleam in her gray eyes; a look that thrilled him on the rare occasions when it appeared.

"No, dear," he answered boldly, "you're not going to bed in your corset."

She pouted again. "I could take it off under my nightgown."

"You could take it off better without being tangled up in a nightgown," he reminded her.

She looked down, submissively. "I suppose I could." Then she sat on the edge of the bed and began unfastening her garters. He saw her out of the corner of one eye while he hastily unbuttoned his undershirt. The miracle was taking place and it was so beautifully, divinely simple. When he ordered her in the right tone she obeyed him meekly and enjoyed obeying. He turned and kissed her smooth shoulder as she leaned forward slightly, loosening her corset lace at the back, and he sensed that she was pleased. But he did not quite have the presence of mind to repeat the kiss.

Dorcas unfastened the clasps of her corset and stood up, slipping out of its iron embrace and pushing down the hem of her knitted cotton shirt with nervous little pats. She was like a bather shivering at the edge of a delicious pool. "Now may I have my nightgown?" she asked, panicky.

"Please, no." He was no longer in such perfect control of himself.

She seemed to sense it and reached for the garment. He recovered his poise and held it out of her reach. "You're not ready for it."

She glanced about the room, sweetly at bay, searching for a means of escape, or only making sure she could not be seen. Then she untied the drawstring and pulled the shirt off, over her head, a little blindly.

He caught his breath. This wasn't Dorcas, this trembling, naked beauty! Or what he usually saw was someone else. The modest skirt that never revealed anything but a little of her black kid shoes that laced half-way to the knee, the high-necked shirtwaist, the uncompromising hair piled on top of her head, and the severe look which overawed him. His mind groped with the miracle. He had undressed a Christian and a member of the W.C.T.U. and found a woman with a woman's desirable body; the unquenchable miracle of the ages. She was straight and a little angular; not quite perfect. But she could be made perfect. Her body needed to be rounded out and softened, not crushed in. She needed the caresses of love instead of the iron-bound embrace of her corset.

"May I have my nightgown now?" Her voice was like the voice of a little girl. "I haven't anything more to take off." She looked a little frightened and proud at finding herself naked and defenseless.

He could not answer her or take his eyes from the cruel corset marks on her white body. Not that. So unnecessary. Without knowing he found that his arms had obeyed his wish. They had encircled her naked body and drawn her close to the edge of the bed where he was sitting. He was kissing her thighs and sides, kissing away the wicked marks of her corset. He was kissing her everywhere, recklessly. What he had dreamed of, dimly, and never dared to think of doing.

She gave a gasping little cry and started back. "Don't! Harry, you mustn't!" Her voice was sharp with alarmed authority.

His arms faltered and let her go. She picked up the nightgown which he had dropped and held it in front of her with one hand. Her face had a stricken look and her mouth was still half open, as if she wished to take back her words. The startled words that had made him let her go, like a fool. She had not been startled at what he did; she had been startled at herself for liking it. He had let her go, like a fool, and she was disappointed.

His mastery was gone, and he began to argue with her. "Why mustn't I?" he asked sullenly.

She shrank farther away and slipped into her nightgown. Her white, fine body was banished in a flash and he became aware of the meanness of the room: the dreary wallpaper with countless thousands of identical red roses crucified on identical lattices; the verdigrised gas jet, the cloudy mirror above the aborted bureau that rustled paper-thin brass trappings under the clanking handles of drawers that stuck; the fat, pious chair that was too heavy to be carried and too weak to be sat on; the mangy, turkey-red carpet. He knew, without seeing it, the exact location of the smug, glassy white chamber pot, with its knobless lid, under the edge of the bed.

Dorcas was standing out of reach, buttoning up the neck of her heavy muslin nightgown. Her lips were set in a hard line and she looked hurt and discouraged.

"Why mustn't I kiss you?" he asked glumly, knowing it was the wrong thing to say.

She looked at the bed with sharp appraisal, probably deciding how she could get in without disturbing him or losing any of her dignity.

"Why mustn't I kiss you?" he repeated, sitting half dressed on the edge of the bed and looking at her belligerently. *Mustn't* was a dirty, stupid-sounding word when you said it a few times.

Her eyes flashed angrily and her lips flew apart. "Oh, because I'm *tired!*" she snapped. "Isn't that enough?" She went to the bed quickly and climbed in, jerking the covers up to her chin.

"You're always tired when I want to love you!" he shot out.

She lay there, breathing hard and looking at him with dark, blazing eyes. "I always will be tired!" she shot back, unexpectedly.

"Thank you!" He started pulling on his shirt again.

When his head emerged from the shirt she was leaning on one elbow, looking at him with withering scorn. "What else do you expect?"

He fastened his shirt hastily, feeling guilty about the missing button.

Dorcas's voice became scalding. "What else do you

173

expect when we have to live in a dirty tenement like this? Look at it! Is this your idea of a home for your wife and baby?''

It was not. Harry's idea of a home for his wife and daughter was a place in Montana or maybe Wyoming, where Martha would run about all day in the sunshine, and where he would work hard with all his energies because there was something real to work for. But he had always been too afraid of his wife's scorn to tell her. At best she would have reminded him sharply to get the money first. And he was sure that if he ever had the money it would go for a mean little house and shoestring lot in the Bronx, which was her idea of a permanent home. So he only glowered at the iron snag on the bedpost while he reached for his shoes.

Dorcas raised her voice. "Why don't you answer me? Is this your idea of a home? Is this what I married you for, when I could have had a decent job and a decent living? Look at it! Is this your idea of a home for your family? I suppose it's good enough for a pants presser. But even a pants presser with any gumption would ask Mr. Lipsky for a raise. You know you do more work than any other two pressers, but you wouldn't ask for a raise. Oh, no! You earn enough now to buy Indian rubbish. It doesn't matter if your wife and child go hungry and without clothes. Why didn't you marry a dirty squaw. Then your wife wouldn't have to wear clothes. . . .''

Harry laced his shoes rapidly, without answering. It was one of his wife's blind spots—to be ignorant of the innate modesty of squaws when she had every opportunity to know the facts. But he knew that when she began abusing the Indians it was time for him to be going. He tied the second shoe and took his celluloid collar and black bow tie from the foot of the bed. He did not need a mirror for putting them on, but he had to stand as though he were in front of one.

The woman's voice lashed out at him from behind. "Do you think you are a man? Sneaking out without answering and leaving me in this dirty tenement. You think I enjoy it, I suppose; you think it is all I am fit for. Maybe you think it is too good for a decent woman. . . ."

He decided to fasten his tie outside, and crossed the room hastily to snatch his coat and vest from the weak, ugly chair, with a hail of bitter words beating over him.

It stopped all at once, as if a door had closed between them, though his hand was only on the knob, going out.

"Harry!" Dorcas called after him softly, in an altered voice. Why did she have to do that—smash everything with hateful words and then call him back to fit the broken pieces together? He closed the door firmly, without answering.

Martha slept on the couch in the dining room, in the uncertain light from the back window. She was uncovered, with one knee drawn up, but did not seem cold. He drew the top sheet and blanket over her again and kissed her on the cheek. Martha turned her face closer to the pillow, without knowing what disturbed her. She was far away and could not help him.

He turned west into Horatio Street, past Murphy's saloon, arguing the case of Harry Bell versus Dorcas

Bell. Fog had softened and changed everything. The damp columns of the Chapel of the Comforter rose before the lighted doorway like old trees in a forest. Across the street the lamps of Jackson Square floated in dripping greyness, lights that were nothing except in relation to themselves, since they illuminated nothing. A line of drays entered the street, with the tops above the drivers nodding mysteriously. Great, creaking drays like sea-monsters, crawling up from the river in the ancient, comforting fog.

Dorcas would think Harry had gone away mad. That was hardly true at all. Except for one burst of impatience he had only been sorry. Sorry and hurt that they got along so badly. It was not entirely his wife's fault, he knew. They had wounded each other too often. And when they tried to love each other one of their hands was almost sure to bruise some sore spot. Hatred and pain.

In many ways he was the more to blame. Dorcas had endured a lot. She had worked hard and made his pay go a long way and not spent much on herself. The time his arm was scalded so badly she had nursed him devotedly. It was his own fault, too. He had been day-dreaming that he was an Indian on the western plains, preparing the nourishing pemican for winter, and he set down his red-hot pressing iron in a pan of water.

Dorcas had done everything a wife should do, except love him. And that made all the difference in the world. She was afraid to love him because of her frozen religious ideas. And because of "The Science of a New Life." She liked to quote the hateful book that said it was vicious and sinful for a husband and wife to have any love-making oftener than once every two years. What could you expect when a man was tied to a woman who believed things like that?

He crossed Hudson Street and continued west in the thickening river fog between walls of decaying brick and vaguely lighted windows. He had to be just. Dorcas didn't always make him wait two years. That week at Rockaway! And once she had taken down the fat, pious volume of authority for him to stand on. . . . What perfect derision. It wasn't that she never allowed any love-making, only that she made it so rare and difficult. Sometimes not for months. Then only when he found the right tone of authority. If he could always be confident and take her without faltering he could do as he wished, and she would love him for it. But he couldn't often find the confidence when she was so stern and forbidding and full of bitter words. Their difference in size was against it, too. When he succeeded, he enjoyed her being the larger; but at other times he was aware of being the smaller, and that was quite different.

Money—that was it. It was always money. If he could earn a decent living Dorcas wouldn't be so resentful and he would find it easier. If he could forget about the Indians and give all his energies to some kind of business. Or maybe he should strike out boldly and do what he was interested in—forget about everything except the Indians and make something out of his enthusiasm. He almost did that, once, only Dorcas threw his chance out of the window. The time he could have been a guard in the American Indian wing of the Metropolitan Museum. With what he knew and his interest in the work he would have become a curator. And Dorcas made him give it up to remain a pants presser.

That was only partly true. When the curator offered to get him the job, Dorcas was in a bad mood; the rent was due and Harry had just bought a mint copy of Catlin's *North American Indians, Volume II*, with the author's superb illustrations. When he told her about the job she pretended not to hear him—until several minutes later when she asked how much it paid. He hadn't received any encouragement to tell her the possibilities of the job or his plans for the future. Dorcas heard that it paid three dollars a week less than he was receiving from Mr. Lipsky, and she asked sharply what they were going to live on. That was all. And he did nothing about it. He didn't have a real opportunity to tell her that he had to decide before the end of the week.

A week later Dorcas surprised him by asking when he was going to start the new job; she had planned how they could live, somehow. The job was gone by then, of course.

That was a fine way for a woman to help her husband —throwing his future out of the window and then being ready a week later to help pick up the broken pieces. Why couldn't she say what she meant in the first place? Or allow him to say what he was thinking?

He crossed Greenwich Street under the death-like blight of the elevated railroad. Deep, unclean shadows under skeleton iron trees, rotten buildings and the smell of death through the fog.

Why couldn't she have said something when it would

have done some good? Or why hadn't he gone ahead and accepted the job? If he had done what he wanted to. . . . A woman wanted a man to go ahead boldly and do things. If a man did what he wanted and took what he wanted, a woman liked it. . . . If he tried to please her, he didn't please anyone. Just the same, Dorcas made it difficult for him to do what she wanted. She resisted him shrewdly and put obstacles in his way and forbade him in a tone of authority. When he obeyed her she was discouraged and disappointed because he did what she told him to do and not what she wanted him to do.

He remembered with anger that she had said she was tired tonight and always would be tired when he wanted to make love to her. He had known that for a long time, but now she admitted it. She tired herself out deliberately with temperance work to disable herself as a woman. And she called herself a wife. He would show her, though he didn't know exactly how.

He turned up West Street, plotting revenge. Whistles hooted and bellowed on the river; inquiries and answers. One blast, two blasts. Four blasts like a quick shout of warning. Three blasts of profane exasperation. It all meant something. Harry understood the tone but not the words. Deep, chill fog. There wasn't much difference between the river and the street. Suppose a steamer lost its way and came trundling over the cobblestones, the captain staring at a street lamp in the fog, trying to decide what lighthouse he was approaching. Bump, bump! Terribly choppy water! Not steering right, either. Something wrong. What could you expect in such a fog?

179

Harry would shout to them that they had strayed out of the river and were blundering down West Street.

"Hear that? There's a man out there, drowning! Or maybe he's in a boat. Better take soundings."

"Horse manure at no fathoms!"

"*What?*"

"Horse manure at no fathoms! The horse has been eating oats."

"Stop the engines! There's something wrong somewhere."

The ghostly ship of Harry's imagination faded into the fog with the voices of its puzzled crew. There were real voices now. Two men reeled toward him, purposefully. How do you know when sailors are drunk? They always walk that way. The men barred his path. He saw their faces dimly. He saw their self-conscious paper collars and readymade neckties. They looked at him with cheerful curiosity.

"Could you tell us where we are, Mate?" the tall one asked. His breath was laden with whiskey.

Harry gave him the information.

"What did I tell you?" the short one observed triumphantly.

The other insisted he had told him nothing at all.

"Listen to him!" the short man said proudly. "We was in Bangkok last, up the river. The watts was wonderful."

Harry began edging away.

The tall man pulled something out of his pocket. "Have a drink with us," he suggested, proffering a bottle.

The short seaman grinned bashfully. "That's right have a drink with us. It's safer than a barroom."

"Thank you, no." Harry backed away. "I just had one."

"He just had one," the short man repeated to his mate, as though it were something to ponder over.

Harry was afraid the men would try to force him to take a drink, but when he glanced over his shoulder, fearfully, the fog had already swallowed them.

Drunk as lords! And Dorcas went around tiring herself out trying to sell vanilla flavoring without alcohol. Why didn't she and her kind take the alcohol out of whiskey first? He would like to come home good and drunk, just to show her how much her temperance work was accomplishing. He couldn't afford it though. The rent was due tomorrow and it took money to get drunk. He couldn't really afford one drink.

Where was he going? Nowhere. And it was time to turn back; one of his shoes was run over at the heel and his leg had begun to hurt. He would turn east at the next corner.

There was a cozily-lighted saloon on the next corner. Mellow, blurred lights in the fog. And he couldn't afford one drink. It would be something to come home with whiskey on his breath. He had only tasted whiskey once, when he was a boy. Then he remembered the quarter he had found in the pair of striped gray trousers. He could acquire the smell of whiskey and still have fifteen cents for Martha's bank. Maybe he would even save the other ten cents out of his lunch. Going through the swinging door had the delicious thrill of a plunge into unknown waters.

The saloon was empty except for a pale young man who was sitting at a table and talking to the bartender. Harry took a place at the next table. He felt awkward, but it was good to rest his feet. "Whiskey!" he called, fumbling for the quarter.

The top of the little table was slopped with beer, as if a glass had been overturned. Would the bartender bring his rag, or should he move to a clean table? He didn't like to inconvenience anyone.

The pale man saw him hesitate. He smiled understandingly and proffered a place at his table, which was clean.

Harry would rather have been by himself, but he accepted because it was a solution of his problem, offered at the right moment. He swallowed the drink which the beef-faced bartender poured for him. A sweetish smell, a sting of heat and one hiccough. After it he felt much as he had before, except for some lingering warmth under his shabby vest. He hadn't even forgot any of his troubles. A lot Dorcas and her W.C.T.U. friends knew about drink. They believed firmly that when a man took one whiskey he was lost to the world forever and descended alive into hell.

During the night it seemed to him that Martha had a vomiting spell. It always hurt him when that happened; she was so forlorn and wretched. Afterward he felt as much relieved as she did. She got over such things very quickly. And she was always so affectionate and grateful because he had held her during her misery and because he didn't scold her for mussing things.

"A little womit doesn't matter, does it, Daddy?" she had once whispered to him, hopefully.

But this was a lot of it, and his head was too aching and heavy for him to get up and find who was sick. Maybe it was himself.

He was awakened by someone vomiting over him. The smell of the room was poisonous, and it reeled about him. He tried to crawl away from the hot vomit that was gushing over his back and found that his legs were paralyzed. He was going to be sick, too. Something was lying across his legs, pinning them down. He tried to crawl out from under the weight, and put his hand down on a hairy face, ice-cold and rigid.

Harry turned violent and sat up, pushing away a body sprawled across his legs. "Good God!" he cried. "Where am I?"

Someone answered with a vomit and a gasping cry of misery.

"Shut up, and let us sleep!" someone else bawled.

There had been an earthquake, or else a plague, and Harry was in some kind of charnel pit, among the dead and dying. He began crawling again, in a new direction, and pawed a stiff, cold trousered leg. He started back, trembling with nausea. Through the filth and vomit there was the unmistakable smell of death. The earthquake was still going on, and he became violently sick.

Afterward they dragged him out by the heels, over a timber that bumped his head cruelly, and threw water on him. The water was ice-cold and bitter with salt when it slashed over his face. He opened his eyes in gray daylight and sat up.

He was on the deck of an immense, untidy sailing ship. Half-furled sails flapped overhead on plunging yards and a tangle of ropes reached in festoons to the littered deck.

"Give the bastard another," a voice directed. A final bucketful dashed over him. He staggered to his feet, squeezing the salt water from his eyes. Near him a gentleman in evening clothes, with a nicely-waxed moustache, lay in the scupper. Blood was soaking through his thick black curls. He looked like a young professional man, Harry thought.

A dark, quiet-looking man grasped him by the shoulder. "Lay aloft, you, and help loosen the upper fore tops'l. Lively, now!" The words ended with a fierce shove.

Harry staggered, regained his balance, and looked blankly at the dark hawk face. "Sorry," he said. "I don't know what you want."

The man struck at him, a blow which he managed to dodge. "What kind of a sailor are you?"

"I'm sorry," he said again, "I'm not a sailor, I'm—a pants presser." It sounded ridiculous to his own ears.

The dark man raged to his companion, who had been kicking the unconscious gentleman lying in the scupper. "Those crimps, those stinking crimps! They've brought us a lawyer and a drayman and two corpses. Now we have a pants presser!" He glared at Harry, with his hands working and his bared chest and throat swelling as if he would burst with anger. Harry was mortally afraid. He suspected that if he opened his mouth to explain there had been a mistake and asked about getting ashore, he would presently lie broken and bleeding in the scuppers.

Another victim was hauled out on deck and Harry was saved for a moment. A short seaman nudged him. "Come on and loosen that tops'l before he brains you! I'll show you what to do." The guarded voice was friendly, and what was more it had a familiar ring. Harry followed the stubby man aloft, weak and giddy. Once he had to stop and vomit. "I don't belong here," he said weakly when he had done. "I've been drugged."

The seaman was not surprised. "You're not the only one. Do you think I'd a joined the *Bloody Harvester* by myself?"

They began climbing again.

"What kind of a ship is this?"

"A hell wagon, bound for Australia."

Australia! That was on the other side of the world, and Harry had never been farther from New York than Rockaway Beach. "How soon will we get there?"

"Four months, if we had sailors. Maybe six in a hard chance like this."

Harry almost fell from the ratlines. Six months— before Dorcas knew what had happened! And Martha! He was crying inwardly. Martha! A year, or longer before he saw her again. Before then her grief would be over and she would have forgotten him. In a year she would be five. She would be someone else who didn't know him. There was death in the thought.

Out on the rotten footropes in the sky his immediate peril drove all the past and future from his mind. If he lived at all, he would have to live like that. Thought would kill him.

Afterward, when they had loosened the sail somehow,

he crept in from the yard and hung in the slings, trembling and sobbing. How would Dorcas and Martha live for a year, or longer, without him? The rent was due tomorrow—this was tomorrow. It was due today and the money was in his pocket. He felt for his wallet, but it was gone. The crimps had taken that, too. He had been drugged and robbed and sold into slavery in the year of grace 1905!

He tried to get a farewell glimpse of New York. It was nowhere in sight. He only saw the Statue of Liberty, dimly, holding up her unlighted torch in the mist. O, Liberty! He was overcome with nausea again and vomited wildly in her direction.

IX

The Sun's Cattle

THE wind had died and while the sea was still rough
it was going down. It hadn't been much of a gale.
The lightship pitched and rolled with abandon in a
dying sea. She rolled with too much abandon, altogether.
There was only enough coal left in the bunkers to take
her into Seattle and she was riding high and flighty. A
bit hysterical, as if the old jade were saying she had
stood about as much as she was able. The crew could
feel the difference made by the coal consumed in the gale.
Coal that was their capital and ballast and safety all in
one—burned to make sure they didn't go anywhere.

Harry was sitting on the galley skylight, looking
toward shore. Clark and Ben and the little chief were
aft, arguing and watching for the *Relief*. Clark got off a
kind of joke, without seeming much amused himself.
He asked Ben why he was looking toward the south.
When the boy said he was watching for the *Relief* the
seaman told him it was the wrong direction. She would
come down from the north, or maybe from the direction
of China. Ben argued the Columbia River didn't lie that
way. Clark finally admitted it but clinched his point by
explaining that Captain Kennedy's navigation was that
way. It was so erratic that once he had approached

from the proper direction and had no end of trouble trying to explain himself. You didn't mind Clark's kind of humor. He only started being funny when things were really bad, and then it was better than nothing.

Harry had given up helping the others watch for the *Relief*. He thought it might come sooner without him. The things he watched for didn't ever seem to come. He sat on the skylight that had once been white and looked at the shore. He was hardly conscious of the seas bursting on the reef between. Blue smoke rose in two places against the evergreen forest. That was the only way you knew the Indians were there. White people would have set white-painted houses against the dark forest and erected flag poles flying flags that celebrated nothing in particular. They advertised themselves with the cheeky confidence of a new brand of cigarette on a billboard: the best ever; the thing the world had come to. And when all was said and done maybe the white, confident race of people wouldn't last any longer in the universe than a cigarette poster on a billboard. Some other race of another color would overrun them, then another and another. Or it might come from inside. Maybe the new horde of barbarians was already upon the world: machines that threw men out of work and thundered arrogantly through the country and cities until one crossed the street in danger and terror among the invading wheels. The confident white race might wake up, too late, and get out extras.

EXTRA!!
BARBARIAN INVASION FROM DETROIT
MILLIONS OF HOMELESS REFUGEES
FLEEING UNEMPLOYMENT AND MORT-
GAGES. NO PANIC, PRESIDENT SAYS.

The Indians had been wiser. They never invented noise-makers or showed off to the stars. They lived on the earth instead of on pavements and had an understanding with other wild things. They lived as quietly and showed themselves as little as the animals. Their tepees were as well hidden as the nests of birds. Confident white people built white houses on hills against the sky and flew flags and made a great noise. And if you went to one of the white houses and asked what it was all about they wouldn't know. They wouldn't know as much as the Indians. The Indians respected the world and when disaster came they knew how to take it. Like Crazy Horse. In those three days and nights on the Rosebud he learned the meaning of life, as much as anyone will ever know . . .

Ole came and sat on the skylight, a little way off. He spat clear of the rail and looked at Harry with the face of a wise old peasant woman. "Thinking about Seattle?" he asked.

"No. I've been here so long I don't think about going ashore. Not cities, anyway."

"They're all right sometimes. I don't care. Only we need supplies."

Harry conceded the point. "It's hard, trying to make meals out of nothing. But if I had my choice about going ashore, I'd go over there." He nodded toward the green shore, with its two columns of smoke. The lightship nodded too, as a cross sea rolled under her wet, red side.

"I was there once," Ole remarked.

"You were? At the Indian village?" Harry's white, thin face lighted up and his eyes became eager. "In fine weather I used to look at it and think there must be some way to get through the reef with a boat."

Ole nodded. "There's nothing to that. In fine weather at high tide you could take the ship in to the beach."

Harry became excited. "Couldn't we take the boat some time, say when we're back in the spring?"

The seaman pouted his long lips and spat elegantly. "We're not allowed to land there any more," he explained. "Part of it was my fault." His small, close-set eyes were faintly amused.

Harry felt uncomfortable. The old, old story: sailors ashore—couldn't they ever behave themselves? "What did you do?" he asked uneasily.

Ole put a fresh pinch of snuff in the pocket of his cheek and proceeded to explain how he had contributed his share to the wrongs of the Indians. He told the story carefully and gravely, without any attempt to excuse what he had done.

It happened years before, soon after Ole had joined the lightship. Mickey O'Rorke was there then, and Oscar, but none of the others. The matter of organizing a shore expedition had come up in some way. They had it from the chief that another crew had done it, years earlier. Mickey had been in the ship from the beginning of time.

They went on a July morning, in settled weather when there had been less fog than usual. Not that you could ever be sure about the fog in summer. As often as not when they went fishing at the reef, it shut down on them and they had to feel their way back to the ship by the sound of her whistle.

Ole had fitted out the expedition. The fourteen-foot boat was stocked with a breaker of water, pilot bread and an extra oar. The cook also made up sandwiches and put in a can of coffee, but that was hardly necessary. The most important piece of equipment was the chief's Winchester rifle, a 44 repeater that took rim-fire cartridges. The rifle weighed all of thirty pounds but it shot beautifully, Ole admitted with regret. They took it to shoot deer. When the expedition was first suggested, they hadn't anything definite in mind. Just a leg-stretch on the beach and look around.

Then someone suggested deer. The crew hadn't had fresh meat in two months. By the time the expedition was launched, they weren't talking of anything else. It had become a deer hunt, pure and simple. There was no end of talk about the habits of deer, their sagacity, how plentiful they were, the superiority of venison over other kinds of meat. Everyone contributed something. One of the firemen had even seen a deer, though he could not recall the circumstances. He was probably drunk at the time.

The shore party was made up of three men; not a large party, but it was as many as could be spared from the crew. Ole went, for obvious reasons. He was a careful seaman, with experience in taking small boats through the surf. And he was a good shot. He impressed the point on the little messman without being boastful. He was a good shot because he had been trained to it thoroughly. In his younger days he had served in the Chilean Navy. Among others things, you were taught to climb up and slide down a long rope, free at the lower end, with a heavy carbine slung on your back. At the middle of the rope you stopped and made a loop for your foot. Then you unslung the carbine and fired at a target which you were supposed to hit in the center. It was excellent training. Ole also admitted that he wanted to go. As a boy in Sweden he learned to say in English: "Many buffaloes roam the plains of America," and he dreamed of hunting them. One way and another, he never got around to it, but he still had the feeling.

The others consisted of a young fireman and the assistant engineer. The fireman was named Larry, a careless, reckless fellow who managed to pick up a dose every time he went ashore. The assistant, Lynch, was also a young man, but very fat. The little chief was jealous of him because he had the greater theoretical knowledge. Mickey may have even encouraged him to go in the hope he would drown or get into some discrediting scrape. He had always been spiteful and jealous of his assistants, as might be expected of an undersized fireman who suddenly became a chief engineer at the age of fifty.

The expedition pulled away from the ship in the morning, with the crew lined up along the rail, cheering and shouting farewell instructions. Oscar was there, not quite so sleek and distrustful; and Mickey, not so gray as he was now and more careful of his looks. In those days he wore his blue coat and brass buttons on all occasions. The others were men who had all disappeared from the lightship long ago. The first casualty of the deer hunt alternatedly waved a bloody handkerchief and held it to his nose. The habits of the deer were still under discussion earlier in the morning, and the seaman had tried to settle one point to his own satisfaction. "Can a deer yump as high as this?" he asked, making a tremendous leap into the air. Someone standing by with a rope tried to lasso his feet, and he was brought up on his face on deck.

The pull ashore went according to schedule, though Ole was rather contemptuous of the fireman, Larry, who sat on the sternsheets, striking heroic poses with the chief's rifle. Ole pulled one pair of oars and the assistant engineer pulled the other, by choice. In spite of being fat, Lynch was a competent, obliging fellow who later became first assistant in the *City of Para*.

The reef? That was much as it looked from the ship: a barrier of stone fangs and grinders. There was more, of course, than you saw from the ship. Plenty of flat stumps and spines, covered with sea growth, just below the surface. Farther inshore, there were broad, dry tables of rock rising from half a fathom to a fathom above the low swells. That was at slack water. Ole had been speaking figuratively when he said you could take the lightship to the beach. A small, handy vessel might feel her way through under perfect conditions, but the chances would be against her ever getting out again. Altogether, you didn't like to think of a ship there under any circumstances.

Larry took a shot at some black sea birds roosting on one of the dry rocks. It was a stupid performance. They were not hunting birds, and the bullet fell fifty yards short.

Landing at the beach was easy, with nothing you could call a surf. They pulled the boat up on the sand, carried the anchor well up the beach and stretched their legs. It was a fine July day and it felt good to be ashore.

The expedition moved inland, with Ole in possession of the rifle. The ground felt unstable under their feet, after they had been away from it for three months, and everything was interesting but not very real. Ole saw some yellow flowers of a kind that had grown on the banks of the Nissa, in Sweden, beside his father's paper mill. He could not remember their name; it was probably something different in English, anyway.

They found themselves in the village all at once, without knowing exactly how they got there. It wasn't much of a place. Shacks you hardly saw until you were close aboard them, and even then you didn't know but what they were deserted. They didn't see anyone at first. A dog came and snapped at them, but went away when Larry gave it a kick. The big engineer found a tree with black fruit on it. They were very good cherries, he said, breaking off small branches and stuffing himself with the clusters. Ole ate one or two. They tasted like cherries, but he doubted if you found them growing out like that. He laid no claim to knowing anything about things ashore.

While the others were about the tree, picking fruit, Ole noticed a girl watching them from across the road.

194

She was brown with black hair. Not bad looking, though her dress was dirty. She might have been sixteen or seventeen. After a minute, Larry saw her, too, and jumped down from the tree, calling to her. He wasted no time in telling her what he wanted. The girl shook her head and started down the road, with Larry after her. When she saw him coming, she jumped over a fence and ran for it, with the fireman in pursuit. Ole called after him to let the girl alone, but it did no good. Then he urged the fat engineer away from the cherries and went on toward the woods. Larry and the native girl were out of sight. The village had a smell he didn't like, and it wasn't safe for sailors ashore to stay too long in one place.

The door of one house was standing open and Ole and the engineer looked in. They saw a blind man sitting in the middle of the floor. He looked like a white man and must have been a hundred years old. When they spoke to him and he didn't answer they went on.

After a little, there weren't any more houses. The trail led through the forest where everything was clean and quiet. There were all kinds of trees and plants. Ole supposed they all had names and would have liked to know what they were. The taller trees were fir or pines, he thought, like the trees in Sweden. Some of them would have made fine masts. The engineer sampled the round, purple-black berries that grew in strings on bushes beside the trail. They were very good, he said. When he stopped to fill up on them, Ole did not protest. It was warm and pleasant in the forest and the trees made shadows so he could look everywhere without having the sun in his eyes. It also looked like a good place for deer. He had the rifle ready at all times.

The engineer was still picking and eating the berries when Larry rejoined them. He was out of breath and had two long scratches on his face, but he was in good spirits. He had plenty to say about the superior qualities of Indian girls. He got the scratches on his face in coming through the woods, he said. Ole doubted the fireman's success with the girl, and his explanation of the marks.

A little farther on, the woods opened and a gate of poles shut off the trail. Beyond it was a grassy place, dotted with clumps of bush. Ole halted the expedition some distance from the gate and held a council. The open place looked right for deer, but there wouldn't be any there if they approached from windward with a great noise. There didn't seem to be any breeze; the leaves of the forest were motionless, but smoke from a lighted match trailed off to the right. They would take a slant through the woods and approach the field from the right, crawling on their bellies when they got near the open, and keeping behind bushes. The engineer and fireman must be careful not to get ahead of Ole. If they were between him and the deer he would have to rise a little and show himself in shooting over their heads.

The engineer decided to stay in the shade on the trail and wait. Since there was only one rifle, he could be of no assistance.

Ole stooped along through the woods until he reached the extreme right of the field. When he looked back, Larry was following on his hands and knees. He had an open clasp knife between his teeth and his black hair hung over his forehead in strings. He looked appealingly at the seaman and pointed his thumb toward a small animal on the branch of a tree; it was about the size of a rat, with a bushy tail. Ole didn't know whether the fireman expected him to shoot the thing or merely wanted to know what it was.

There was a fence at the edge of the open place, and Ole wriggled under on his belly, pushing the big rifle ahead of him. He brought up behind a bush, where he could see only a little of the field. There was nothing in sight, but with his ear to the ground he thought he heard animals walking. He crawled to another bush. The field opened out before him and he saw one of them: a white animal the height of a man's waist, eating grass about fifty yards off. It was the right size for a deer, the seaman thought, but it didn't have horns and the color seemed wrong. Before leaving the ship he should have got a better description of a deer; he was a little vague as to what one looked like. Most of what he had heard was about the animals' habits and sagacity. They always fled on the approach of danger, going in high, stiff legged jumps that made them impossible to hit. Yet they were curious by nature and could sometimes be lured back by a white rag waved on a stick. The cook declared they were partial to the smell of anis seed and would brave any danger to get it. One of the firemen was of the opinion that a cooing sound made through a megaphone would bring all the males within miles. None of the information promised to be of much help in identifying the animal. Had it been bounding across the field, Ole would have known it for a deer, but it grazed pretty much in one spot, only taking an occasional short step. It seemed unlikely that even a deer would leap ten feet into the air in moving to a clump of grass six inches away.

The white animal noticed something in the grass and capered about it awkwardly, with its head down and tail sticking straight out behind. It ended by stopping on all four feet at once, in a stiff-legged prance. That decided Ole. He believed it to be a deer, but since the animal showed no intention to cut and run he would wait for another opinion. He motioned for Larry to join him, and covered the deer with his rifle. The black sights showed up nicely against the white forehead.

The fireman crawled up behind the bush, with his knife between his teeth. A bee had stung him while he was going through the grass and his hand was already beginning to swell, but he had made no outcry. Altogether, he had shown up better than might have been expected.

"Is that a deer?" Ole whispered, drawing a bead on the animal again.

"Sure," the fireman answered. "Knock him down!"

Ole doubted if his companion had taken a good look. "Are deers white?" he asked.

"Some of them," Larry said. It didn't look as if he would be of much help. Then he had an inspiration. "In the north, all the animals are white in winter."

They were not very far north, and it was summer. Ole reminded him of the fact.

"They can't all change back when they want," the fireman opined.

"You think it is a deer?"

"Sure. What else would it be?"

The final decision was up to the seaman. Larry probably knew nothing about it. Ole at least thought it was a deer. He spread his legs comfortably and dug his left elbow into the ground. It was a matter of several minutes before he managed the shot he wanted: the deer with its head raised, looking in his direction. He brought the sights in line with the center of the forehead and squeezed the trigger.

BANG! Blue powder smoke veiled the results. The rifle was so heavy there was no noticeable recoil. It felt like a perfect shot.

The smoke thinned and they saw the deer collapsed in its tracks, just vibrating a little. Larry leaped up with a yell and rushed across the field, knife in hand. Another deer, white with black spots the size of a hat, looked at the men doubtfully. Ole thought it might be a spotted fawn, but was disturbed at seeing it so tame. The fireman was evidently going to distinguish himself by killing it with his knife, single-handed. The deer waited until he was within two fathoms of it, with its head down and legs splayed out, ridiculously. Then its nerve failed and it turned and ran, its tail sticking out stiffly behind. Some larger animals got up from the shade and ran. One of them had a bell which clanged frantically as the fireman chased the herd about the little field. The bell didn't sound right, and Ole called sharply for Larry to avast chasing. Then he examined his kill. The deer had been hit between the eyes. A perfect shot. He picked it up, experimentally. It weighed well over a hundred pounds; a fine lot of meat.

Larry was still pursuing the others. The clang of the bell was annoying. Ole shouted again, but the fireman did not stop until the rifle was pointed in his direction. Then he dropped back under the impression that the seaman was going to shoot another deer. When he saw how matters stood, he returned, mopping his face disgustedly.

"Jesus Christ!" he panted, "why did you stop shooting? The deer are caught in this place and can't get out! I almost got one of the big ones with my knife. Nicked him, but he got away." There was a smear of blood and some hair on his clasp knife.

The assistant engineer had been aroused out of a nap by the shot and the clanging bell. He came lumbering across the field, smiling with uneasy indulgence. "Were you boys chasing the cows?" he asked.

Ole had begun to suspect something of the kind. "Isn't this a deer?"

Lynch saw the kill for the first time, and whistled. "It'll do," he observed. "Only I think we ought to get out of here and head for the beach!"

They took turns carrying the deer and the rifle, from which Ole had extracted the cartridges. On the way through the village they had the feeling of being watched, but no one molested them until they were abreast of the cherry tree, where the leaves of broken twigs were already withered in the hot sun. Then an old Indian in dirty blue jumper and overalls came to meet them. He looked sorrowful.

"You have broken my cherry tree and killed my calf." He looked at Ole, who was taking his turn carrying the deer. "You must pay me."

Ole turned to his companions, troubled. "Is it really a calf?" he asked.

"Keep walking and don't pay any attention to him," Lynch advised in an undertone.

"It is my best calf," the Indian explained, shambling along beside the seaman. "You have killed it and now you are taking it away. You must pay me."

"Go away, you old bellyache," Larry suggested.

"Pipe down," the engineer muttered. "You might make him mad." He fumbled in his pocket and found two silver dollars, which he put in the Indian's hand. "Run along," he advised, "and forget it."

The Indian put the money in his jumper pocket, without being appeased. "It is my best calf," he repeated sorrowfully to Ole "It is worth thirty dollars."

Ole didn't know whether it was a calf or a deer, and he had no money with him. He walked on, saying nothing, with the Indian dogging along beside him. They came within sight of their boat, undisturbed on the beach, and the lightship lying motionless on the blue summer sea, a long way off.

The distant ship inspired Larry with more confidence than ever. He stopped abruptly in front of the Indian, with a shooing motion. "Go away; clear out!" And he advised the old man to perform with himself an act which was physically impossible.

"Pipe down," Lynch growled uneasily. "Let him alone."

The fireman was still obstreperous. When the Indian faced him, injured and unmoved, he cocked the rifle and pointed it in the direction of the old man's legs. "Go on, beat it! Go wet your back!"

The engineer tried to wrestle the weapon away from

him, and the trigger was pulled in the scuffle. It was a good thing the cartridges were in Ole's pocket. Larry gave up in disgust and allowed the engineer to carry the heavy rifle the rest of the way, while the Indian went on with sad stubbornness about his wrongs.

"You were not asked to come here," he reminded them. "We never asked you. We didn't bother you. You came and broke the cherry tree. You chased our cattle in the field with knives."

"Why, the old son-of-a-bitch!" Larry remarked admiringly. "He knows about that, too."

"You killed my calf that is worthy forty dollars—"

"Thirty," Larry corrected.

"You carry the calf away and give me two dollars that do not pay for the cherries. Then you call me bad names and try to shoot me with your gun."

The tide had almost reached the boat, which Lynch and the fireman managed to launch without asisstance. Ole was streaming with sweat in the hot sun and the weight of the calf was breaking his back, but he didn't want to put it down where the old man could pounce on it.

"The calf is worth fifty dollars," the Indian decided. "The milk of our cows will dry up because you chased them. You must pay for what you have done here. I am Chief Morning Sun."

The engineer and fireman had launched the boat awkwardly, stern first. They chose the wrong moment for turning it bow-on to a slight surf which had come up. They managed, but got wetter than necessary in the process.

Rising Sun followed Ole into the water. "The White Uncle in Washington will hear this," he said as the seaman was stowing the calf. "You will be punished for this. You men from the ship that goes nowhere will not be allowed here any more. You will not come back until you are washed up dead on his beach. Pay me thirty dollars—twenty . . ."

They waded out a few steps with the boat, then jumped in and took to the oars. Larry was on the sternsheet again. He turned round, with his arm in his mouth, and made a derisive noise for the benefit of the Indian on the beach.

The engineer was disgusted with him. "You'd think you were a whole black-gang," he said, "the way you stir up trouble. And you came near killing the fellow."

Larry made a final horsey noise against his arm. "I would only have shot him in the foot," he retorted. "Anyway, I knew the gun was empty."

Near the outer edge of the reef a seal came up close beside the boat. They didn't know what to make of it at first. The fireman fondled the empty rifle and begged for a cartridge. Ole thought there had been enough shooting for one day, and he hoped the seal would leave. But it swam along beside the boat, between the gunwale and the moving oars, with its slippery head raised and its bead-eyes turned toward Ole, as if it had a mind to come and sit in his lap. It gave him a queer feeling, the seaman commented, not but what there is a reason for everything.

Afterward, he decided the seal was there on account of the calf. It was stowed thwartship in the boat, with its head over the gunwale, and the seal had been attracted by the smell of blood.

When he saw the thing wasn't going to leave them, Ole shipped his oars and asked for the rifle.

Larry was aggrieved and sarcastic. "Don't shoot it," he said. "It may belong to Chief Rising Sun."

The seaman put one cartridge in the ancient rifle and shot the seal through the head. The fireman tried to pull it in to the boat with one of the oars, which he had no business to touch, but it sank immediately. By that time, Ole noticed that Lynch had quit rowing and the boat had sternway. While he was getting his oar away from the fireman, a swell carried them over a blunt spine of rock which rose from nowhere. The keel just kissed it, but it was a disgraceful performance—running onto the reef in broad daylight with a boat drawing a foot of water.

On board the lightship there was a sharp division of opinion. The crew thought the expedition had done very well indeed, and the men feasted on fresh veal. Captain Williams was furious and forbade the cook to serve any of the meat aft. He hinted at loggings and wholesale firing of the crew; he was even more upset than you might expect of a conscientious and hot-tempered man.

The little chief, who inspired the expedition and furnished the riflle, followed a middle course. As long as Mr. Lynch was on board, he made sarcastic remarks about assistant engineers who were too ignorant to know a calf from a deer. On the other hand, he was surprised in the fidley in the act of gnawing a forbidden veal cutlet.

Out of hearing of the vexed captain, Larry repeated his story about the Indian girl. No one believed him, however, because he failed to clinch the matter by coming down with the gonorrhea, which he always did after having been within hailing distance of a woman.

That was the story, as Ole remembered it. The next mail, a month later, brought a letter from the lighthouse inspector which completed the ruin of the captain's temper. And among other things, the crew of the lightship was forbidden to land on Indian ground.

That was ten years ago, and the order still held. It would probably hold until everyone had forgotten. Or until seamen learned how to behave themselves on shore.

Harry thought that time a long way off.

Ole did not see it so. The day was coming when people would learn all the secrets of the world. Religion and other superstitions would go overboard. Science would be God, but science used for the common good. The world was like a ship. Things could not be right while there was disease and ignorance and superstition on board. Until now, people had only played at being alive. It had all been dress-up and foolery. People had tried to make themselves angels, devils, monkeys—anything except men and women. Now men and women were going to have their chance.

X

The "Relief"

"RELIEF ahoy!" Clark's pleased voice, like a deep bell, put an end to Ole's plans for the future of the world.

The seaman and messman left the galley skylight and went to the rail for a look. A small steam vessel was coming up from the south, about twelve miles off, head-on for the lightship. A narrow pyramid shape in a brown smudge of coal smoke, rising out of the troubled immensity of the gray sea. Harry could not tell whether or not it was the *Relief*, but the others looked as pleased as if it were a certainty.

Ole squinted gravely at the distant smudge. "That's the *Relief*," he said without emotion.

Captain Lindstrom came on deck, followed by the little chief. He studied the approaching vessel for a minute. "Get steam on the windlass, Chief," he directed, "and commence heaving." He was gravely and profoundly pleased.

The old chief looked round with his cat's smile. In a few hours the ship would be under weigh, and in the excitement he would be firing his men right and left. His eyes fell on Ben and he licked his chops.

"Ben, Ben, me bye, come and show what you're good for!" His exultant voice announced to everyone that Ben would be fired at least once before the mooring was up.

Ben followed the old leprechaun below with scornful willingness. The captain watched the two down the reeling companionway, his face relaxed in an amused grin. There was zest in the old comedy when it meant getting in from station, out of a tight pinch. They would make Eagle Harbor on the last of the bunker sweepings, but they would get in, unassisted and with a clean record in spite of a hard chance and the charming human frailties that made life bearable.

The cook came up in his green overcoat and sat on the cabin skylight, moaning and staring at the horizon with animal eyes. He had lost a good deal of weight and might have been sick as well as insane.

The others looked at the approaching craft and at each other, unwilling to admit how pleased they were. Oscar came on deck and looked suspiciously, then belched and grunted in contempt, as if the *Relief* were not as fine or useful as she should have been.

"I'm wise to you, Oscar," Clark announced. "When we get to Seattle you're going to eat at a nickel coffee house and then stand in front of the Pig n' Whistle and pick your teeth."

It was a very old joke, but it sounded good because it made going in from station seem real. Oscar only made an obscene noise and stamped away on his slippered feet, muttering darkly. He was under the impression that Clark had said he was going to be put in a pig pen.

A shovel clashed energetically on floor-plates below. Fire-doors banged. Steam cracked and thumped in long-cold pipes. The windlass awoke with a heavy whine and there was "clank, clank," from the great mooring chain coming in, link by link. They were the good sounds of quitting station.

The *Relief* was coming up fast, with a bone in her teeth. She was in such a constant cloud of smoke that her firing periods seemed continuous and she rolled wildly in a heavy beam sea as she stormed along. It was like Captain Kennedy to do something dramatic, racing up the coast as though *Lightship 167* were in flames or going on the reef. Now, even Harry was sure of the vessel's identity; he could make out the black balls of her day marks each time the masts reeled out of the belching smoke.

There was nothing more to be done just now. It would take hours for the cable chain and immense mushroom anchor to come up from the bed of the sea. The windlass would be whining and clanking long after the *Relief* had let go her anchor nearby.

The crew relaxed still more, standing about the captain in a pleased group, poking fun at each other about what they would do ashore. Mr. Gill came up from a nap below, with his pipe and spectacles in his hand, and looked approvingly from the rail.

"Good," he commented heartily. "That's good! Look the way the boys are firing her; she's blowing off. Good men to keep her turning up in a sea like that, with one bunker and then the other hanging over you, and the coal and slice bars shooting back and forth around your legs. A good man at the wheel, too. Captain Kennedy's the man to get there in a hurry."

The other members of the crew had an obscure prejudice against the captain of the *Relief*, without knowing him, but Mr. Gill wished everyone well. And he believed in bestowing praise wherever it was due.

Mickey reappeared, buttoning the brass buttons of his blue coat with the propeller insignia on the lapel. He wanted everyone to know he was a chief engineer. He was full of energy and did not seem at all like a man of seventy. At times like this he was particularly fond of joking, but his temper was unreliable. He sidled up to Ole, with a confidential leer.

"Ole, me bye, are you *thinkin'* of gettin' married this trip?"

Ole said he wasn't. It was a very, very old joke of the chief's.

Mickey looked dramatically downcast. "I was *thinkin'*, Ole, that if you were gettin' married your wife might take me for a boarder. Tell her I'm a *kindly* old man." He ran out his cat's tongue and licked imaginary canary feathers from his whiskers. Everyone smiled appreciatively.

They smiled again at Harry's hopeful eagerness when he asked if the *Relief* would put supplies on board. He wanted to give the crew the dinner of their lives.

Captain Lindstrom answered gently. "I think not. It's still too rough to lower a boat. They'll throw the mail on board if Captain Kennedy can get close enough, but that's the most we can expect."

The little messman was crestfallen. "We haven't much of anything," he said.

The captain knew that. "Serve what there is," he said, "and we'll eat decently when we get in. It could be worse."

Harry didn't seem to think so, from the upward look

of suffering in his eyes. Then his fragile gray face lighted up bravely, and he limped below to plan a worthy dinner out of practically nothing.

Ben came on deck and stood at the rail with an air of sullen negligence, wiping his long hands on a piece of cotton waste. He had put on a sweater, with the collar turned half way up the back of his shaggy head, long overdue at the barber's, and he looked quite like the trained bear.

The *Relief* was coming up fast, rolling prodigiously and spouting smoke. When she yawed a little, she showed a glimpse of white lettering on her wet, red side. Captain Lindstrom thought one of her boats was missing.

"They must have taken a terrible beating on the Columbia Bar," he told Clark. "I didn't expect them before tomorrow, at the earliest."

Clark answered with a dreaming look. There was some kind of an understanding between them about the great river. "Th' bar is terrible when it kicks up at low tide," he said in a hushed voice, "all breakers with no water between. The first time it's enough to deafen you and scare you to death."

The captain nodded. "Did you ever see Matthews take the *Rose City* out when it was like that?"

Clark had. "Hitting bottom, solid, in every trough. How he did it! A man like a fussy old woman, taking a shipload of passengers, women and children, through that hell when nothing else dared to cross."

"Quite so. She didn't sail across; she walked, from one spot on the bar to the next. The engineers said it was enough to jar your teeth out, below."

"How he did it, year in and year out! That old lady taking chances a madman wouldn't dare. And he never slipped."

"That was the strange part of it; he never slipped. It seemed he couldn't, somehow, and he knew it. But others did try. That big new freighter—"

"That was at high tide."

"I saw her go. I had a week at home, when my oldest was born. She was half-way across when a sea went clear over her stack and put out the fires—at least it looked that way. Even then they would have been saved if they hadn't let their anchors go. But a man can't foresee everything when he has to make a decision in a second, or thinks he has to. What might have been salvation came from the most unlikely place. The sea had piled up so they would have been carried clear over the jetty. Would you have expected a chance like that? I played with the idea, watching the ship and figuring what I would do in her master's fix, but I wasn't sure. A great sea favored them, too. The ship took the jetty stern first, in a clear swoop. She was almost over when she brought up short. It wasn't until then we knew about the anchors. The rest was dreadful."

"One fireman swam ashore," Clark said.

"A fireman and the master's Airdale dog. The man died of consumption. All that sand in the water did for his lungs."

The captain and the big seaman talked in quiet voices. The others heard and there was nothing new in what was said. It was all an old story, but there was a different meaning in their voices. They talked about the bar, but their minds were already past it, on the great river. The bar was the dangerous gateway to peace. Captain Lindstrom's wife and young children lived at Tongue Point. What the river meant to Clark, the others did not know.

Ben stood near the two, listening intently to their words and trying to grasp the meaning behind them. He was no longer a child, but he was like a child trying to see through the veils of adult conversation. After a while, his intentness attracted the fire of the little chief.

"Ben, Ben!" he chided sharply, "Why are you standing there like a tourist? Are you a fireman, or aren't you? Go see that the oil cups and swabbing cans are full."

"They are full," the boy answered.

"And what of the grease cups in the shaft alley?"

"All filled." Ben turned comfortably to the rail and studied the approaching *Relief*. He was as anxious as anyone to get in from station, and with Allen's help below he had done a thorough job.

"Ben, could I have a minute of your time?" Mickey asked sarcastically.

The boy turned slowly and looked at the irate little chief. "What?"

"Go pull some coal from the port bunker. We'll be under weigh soon, and you'll be the one to bellyache with no coal handy in your watch."

"That's done already," Ben observed, turning his back again. There was a rubbery quality to his resistance that particularly exasperated the chief.

Mickey's faded eyes shone with a wicked light. "Ben, me bye," he said with treacherous mildness, "could I have another minute of your time?"

213

The boy turned toward him again. "What?" he asked wearily.

"Ben, you're a bright lad, and a fine lad. I have a fine job for you. Come below for a minute, will you?"

Ben followed the old imp in silence. For the time being, the chief had the last word. The crew smiled, the captain a little wryly. It was a toss-up as to whether the young fireman would be set to cleaning bilges or chipping rust in one of the empty bunkers. Whichever it was, he would not do it and nothing would come of it but grievances on both sides.

The drone and clank of the windlass ran on like music, and the lightship rolled and flourished as she inched farther away from the reef. But the crew was unconscious of any motion. It was a raw mid-November afternoon and a squall was making to the west, across the gray, sharply-rolling sea. There was comfort in the gathering squall because it stood for everying the men were leaving. When their mooring was up, the *Relief's* would be down. There would be no precarious plying of small boats between the ships. Nothing to do but head for a safe harbor under the hills of Bainbridge Island. The squall would probably break over the lightship steaming toward the shelter of the Straits.

"She has taken a beating!" Captain Lindstrom observed to Clark. "Look at that stack."

The high, black funnel of the *Relief* was streaked gray with salt. Her small boat was gone, they noticed, and an empty davit bent at an odd angle.

"They're getting the mail ready," Ole observed.

On the port side of the wheel house, a seaman was

going through the motions of overhauling a heaving line.

"Letters from our sweethearts!" Mickey crowed. He sidled up to the messman, who had come on deck in his apron. "If you're *thinkin'* of gettin' married this trip, Harry, ask your wife if she wants a *kindly* old fellow for a boarder while you're away again."

Ben came up the companionway in unobtrusive rebellion and watched the *Relief* from farther forward.

Captain Kennedy brought his ship up with a flourish. She came on under full steam, headed for the middle of the lightship as if determined to cut her in two. A hundred yards off, a bell clanged and she lost some of her way. She still came on, unswerving, but edging a little to leeward. The seaman forward twirled the weighted end of the heaving line tentatively. Others of the crew were grouped at the rail, further aft. The *Relief* was no bigger than *167* and little different in build, but her globular day-marks gave her a more modern look. Ben also knew that she had a double-expansion engine which reversed by steam— very different from a single-cylinder mill that looked like a cream separator and reversed with a six-foot wheel that had to be spun by hand. The crew also looked trimmer, more alert and urbane; they were barbered like people ashore. The boy was acutely conscious of his wild, shaggy growth of hair. Some of the men grinned. It seemed to Ben that he and the other members of the crew, the lightship itself, appeared a little ridiculous to the men of the *Relief*.

She slid up to the lightship, pointing directly at her but moving sideways with the scend of each sea until Ben saw she would clear the stern. The wheel house door was open and Captain Kennedy stepped out, a broad-shouldered, dramatic figure with a megaphone in his hand. He barked an order. The seaman twirled his heaving line and let it fly. It whizzed through space, high and clear of the lightship's taffrail. Clark reached up a long arm and caught the line smartly behind the weight, and began to pull it in.

"Look out for him!" Mr. Gill's voice boomed.

The cook came leaping aft, a great, mad figure, with his green overcoat unbuttoned and flapping about his legs. Some of the crew drew back, instinctively, but Ole stood his ground and as the cook went by he thrust out his foot and tripped him. At the same time, he got one hand on the coat, between the shoulders. The coat split down the back, but the force of the charge was broken. Mr. Gill raised the fallen giant by the arm, talking to him soothingly.

Captain Kennedy trained his megaphone on the lightship. "Hold on!" he thundered. "We're going to Swiftsure Station! Th' *Columbine's* bringing you coal."

Captain Lindstrom was agitated, non-plussed. "What?" he shouted his disbelief.

"We're going to Swiftsure Station. She went—" The safety valve of the *Relief* blew off, and the hollow, metallic roar of steam drowned out the rest. Captain Kennedy made the deprecating gesture of a general apologizing for his snorting steed, and lunged into the wheel house. The engine room gong clanged "full ahead." The *Relief* rolled, quivering, then lifted grandly above the lightship's stern with a big sea. As she rose, she swung a little and bore away, with her safety valve still roaring.

The men looked at each other, blankly.

"They're going to relieve *Swiftsure*." Ole thrust the statement into an atmoshere full of questioning.

"*Swiftsure* only got back on station!" Ben objected angrily.

"Yah, what of that?" Oscar put in. "Who cares for us?"

"There must be a mistake," Harry insisted hopefully. "Why, we haven't any supplies left!"

Mr. Gill was leading the cook to the companion-way, saying mildly, "There, lad, it won't be long! You're going home soon. It wouldn't do, jumping overboard."

Captain Lindstrom said nothing, but cut the lashings of the wet bundle Clark had pulled in on the end of the heaving line. There were a dozen or so of letters, official and unofficial, and a few papers. Ben saw a letter from his mother, but did not want to ask for it just then. The captain caught up one of the unofficial letters and held it tightly in his hand while he ripped open a long envelope with a lighthouse printed on the corner. He read its contents quickly, moving his head a little as he glanced from line to line. When he had finished, his face looked settled and sad.

"*Swiftsure* went adrift in the gale," he announced quietly. "Pulled her snubbing gear clean out through her nose. She'd never have made the Straits except that she was able to run before it."

"We should have thought of doing that," Oscar commented. It was the first time anyone had suspected there was any humor in the man.

The others stood about, disgusted, crestfallen or annoyed, according to their natures. The windlass still whined and clanked, stupidly.

"Chief, stop that windlass and let out the cable again." There was no longer any music in the clanking of the great chain that held the lightship to her station, and the captain wanted it silenced as quickly as possible.

"Stop the windlass," Mickey repeated in a voice of disgust. As he turned to the companionway, his disappointed gaze fell on Ben who stood disconsolately in the group about the captain. "Ben, Ben," he growled, "is that where ye are? Come below, and I'll have a word with ye." The look in his eye was explosive.

The boy followed him with the air of one on whom new misfortunes would be wasted.

Oscar peered to windward, where the rain squall had obscured the horizon. "Start the bell," he muttered to Mr. Gill, who had just come on deck.

"Right, Oscar," the old fireman answered cheerfully, and lumbered below.

Ole opened his hand and showed the others a shred of greenish cloth. "Rotten," he commented, looking at it with a kind of cold wonder. "Rotten, long-shore stuff. Couldn't stand up at sea." They didn't know whether he referred to the cook or his overcoat. The seaman dropped the fragment over the rail and dusted his hands.

Forward, the windlass stopped, then began again in a higher pitch as the cable ran out. Below, the bell began its cold clanking in the sea. Oscar peered to windward again, then went to the companionway. "Gill," he called down, "start the whistle!"

Captain Lindstrom gathered up the mail. The others were trailing below as the squall shut down and came hissing over the sea. It blotted out the *Relief*, racing north toward Swiftsure, and gathered *167* into its grayness. She rose and fell and reeled in the gray, rain-pelted seas, flourishing her day-marks aloft, beating out her number on the submarine bell, wracked at two-minute intervals by the great cry of her steaming whistle, like recurring pain in some lonely travail.

Clark and Ben were the only members of the crew who shared in the mail brought by the *Relief*. In another six months, perhaps, Ole would have a letter from his enduring mother in Halmstad. The others did not expect to hear from anyone.

The big seaman's letter was from Cousin Grace, who wrote to him at intervals—much oftener than he wrote to her. Directly or indirectly, all her news led to dairy. John had been ailing since summer, and the doctors hadn't found out what was wrong. He only came in on days when he felt a little better but Grace had no trouble keeping the business on its toes. Young John had taken charge of the trucks, in addition to driving one of the Macks. The bills for maintenance had gone down remarkably since he had his own shop. Grace's oldest daughter, Virginia, was going out with a young man from Eugene. It looked like a serious affair and Grace wouldn't be surprised if they got married any time now. She was disappointed because she had counted on Virginia to help look after the accounts. Oh, well, we're only young once. Lawrence was a nice, steady fellow who had a good job with the power company. As for Virginia, girls would be girls. And everybody knew Grace could run the whole damn dairy business without help from anyone.

When he had read the letter and put it away in his shirt pocket, Clark continued to lean against the end of the carpenter's bench, watching the rain trying to smother the gray, breaking sea and listening idly to the mechanism of the bell and whistle, and the windlass letting the links of mooring chain slip back into the depths like the minutes of an unprofitable life. He felt that something was amiss, but was not sure what part of the letter disturbed him. Too bad about John. He hoped the doctors would find what was wrong in time to do something, and he hoped it wasn't cancer. John had been a quiet hero. Clark felt sure he knew about Grace's past when he married her, but with John you would never actually know.

It was pleasant that the girl was going to marry such a fine young fellow; it was good that Grace took it so sensibly even if it didn't fit her plans. And still Clark felt there was something amiss, a kind of inner jealousy. Something about the girl. She had looked Clark up in Seattle the year before, when the lightship was in from station, and he had become fond of her in their first meeting since she had grown up. It might only be her name that troubled him; he wished they had called her something else. She was rather short and dark and shapely, with a lively face and wicked eyes. The name of Virginia seemed like an obvious mistake. . . .

Ben hunched on the carpenter's bench, reading a two-weeks-old letter, written in his mother's fine, copperplate hand:

Father and I are alone on the farm, as we were in the beginning. Frank and Arthur decided to go back to the "U" for the fall semester, though I'm afraid they will have a hard time working their way, with conditions as they are.

I don't know how recently you have heard from Jim. In his last letter to us, about ten days ago, he told us he had become president of the debating society at Baliol. It seems only a year or two since the morning I found him trying to make friends with a wildcat that was watching the chickens from the edge of the woods.

The Burtons have bought a new Ford. I wonder when it will be our turn? Your Father seems to be satisfied with the spring wagon, though I don't think it looks well with our old horses tied back of the church on Sunday. Last week, the Erickson boys arrived home from Alaska in the sloop they built. They had been gone three years. They didn't bring back any gold, but all look well. I am sure the experience was good for them and taught them self-reliance. I thought they might have passed your way, but Carl told me they went through the Georgia Strait, on the other side of Vancouver Island.

Autumn is here again. Every day the wild geese pass over, flying south. We have gathered in all the apples. The rains have begun. When the weather permits, Father works at clearing a new piece of land east of the barn. When it is done, it will mean thirty acres under cultivation. That does does not sound like a great deal for twenty-six years of labor, but when I see how hard the work is I wonder that he has been able to clear so much. . . .

Near the end of the letter, the boy read a passage twice, with a look of complete disbelief. Then he made an inarticulate sound in his throat and slid off the bench, with his eyes showing a need for action. He strode aft and into the cabin, where Captain Lindstrom sat at the table, under the swinging, unlit lamp, studying a letter of his own with grave concentration.

"What do you think of this?" Ben demanded. Then he read belligerently:

P.S.   Cousin Willie is taking this letter to mail. He brought the *Alki* down for a tow of logs and had to wait over a tide. So he hired one of the Norton boys to drive him out from town. (Like a true sailor, he has never been able to find his way here on foot, although there is only one road.) Willie said the *Alki* was off the Cape about ten days ago, looking for a barque which had been reported. They passed near the lightship but did not try to come within speaking distance because of the rough sea. Through his glass, Willie saw you come on deck in dungaree trousers and undershirt, although it was cold and raining. He said you looked well, but I fear you won't remain that way if you expose yourself to the elements. Please remember to put on your coat or warm sweater before going on deck.

Your loving Mother.

XI

Mickey's Wedding

IT WAS Allen Ross who got Mickey to tell Ben how he became chief engineer of *167*. There had been friction between the two since the visit of the *Relief*. Mickey had directed Ben to chip paint in the fidley while all the excitement was going on above, and the boy rebelled. The moment the chief left him, Ben put out the little, naked hand lamp, threw down his chipping hammer, and went on deck. Mickey had told him he was fired, and Ben retaliated by saying he was going to quit anyway when the ship got into Seattle.

It was the one unpardonable sin, for a fireman to quit, even after he had been discharged. Mickey had grieved for two days after reporting to the captain that Ben had thrown his job up in his (Mickey's) face. The chief made Ben's hypothetical quitting an act of mutiny. He said nothing about the boy having refused duty. That was a matter of slight importance. Ben had said he was going to quit, and the old engineer's pride was wounded deeply. Captain Lindstrom talked to Ben, who immediately told him about having refused to chip paint in the fidley. The captain was amused, but he was also a little troubled. With the ship long overdue for relief and low on supplies and coal, things were naturally tense. He had his own worries, too, including a family matter. It wasn't the time to make things worse with a low comedy of quitting and firing. No one could quit or be fired until the ship got in, and by that time the matter would be forgotten.

The captain told Ben it would be only natural for him to quit and join a ship that went somewhere; the lightship wasn't much of a life for a boy. But he musn't do it on the basis of a quarrel with Mickey. The chief was old and getting a little childish, and he had always been jealous about his position. The lightship was his life, and he couldn't bear to have one of his men quit in anger. It was like walking on the thing he treasured.

Ben agreed at once that when he quit he would make it plain to the little chief that there was nothing personal about it; he only wanted to see some of the world. The captain's talk influenced him a good deal and gave him a sense of responsibility. But his pride would not allow him to apologize in words when he did not feel in the wrong. And the chief continued to grieve.

That afternoon at four, when Mr. Gill had taken over the fire room, Ben went forward and found Mickey visiting with Allen Ross. The little chief was sitting on the bench, his brass buttoned coat giving an air of distinction to the firemen's dingy room. Allen was on the edge of the lower bunk, with a cigarette between his fingers, nodding his head in cheerful agreement with some remark of the chief's. He knew how to get along with people and he, too, felt a kind of responsibility for his old superior. He was also fond of him.

"Ah, Ben, me bye!" Mickey said a little suspiciously,

as Ben looked in. The boy guessed that the chief had been lamenting over his defection, and Allen had been telling him it was nothing at all. It was nothing at all, but once the chief's suspicion had been aroused it was the devil and all to get him over it.

"Come and join the party, Ben," Allen said, moving over.

The boy went round the end of the bench and sat down, tossing his padded black cap onto the shelf behind his bunk. He did not feel specially festive. Outside it was raining and blowing. Above and below the whistle and bell made their everlasting racket. And there was a sharp crash from the forepeak as the ship reared back on the chain with each sea.

"Chief," Allen said, "tell Ben about the time the lightship went adrift. He's never heard it."

"Sure you have," Mickey said, looking hopefully at Ben.

"I haven't," Ben assured him. "I'd like to hear it." He had heard an outline of the famous story from others, but never from the man who had played the leading part.

Mickey smiled his old cat's smile. "Well, Ben," he said, "if you're *thinkin'* you'ld *like* to hear it. . . ."

He did not begin the story at once. He wanted to have his audience with him when he did. He started by saying that Ben wouldn't find him a bad chief. (He couldn't bear the thought of changes in his department; he visioned Ben staying with the lightship for the rest of his life and learning the good qualities of Mickey O'Rorke as the years passed.) Ben would find out he wasn't a bad chief. "Some ways," he said, "it's a dull life here, but we get along. We're like one family."

No, Mickey wasn't a bad chief. He spoke of himself as Mickey. Twenty years chief, and in that time he had only really fired one man. That was Larry, the one who went ashore with Lynch, the stupid assistant engineer, and killed the calf and chased the Indian girl. Not that he fired him for that. It was all Lynch's fault. And he called himself an engineer. Maybe he had an eye on Mickey's job, but he didn't last long in the service after the lighthouse inspector heard about *that*.

But he was talking about Larry. Larry was a young devil. Every time the ship got out on station he was laid up with the pox. (Every sailor's ailment was the pox to Mickey.) Not that he fired him for that. Larry was a terrible one to drink. Not that Mickey minded a man having a good time. Ask Ole. He would tell you about the old days when Mickey went ashore, and the lightship in from station. Mickey cashed one month's pay check in a saloon and held the money in his left hand, and shoveled it out with his right until it was spent. He showed Ben the stubby-fingered old hand that held so many pay checks until they were gone. It was a big hand for such a small man. None of the first pay check had ever gone into Mickey's pocket in those days. It was a ritual. One month's earnings to wash away the loneliness of the sea.

No, Mickey didn't mind a man having his drink. But Larry was always drunk when the ship was in from station. There was no work in him at all. And after a while he got abusive. Once he came on board drunk, after having been away from work two days, and came aft to beat Mickey up. That was the last straw. Mickey arranged for him to be paid off.

He came back, drunk, for his pay check when the lightship was lying at the coal dock in Seattle. When he got the check he became insulting in his language and made a scene on the dock.

"I wipe me arse on your pay check," he proclaimed, suiting the action to the word. "I wipe me arse!" There was no getting rid of him. Mickey thought a man who put a Government pay check to such a use would come to no good end.

About that time the lightship went adrift. Mickey was a fireman then. But he had to go back farther than that, through the dim years. The first thing he remembered was falling among burning peats when he was a child. It was in the morning and the smouldering peats had been pulled out of the fireplace to be replaced with fresh ones. In running about Mickey fell among them. He had nothing on but his little shirt and was burned cruelly. Perhaps that put it into his mind to become a fireman. Mickey would have been a big man if it hadn't been for the Potato Famine. His mother had been a beautiful tall woman.

While he was still a boy, Mickey rode in an ass cart to Queenstown with a neighbor, to become a fireman in a transatlantic liner. Members of his clan were already in the ship and they held most of the jobs below: storekeeper, firemen, greasers. And they got Mickey in. Mickey had to stand on the shoulders of his clansmen to fire the upper doors in answer to the everlasting cry for steam, but he didn't ask odds from any man.

The boilers they had in those days, and the engines! Builders were only learning. Manhole plates were on the outside of the boilers, with the steam always trying to force them off; always leaking. The engineers always tightening up on the nuts until the threads on the studs let go and someone had the flesh scalded from his bones. It wasn't until years later that someone thought of putting the manhole plates on the inside, where the steam pressure held them on instead of forcing them off.

And the engines! His first ship had been built before the crosshead was invented. The piston rods were solid columns of steel, from piston to crank bearing. The cylinders were hung on trunyons and the whole clumsy, monstrous engine rocked back and forth with every revolution. You'd think the whole engine room was coming down on your head, Ben. It was a living nightmare an engineer had on his hands in those days. And the bridge always calling for more revolutions. Speed across the Atlantic!

Afterward Mickey was in the *Mariposa*, to Australia out of San Francisco. She was a fine ship; a beautiful big ship, touching at the islands of the South Seas. He didn't say how he came to leave the *Mariposa* and join *Lightship 167;* there had been many ships in his life. But it was on the lightship that he got his chance.

Mickey was fifty when he joined, still a fireman. The chief didn't think much of the middle-aged Irish bantam. The assistant was on board when the ship went out on station. He didn't think much of Mickey. Mickey didn't think much of either of them. No one on the ship thought much of anyone else. It was a cat-and-dog kind of crew, with a broken-down master in charge. Good men didn't stick in those days, and the other kind, the leavings, got enough of it in no time. There was a new crew every time the ship went on station, and when the men went on leave, a seaman and a fireman at a time, they never came back. It wasn't until the days of Captain Lindstrom and Mickey O'Rorke that the good men stayed, and the crew like one family.

Mickey's story was told to the accompaniment of the clanking bell, the rush of seas and the crash of recoil springs in the forepeak; punctuated by the iron shout of the whistle which shook everything with a fierce insistence that it be heard.

Mickey had the bunk that Allen and Ben were sitting on. Allen's bunk was occupied by a fireman with white chin-whiskers. He must have been near eighty; a man who had been fireman in the *Atlantic* when that little paddle-wheel steamer was the crack ship of the Collins fleet. The old fireman may have been good in his day, but on the lightship his value was mostly historic. He gave Allen's bunk hard wear. One of the bunks in Mr. Gill's room was occupied by a scared boy whose experience had been limited to firing on the *Flyer*, between Seattle and Tacoma. It didn't sound like a happy crew for wintering on a stormy station. The ship went out in November, and it threatenin' to be fine weather.

The ship didn't stay on station for long. The threat of fine weather faded and it blew a living hurricane from the north. The boy lay retching in his bunk and was of no use at all. The old fireman stood his own watches for a while, and spent the rest of the time clinging to his bunk like a crab. The devil could take care of the boy's watch.

They kept the engine going at half speed for a while, to take some of the stress off the cable. Afterward they had it going at near full speed.

Mickey stood an eight-hour watch, with coal, shovels, slice-bars and hoes jumping at him from all directions as the ship lept and plunged and lay down on one side and then the other. Once he was thrown against the red-hot fire-doors and could not get away promptly because the ship was standing on her head. The chief clung to the reversing wheel, now and then managing to give the engine a dahsh of oil. He didn't look like a man who enjoyed the work he was doing.

After eight hours of it Mickey decided some one else could have his turn at firing. By that time the ancient had decided the devil could take care of his watch, too. Mickey dragged him away from his bunk, but it was no use. In the end he had to leave him lying near the fidley, like a balky old mule. Mickey went aft and found the assistant engineer in *his* bunk. The man wasn't sick, but he looked white in the gills and made excuses. The little fireman was savage after his eight hours of hell, and the excuses didn't help. He hustled the assistant below and left him vomiting over the clinkers Mickey had just pulled from the fires.

The ship went adrift about an hour after he turned in. The assistant hadn't kept up the steam and there was too much stress on the cable. The excitement seemed to help at first. Men who had been scared out of their wits saw a chance of getting in from station, where they could quit and take up farming. They even got the eighty-year-old fireman below. Mickey cleaned the fires for him and went above for some sleep.

He woke in the early morning. The ship wasn't slamming into it any more, but going off before tremendous seas. The motion was a little easier, but even before Mickey was fully awake he got the feeling that something was terribly wrong. The engine! He didn't hear it stamping and didn't feel its vibration. The engine had broken down and they were driving off to hell before the hurricane! He piled below in a hurry.

There wasn't anything the matter with the engine or anything else, except that there wasn't a soul below! The boiler was still warm, but the steam pressure had dropped to zero, and when he opened the doors the fires were out. At first he thought the crew had gone overboard in some unaccountable manner. Well, God rest them; they hadn't been much of a crew.

Mickey cleaned out the dead fires and the choked ash pits and found wood and waste, which he soaked in a great dahsh of oil before lighting it. The fire-doors weren't so hot that they hurt when he was thrown against them. While he was working with the fires the ship was pooped, and he waited a minute to see if there was any sense in going on. She seemed to be going under, surely, stern first. The ship came up, though Mickey was all but drowned by water that came down the smashed ventilator, and his matches were soaked. He went above and got more from the galley. On the way he noticed the body of the assistant engineer crouched in a curious posture under the carpenter's bench, but he didn't have time to investigate. Through a portlight he had glimpsed the sea spouting against a rock not far to port, and no telling what lay ahead. He touched off the oil-soaked waste and wood, and pried up the starboard bunker gate to get at some clean coal. The stuff underfoot was mixed with clinkers and ashes and stewing in sea water.

He got coal, and plenty. As he pried up the gate the ship was knocked on her beam ends by a cross sea and Mickey went away to port with tons of coal on top of him. After a minute or so he came to and dug himself out and took his revenge on the coal by feeding some of it to the newborn fires.

While waiting for the fires to burn up, he oiled and swabbed the engines and auxiliaries and scooped stray coal out of the crank-pit. He had a bad minute filling grease cups in the shaft alley, with the ship getting pooped hard. It was enough to frighten a man, he said, down in that narrow prison like a trapped rat, with the whole stern under the sea and maybe never coming up again. But the ship came up, and Mickey came up. He nursed the fires until they became raging furnaces, always with the threat of being put out by the water that washed about the fire room. It wasn't knee deep, but when the ship stood on her head it ran into the ash pits and touched the forr'ard grate bars, Ben. And more came in every time the ship stopped a sea with her stern. If they didn't head up into it soon, they would never head up at all.

Mickey fed the raging furnaces until the steam began

232

to rise in the Scotch boiler. When he wanted a slice-bar or hoe, he had to watch until one appeared out of the avalanche of coal and tools and pursue it before it disappeared. The ship was rolling too much to keep the implements on the hooks. If a slice-bar had fallen on his head, that would have been the end of Mickey.

When the steam pressure reached forty pounds, he got the air pump and circulator and bilge pump going. He was a fireman, mind you, but he hadn't been a shipmate with machinery for nothing. The steam rose to fifty, and he got the main engine turning over, the first dahsh out of the box. He closed the throttle at once, stopping the engine neatly off dead center. If the ship was headed for the rocks it was no use getting there faster. The time had come for the navigating department to show what it could do.

In the officers' quarters aft Mickey found the captain, who had taken to his bed some time during the night, and reported that he had steam up. If the captain would send a *man* to the wheel—.

"Go to the devil!" the old fellow told him. "I'm a sick man!"

"Sick! You're going to be dead if you don't do something!" Mickey told him.

The captain fell back on his dignity. "Go away," he said. "What do you mean? A fireman coming aft and insulting the captain!" He looked as if he were about to cry.

"Captain, me arse!" Mickey said. "You're a broken-down old washerwoman!"

He left the captain in tears and found the mate in *his*

berth, lying face down and holding on with both hands. When he had torn the man loose and turned him over he could get nothing out of him but groans and retchings. The mate, too, had composed himself to die and could not get back into the spirit of working a ship. After a bit Mickey gave him up and ran below to put more coal on the fires. The steam which no one seemed to want was still coming up; it was near sixty now.

Mickey went above again, and forward to the crew's quarters. When he was passing the carpenter's bench the assistant engineer's body came to life and caught him by one leg.

"Save me!" the assistant implored. "I'm a family man. My wife and children!"

"Your wife and children aren't on board," Mickey reminded him. "If you drowned every day in the week they would be losing nothing!" He jerked away and continued forward, with the assistant sprawling after him. "Me wife and children!"

In the sailors' quarters it was the same thing over again—like trying to raise a crew from the dead. A big seaman alone in one stateroom did nothing but moan, "My head, oh, my head!"

And when Mickey spoke derisively of some other part of his own anatomy and asked if he wanted to drown, the fellow indicated that he would dearly like to drown. There was a bit of water dahshing about in the messroom outside and coming in over the door coaming when the ship fell over on her port side, and the bould sailor would have it that they were sinking already, and a good thing, too!

In the forr'ard stateroom there was a seaman clinging to a bunk with all his arms and legs, while another, a little, fair-haired Finn, lay on the floor, bleeding from a great gash on his cheekbone. He had been thrown from the upper berth in one of the wild rolls of the ship and hadn't bothered to pick himself up again. For a good five minutes Mickey shook the man on the bunk, cursing him and shouting that there was a good head of steam. If there was one man at all on board to take the wheel they would be saved! It produced no effect except that the fellow began vomiting.

Then the little Finn sat up on the floor and began to cry, with tears and blood streaming down his face. "I don't care!" he sobbed. "I don't care for those folks. They quit, the folks! They should be drowned, but if there's steam, I'll steer!"

Mickey thought better of the seaman when he saw that he had only been crying because he was angry, and when he offered to steer he was ready to cry himself, with gratitude.

With the companion slide cracked enough to stick his head out, Mickey saw the little Finn reach the wheelhouse. It was blowing a living hurricane, he said, with monstrous big seas, enough to frighten a man, and there was wreckage and lumber about.

Ben wanted to know how high the seas were.

Mickey couldn't tell him that. Fifty feet, or a hundred feet. That was the business of the deck department. On deck, things were done by guess and by God. If a navigator came within a mile of what he shot at, he spoke to no one for days. An engineer measured things in *his* department by a thousandth of an inch, and didn't think anything of it.

When Mickey saw the man gain the wheelhouse, he scuttled below and coaled the fires. There was a grand head of steam, near ready to blow off. He warmed the engine and got it turning over, with the water service turned off at first, so it would warm the quicker. When he had closed the drains, he blew into the speaking tube by the log desk.

"Are ye there?" he asked.

The little Finn was there.

"Say the word!"

"Full speed ahead! There's rocks—"

Mickey didn't wait to hear any more. He opened the throttle full, but gently, Ben, gently. Then he went back to the fires and opened the drafs wide.

The Finn didn't do things so gently. One wave may have looked as big to him as another, and with the sea dahshing and spouting against the rocks ahead he may not have had much choice. However, that may be, he put the ship about the minute she had good steerage way on her; just wrastled the wheel hard over and kept it in a becket until she came about.

The lightship fair lay down on her side and kicked, with more water on top of her than underneath. Mickey was torn loose from the damper chains and went away to leeward, with everything but the engine piled on top of him. Through it all, he heard things breaking loose all over the ship. A ton of water came down the ventilator, but by the grace of God it rushed aft, into the shaft alley and the bilges.

You'ld expect a Finn to do a clumsy thing like that. But he brought her about. The ship came up, with her own weight of water sluicing off her decks, and began slamming into it. Mickey dug himself out and found the engine still stamping away and the fires burning.

The thing was as good as done, Mickey said. There wasn't anything left to do but force the ship through the hurricane with her fifty horsepower engine and get inside the shelter of the Straits. Always providing, of course, that nothing really heavy fell on Mickey, and the little Finn didn't bleed to death at the wheel.

It was no excursion, though. The motion of the ship was ten times worse, and she slamming into it. The Finn didn't ring for half-speed, with a big one coming— the way they would on a well-manned steamship. He never touched the gong-pull and took the seas as they came, on the nose. There were some terrible rough jolts, but perhaps it was as well, Mickey decided. Besides being engineer, he was fireman and oiler and coal-passer and water-tender. There was no one at all to stand like a bould hero, with his hand on the throttle, when Mickey was grubbing ashes out of the pits or sitting up with a sick auxiliary, or maybe picking himself up from a corner, and the engine room tools on top of him.

In his spare time Mickey ran above and abused the officers and crew, the ones on the port side still lying where they had been thrown by the rough hand of salvation when the ship was put about. For a while he clung to the idea of getting someone to relieve the fire room or wheel. But it was no use. Everyone was sicker than ever with the great motion of the ship. Everyone but the boy fireman, who didn't seem sick at all any more. He just lay in his bunk, laughing, with a light in his eyes that made your hair creep. Mickey closed the boy's door, not wanting to hear him or see that look.

Another pest, of a different sort altogether, was the assistant engineer in his refuge under the carpenter's bench. When Mickey went by, he grabbed at his leg and pleaded. By this time the man had his wife and children on board, and he appealed to Mickey gallantly to save them.

Mickey didn't know whether he was tired or not. He carried on the duties of a whole engine room and fireroom crew all day, under impossible conditions, and he the smallest man on board, not five feet high and not a young buck any more. And he didn't know whether he was tired. He drank some water now and then, with the engine room thermometer at 120, and ate a few rounds of pilot bread. He became like a god, or an imp with all hell to himself.

In the afternoon he remembered about the little Finn in the wheel house. He hadn't heard from him all day, and only knew he was alive because the ship was still bucking the wind and sea, head on.

He didn't know whether he should risk going on deck, but he feared the man might give up or go mad with thirst, and him with nothing to eat or drink all day. Mickey took the chance he had to take and reached the wheelhouse with pilot bread and a can of water and sticking plaster. Now he was ship's doctor and messboy, besides being three firemen and a few engineers.

The Finn was something to look at. He had a handkerchief bound round his head, with his yellow hair sticking up at the top like hay pulled out of a scarecrow and half his face, from the eye down, was caked with blood, like a great birthmark. Mickey thought the handkerchief was a misplaced bandage, but the man said it was to keep the hair out of his eyes. Mickey stopped in the wheelhouse only a minute, long enough to add some sticking plaster and soot marks to the helmsman's patchwork face. And he wrastled the wheel while the Finn drank half a gallon of water. Mither of God, what seas! The light of day went out when they took a breaking one on the nose.

The Finn thought they had made good six miles in the twelve hours, but he was vague about where they were. He would steer till Christmas if the steam held. For all he cared, Mickey could use the crew for fuel, the dirty folks!

Mickey got to the companionway between seas, and below in time to save the condenser from bursting, the air pump having stuck. When that was attended to he looked after the fires and the engine and made a trip through the shaft alley and filled the lamps which had burned out the night before. At half a mile an hour, it would take thirty hours from the station to the Straits, and no telling how far south they had drifted before Mickey O'Rorke took charge.

During the night Mickey decided he was tired. For eighteen hours he had done five men's work, and something extra, and he couldn't stay awake any more. So he gave the fires a monstrous big stoking and the engine a great dahsh of oil, and he went above to lie down in the fidley for a minute. All bruised and skinned as he was, the iron grating was like a bed of roses, Ben.

He came to with the ship rising side-on to a great sea and dropping fifty feet into the pit of hell. The engine was stopped and the gong clanging like mad. Mickey lept below and found the boy fireman laughing in a cloud of steam, wetting down hot clinkers with a hose.

There was no laughing for Mickey when he opened the doors; not a coal left! With some insane idea of helping, the boy had pulled the fires and wet them down. Mickey chased him above, still laughing, and found wood for new fires. The boy's brain had burst, he said; he died in the hospital in Seattle a day after they got in.

Mickey didn't remember the rest too clearly, only that he kept things going, somehow. He managed some sleep, coiled like a serpent on the engine room ladder. He awakened whenever the mad boy was stepping over him, and him trying to get at the fires.

Around noon of the second day he went to the companion hatch and saw Tatoosh Island, close aboard the port bow. He also saw a passenger steamer turn in toward the Straits and disappear. With the first sea on her beam she lay over on her side, quite gently, and never came up again. Nothing came up but a burst of steam, and the sea getting at her boilers.

All told, it took Mickey and the little Finn thirty-six hours to bring the lightship into the Straits. When he felt the ship in calm water, and all the noise and tumult ending, Mickey stoked the fires for the last time and crept up to sleep in the fidley.

He woke with the ship being worked into Seattle.

The others had come to life and were bustling about, feeling that they had done pretty well, after all. Mickey lay on his luxurious iron grill and heard the assistant engineer bawling in strident tones: "Where's Mickey? Where's the little Irish son-of-a-bitch!"

After a while Mickey went out to meet him. It seemed the assistant wanted him to stand his watch in the fire room, short-handed as they were with the boy gone mad.

"Was I a son-of-a-bitch yesterday, with you on your knees, begging me to save your wife and children?" Mickey asked in justifiable spite.

But the assistant didn't want to talk about his wife and children at all.

That was the story, Ben. There wasn't much more to tell. After repairs had been rushed, *Lightship 167* went back on station with a brand new set of officers and crew. Mickey was there, but he was new, in a way of speaking, because he went as chief engineer. Some of the Department thought he should get it, and some thought he shouldn't. He had never even been an assistant, and he was shy on book knowledge and mathematics. But he had remembered that two and two made four when he was standing on his head with the whole engine room on top of him, and that counted for something.

The thing had brought Mickey a kind of fame. It was written up in the newspapers at the time. Mickey'd had a clipping from the *P.I.* which he used to keep in the top of his derby hat, but he'd lost it since. And a writer for the *Saturday Evening Post* spent a week in the ship on station and made Mickey the hero of a series of stories. Only one about the lightship, however. There hadn't been enough in the life for more than a short story. In the others he was an engineer in ships up North and one place and another. In one Mickey was in a ship with another engineer and a beautiful woman, and no one else at all. And in the end Mickey married the woman, or maybe the other man did. But that was only a story. In a way of speaking, Mickey's wedding was with the lightship in the storm. He'd been faithful to her, as men went, these twenty years. You've read those stories, Ben.

Ben had read them aloud to the little chief when the ship first came on station. They had been offered to him as the real Mickey O'Rorke. "They didn't do justice to you, Chief," he said.

"Ah, they're grand stories, Ben."

"But they're not Mickey O'Rorke," Allen put in.

The little chief looked at his firemen affectionately out of his old cat's face. "Ah, me byes, a story is only something to read, and you with some time on your hands. You couldn't expect it to do a man justice."

They tried to induce Mickey to enlarge on other incidents of his career, but he was against overworking the truth. He substituted fiction and began telling about the time he went to Rome to become a priest—a story the firemen had heard several times before.

Mickey reached the point where, in the midst of riotous living, he wrote home that for five hundred pounds more he could become a bishop. "And me not knowing a word of Latin after two years, what with drinkin' an' carryin' on and not going near the college—"

Ole's, wise, homely face and stocky figure appeared in the doorway.

"Th' *Columbine's* alongside." His tone suggested that while it made no difference to him, it might interest the others.

The chief dismissed his story instantly. "Coal for our bunkers!" he proclaimed gleefully, scrambling to his feet, "and maybe some 'Tom and Jerry!'" It was his pet name for the special oil used by the bell machine, and he welcomed the torpedo cans of gray lubricant with an hilarity past Ben's understanding.

Ole went on to his stateroom, while the firemen and chief straggled aft through the lurching ship.

"I doubt though," Mickey observed, "that there'll be any coaling at sea on a day like this."

Ben had the same fear, but he thought it a little heartless of the chief to put the matter into words. It seemed to lessen their already slender chances.

The trio went to the head of the companionway, where they were partly sheltered from the wind and rain, and contemplated the *Columbine*. The tender lay wallowing in the sea, hove-to, about a hundred yards off. She was an old wooden steamer a hundred and fifty feet in length, with the determined ugliness of a craft built for one special purpose. The forward three-fifths of her consisted of practically nothing: an insignificant foc'sle head and a low, naked well deck for buoys. For the remaining two-fifths the designer seemed to have gone into a panic over his slender accomplishments for-

243

ward and uttered all the elements of a steamer in one breath. Derrick, wheel house, smokestack, ventilators, boats and accommodations for officers and official passengers were crowded together and heaped up at the stern. The unbalanced craft gave the impression that at the slightest hint she would sit down heavily on her tail and be unable to get up again.

There was nothing particularly cheering in the ugly gray craft floundering in the gray, rain-plagued sea. Particularly when conditions seemed poor for transferring coal and supplies. It was blowing, not a gale nor half a gale, but hard enough, and the seas were heavy and breaking. The empty lightship rolled wildly along with her pitching, and the tender's whaleboat would be hard put to it while the crew passed bags of coal through the half-doors. Ben had been through one coaling on station, in easier weather, and then it was bad enough. One moment the men in the whaleboat had been around the turn of the lightship's bilge, fighting to be clear of the murderous guard when it bore down with the whole weight of the ship behind it, and the next moment they were swept up out of sight, with the sea gushing in through the open half-doors. What it would be like in this weather he did not know.

Captain Lindstrom and Oscar and Clark were standing aft in the rain, alternately looking at the wallowing *Columbine* and talking among themselves. Ole passed around the group at the head of the companionway, clasping his slicker.

"Ah, Ole, me lad," Mickey said cheerfully. "Are ye going over for the coals?"

Ole glanced back. The face under his sou'wester was like the face of a shrewd old peasant woman under a bonnet. "If I am sent," he answered gravely. "But we will not be sent. And they do not expect to come over today. Their boats are on deck."

The old commander of the *Columbine* showed none of Captain Kennedy's fire in arriving at the station. He did not attempt to come within hailing distance, but steamed a little further up to windward and let go an anchor. Then he veered out on the cable and let go the other. Thus moored, the tender brought up about two hundred yards from the lightship, heaving and rolling in a manner that startled Ben. Though Mickey assured him it was nothing compared with the motion of the lightship, which he hardly noticed.

There were no further signs of life from the *Columbine*. After standing about for a while longer, the others came below, leaving Oscar's yellow-slickered figure alone in the wind and rain, like the last haystack of summer.

Captain Lindstrom seemed neither elated nor depressed when he came down the companionway; he only had an even look of waiting.

"Tomorrow, I hope," he said in answer to the little chief's appeal for coals. "We have a rising barometer, and I don't think this dirt will last. Captain Richardson probably has orders to stand by until he can coal us."

At the foot of the companion steps, the officers and crew scattered. Allen Ross was very cheerful as he and Ben went forward.

"Mickey's coals are at the door," he observed. "Let's

forget the *Columbine* until morning. How about reading me some more of 'Tess'?"

"All right."

Reading aloud to Allen was the only way Ben could forget the lightship completely. Allen's acquaintance with literature had begun when Ben unpacked the books from his cardboard suitcase. He was virgin territory, but fertile, and his tense interest and shrewd comments gave every book a new edge. There, too, he had the advantage over Ben. He had experienced and observed a great deal of life in his thirty-odd years, and when he saw the familiar material in a work of art his flashing recognition was splendid. Ben had been well-read at twelve. At eighteen, he was beginning, painfully and gropingly, to recognize some of the familiar material in the slow complications of life. Really, his literary education had begun with Allen Ross.

"We got as far as where Tess told Angel she'd had a baby, and he was sore about it," Allen reminded his roommate. "I knew a girl in Seattle who had something the matter with her so she couldn't have one, and she didn't tell the man until after they were married. That was worse, because it was really gyping a man out of something. He was sore, all right, and I don't blame him. But what this other girl had done before was none of the man's business, when she was on the square. I guess old Hardy wasn't so keen about religious people, either, when he named the fellow Angel." Allen seemed particularly ready to shut Ben off from his surroundings.

Ben, for the first time, was beginning to sense a shadowy significance in the lightship on her lonely station. With the book in his hand, he stood on the rail of his berth and gazed through the porthole until the rolling ship gave him a glimpse of the lighthouse tender, wallowing in the gray, rain-smitten sea. Things were coming to a point. Always before, when conditions weren't right, the tender steamed on about her other business and tried again later. Now, it had become an emergency. It might be a month before the damaged *Swiftsure* got back on station and released the *Relief*. Until then, *167* would have to hold on. If the tender failed to transfer coal and supplies, the dreary lightship might do something unexpected. There might even be an end to dreariness. By persisting in it too long, *167* might become something spectacular: a hungry and empty ship, defying assistance; saving others without being able to save herself.

"I've found the place," Allen announced cheerfully. The book was open in his hands. "Come down from your perch. I want to find out if Angel still thinks he bought the rights to the girl's past when he married her. If he does, we'll fix him; we'll start by sending him a bill for her baby clothes and schooling!"

Ben stepped down from his bunk, reluctantly. He could not see why his cabin mate was so anxious to make him forget. Something exciting was making up at last, and he was too young to consider the possibility of excitement passing the bounds of safe entertainment. His heart never doubted that in the end everything would turn out well.

XII

Ole's Bible

IT WAS Saturday morning and Harry was making his rounds of the cabins, a duty he liked. The crew found some comfort, he thought, in fresh sheets and towels, new little cakes of soap and boxes of safety matches. If it weren't for the cook's illness and his own double work, he could do much more to make the ship comfortable.

For the present, there wasn't anything left but the small comforts. It had blown up during the night, and in Ole's watch the *Columbine* got up her anchors and steamed south. She was beginning to drag, he said, and got under weigh a little after three bells.

It would never have occurred to Harry to blame the cook for being sick, or resent his extra work, but the crew seemed to have reached that state of mind. Mr. Gill lay solidly in his plunging upper berth, with his mighty bulk defying the messman's inclination to change the sheet.

"Leave it, Lad, leave it!" The old fireman looked down from his seasoned copy of the *National Geographic*. "You have other work. I'll change it when I'm ready and bring you the old one." He turned his mild, spectacled gaze on the magazine again, and the substantial fact of his two hundred and fifty pounds won the argument.

In the other starboard cabin it was the same story. Ben collected his towel and Allen's, gingerly, and pulled the grimy sheets from the bunks, throwing them down by the door for Harry to take on his return trip.

"I'll put on the clean ones," he said gruffly, taking them from the protesting messman, "—unless the cook does it."

On the port side, Harry met with more of the conspiracy.

"I fix my own bunk," Oscar told him darkly. He took his allotment, jealously, put it on the bunk beside him and opened his box of matches with suspicion, as he always did. Once, he explained, he had been dealt an empty box and did not discover the fact until afterward. It was not clear whether he had been seriously inconvenienced by the omission, but his tone put it in a sinister light.

In the next little cabin, Ole was sitting in his upper bunk with a copy of the *Oregonian* which the *Relief* had brought, his hair-cutting shears and a pot of paste such as children use in school. He looked down gravely at the messman.

"Leave the sheets there," he advised. "I am not too proud to make the bunk I sleep in. Clark can make his own, too." When the messman protested it was no trouble, he went on cutting, without comment.

Harry stripped the sheet from Clark's bunk, and shook out a fresh one. He was glad Clark was on watch and Ole otherwise occupied. There would be no more clean sheets until the ship went in from station. He wanted the satisfaction of performing his duties as long as he had the materials to do it, and the helpful spirit of the crew baffled him. However, one bunk to make up was better than none.

"The cook is like an animal," Ole's voice remarked from above as Harry smoothed Clark's blanket. "He sits like an animal in a cage and doesn't work." There was cold wonder and contempt in the seaman's voice.

The messman patted Clark's thin pillow into shape and sat on the wooden bench, looking up at Ole. "I don't mind the work," he insisted. "I only wish we could do something for the cook. It is terrible for a man to go insane like that."

"No, there is nothing terrible in it." The seaman's face was all wooden gravity as he pasted a clipping in a thick notebook. "It is only a disgrace. He is going out of his head from loneliness; they said that about the others. Loneliness in a ship with nine other men! I have this upper berth to keep people out from under my feet, and I don't ask everyone into my cabin.

"The cook is not going out of his head because there is no one to talk to. You know what he thinks about: movies, automobiles, crowds of people he doesn't even know. He would not be crazy if he could look at electric light signs and crowds of women going in and out of Frederick & Nelson's. He would be all right if he could stand on Second Avenue and listen to a player piano in a store window." Ole spat into the distant cuspidor with contemptuous accuracy. He put away his shears and little pot of paste. "It is not terrible," he repeated. "It is disgusting for a man to have nothing of his own in his head." He looked down at the messman with grave appeal in his little eyes. "Maybe you could tell me; I have thought about it often, but I know very little. Do cities make people like that? Sometimes I tell myself people go that way because there is so much in a city they think they have everything. And when they get by themselves they find they are empty because none of it was their own."

Harry was glad to discuss the side issue. His feelings protested against Ole's unsympathetic view of the cook. But the seaman's opinions had a cold justice that made argument difficult. Where he was not sure, he admitted his ignorance and appealed for information without any false pride.

"I don't think cities do it," Harry told him. "I was born in New York, and was never really out of it until I was thirty. Then I was away for over a year, at sea and in a hospital in Sydney with my broken leg; it never mended right. When I went back to New York, I only stayed three days. I loved New York, it was wonderful!" The upward-looking eyes in his fragile face flashed with glory and pain. "I think about it like I do about living. It was wonderful, but I couldn't do it over again. It would be too much!" He blinked and worked his small, thin hands together as if he were washing them. "I don't want to live in any city; I'm not lonely here."

The seaman looked down solemnly, like an owl from a branch. "You have something of your own in your head," he observed. "When you lived in New York, you had something of your own. You didn't just go to movies and listen to player pianos.

"No." Harry said, painfully. "I was interested in the American Indian."

Ole pursed his long lips. "I know nothing about Indians," he said with regret, "except what I told you—the time I killed the calf. I didn't think well of them because I had done them a wrong. Really, I was angry with myself because I was so ignorant. Some time you must tell me about the Indians. We could learn from people like that."

"We could learn a lot!" Harry answered vehemently.

"When I was on the Gold Coast of Africa," the seaman recollected, "I learned something from the natives. After eating, they would take rice, or whatever food was left, and put it on their fingers and rub their teeth and gums. They had fine white teeth, too. I didn't think the food helped, but there must be something in what they did. So I rubbed my teeth and gums with my finger every day. Now, the magazines tell you to do that. But I have been doing it for twenty-six years. See what good teeth I have?" He drew back his lips, baring his strong, yellow teeth.

Harry murmured admiringly.

The seaman folded the newspaper and opened a bloated note-book, which he examined critically. "I have been working on my bible," he explained.

"Your bible?" Harry was mystified. "I didn't think you had any use for religion."

"Not the Sunday school kind," the seaman explained contemptuously. "People like that are hypocrites. But I have my religion. For a while after I gave up the Sunday school kind, I didn't have any, but now I have my faith.

People are my religion. They may be a little dirty and crooked, but they are all we have. They are better than the kind you hear about in church because they are real. America is my special religion; I am an American citizen. Americans are good people. They aren't perfect, but they believe in people and they go ahead and learn the secrets of the world. They want to learn, and when there is so much to find out that is better than being perfect."

Ole looked down from his plunging bunk with unconscious, wooden gravity. "Sometimes I have been angry at what some of the magazines say about America; they make fun of nearly everything. But now I think that is good, too. Politicians tell the people everything is fine, but people who care say the hard things. People who are learning want to know their faults. I read the magazine that made fun of every state, and I told myself: 'That is good, too.' But I didn't forget my religion. America is a good religion because it is people from every country in the world learning how to work together and not kill each other." He paused in his sermon to open a little round tin of snuff.

"It is a good religion," Harry agreed, wishing he could have Ole's steadying faith.

"Would you like to look at my bible?" The seaman put a pinch of snuff in his cheek and capped the box. "I don't show it to everyone." He handed down the notebook and looked on with grave anxiety as the messman opened it, after wiping his hands on his apron.

The notebook, swollen with clippings to thrice its normal thickness, was the ordinary school kind, with a tough paper cover and ruled pages. On the first page was a lithographed American flag, neatly cut out and pasted; the symbol of the seaman's faith. Harry held the book flat on his knees and turned the pages with a connoisseur's hand. He knew from experience that a man sees his collection with double pleasure when someone else is looking at it. He turned a page and paused before a large newspaper picture of Robert La Follette.

Ole was leaning over the edge of his bunk. "I like to look at his face," he explained. "He is a part of my country. His name is French, but he is a great American. He lived in the middle of the land, but he knew what went on at sea, and he passed the Seamen's Act. If you had gone to sea as long as I have, if you had been treated badly and sold like a slave, you would know what that meant."

The little man on the bench was shaken. "I know," he said, without looking up. "I was sold into slavery."

On the next double page, a picture of Roentgen and the first X-ray machine faced the story of a telephone operator who stayed at her switchboard, warning others of a flood, until she was drowned.

"Things aren't in any special order," Ole pointed out. "They are put in the way they happen. When I find something that should go in my bible, I put it in without knowing what will come next. The X-ray was a great invention because doctors can see inside of people without cutting them open. That was a great secret to learn. But the telephone girl has a place in my bible, too, because people like her make inventions mean something."

The messman turned another page and started at the picture of a grave, handsome gentleman in dark clothes and clerical collar. He looked closer, thinking there must be a mistake. There was none. Under the picture was the man's name: the Reverend Archibald Mansfield.

Ole moved uneasily on his bunk. "He is not there because he is a preacher," he explained. "He is there because he is a man. He stopped crimping in New York City. It took him a long time, and it was hard work. The politicians and ship-owners were against him, and the crimps tried to kill him. But he started his own shipping offices and drove out the crimps. You should know him; you are from New York."

The messman answered with a sigh. "I don't know him. He was after my time."

Ole was annoyed by the sadness and regret in Harry's voice. There were so many sad people in the world. They slowed things up by looking back when they should look ahead. Also, he hadn't liked the way Harry looked at Mansfield's picture. Maybe he should try to make himself clearer.

"I don't say a man is no good because he belongs to a church," he explained. "I only say he is in bad company that wastes his time. But if he does something good, he goes into my bible just the same. You will find the Molokai priest in there, too. Most religious people are hypocrites, but a hypocrite doesn't live among lepers and die of their disease."

Harry turned the page and saw the picture of a powerful, business like craft; a solid heroic old ship, that caught his eye like a familiar figure. It was the Coast Guard cutter *Bear*. He had often seen her in Seattle Harbor, between her trips to the Arctic. And once when he was messman in the *Nome City*, the steam schooner anchored near the *Bear* at Point Barrow. Earlier, there had been the *Bear* and the *Beaver*, both famous in their way. But he had seen the *Beaver's* Scotch boilers lying on the beach at Valdees, and the *Bear* went on. She was one of the ships Captain Lindstrom liked to talk about: ships that couldn't fail. There was a mystery about them, he thought, something that couldn't be explained away. For forty years the *Bear* had brought spring to the far north. She had brought news of the outside world, food for starving villages, medical attention, law and order. She had rescued lost Arctic explorers and the crews of countless ships. The old *Bear* had steamed the better part of a million miles, most of it on a badly-charted coast and among Arctic ice.

Ole was leaning down, with his small grave eyes on the picture. "The *Bear* is part of my religion," he said. "She is a fine part of America. School children should learn about her as well as about battleships. And if people learned how to get to one of the other worlds in the stars, where people live, they should send the *Bear* first. She would do a good job."

"Yes," Harry agreed, "she would do a good job!"

He went on through the neat, homely notebook, looking with respect at the stories and pictures of people who had given their best. Pasteur, Dr. Wiley and Madame Curie were there among obscure men and women who gave what they had and had been forgotten by everyone but the grave little recording angel, with his turned-down Asiatic hat and a quid of snuff in the side of his homely face. Count Marconi's picture shared a page with the story of a ten-year-old Iowa boy who was drowned while rescuing two smaller children. He had saved one, and was lost in going after the other.

"He was a good boy," the seaman commented, "He did his duty and wasn't afraid."

"Is your picture here?" Harry asked.

"No." Ole was surprised. "Why should it be?"

"Clark told me you once saved a woman from drowning."

"Oh, that time." Ole was annoyed that his cabin-mate had mentioned it. "That was nothing for my bible. I didn't take any chances. Anyway, I expected to get something out of it."

"A reward?" The messman couldn't believe it of Ole.

The seaman wrinkled his forehead, wondering if that was a proper name for it. "Something like that," he decided. "But she turned out to be an old lady."

"I was in a three-masted barque," he explained, "lying at a dock in Liverpool. It was at night, and I was going ashore for some fun. I had my good clothes on and a gold ring on my finger. I always go to a whorehouse like a gentleman. When I was on the gangplank, I noticed something moving in the black water a little farther for'ard. When I looked closer, I made out that it was someone overboard, and I knew what had happened. It had been raining. (That was why I happened to go ashore late; I waited for it to stop, so as not to spoil my good clothes.) We were lying at a stone pier, with a flush edge. The lights reflected on the wet pier and made it hard to tell where the stone ended and the water began. Someone had walked off the edge; a sober person could have done that.

"It would have been no trouble to save the person in some lubberly way, but I had to think of my good clothes. I found a coil of new rope on board—it was quite clean—and worked it into chain knots, with a round turn and half hitch in each one. That took only a minute, and I had a rope ladder that reached to the water when I made the end fast to a bollard. It was an inch Manila, and even a heavy man would not have pulled it too tight to get his feet in the loops.

"'There's a ladder, dead ahead of you!' I sang out. 'Grab it and lay aloft.' I had fixed things so nice that I wouldn't get a drop of water on my suit. But he kept right on paddling in one place.

"Then I made it out to be a woman. 'Here's where I have some fun without having to go ashore,' I said. And I walked down my rope ladder, right to the water, without even getting my shoes wet.

"The woman wasn't a fathom from me. When I hailed her again, she came over, paddling away like a cat and not saying a word. Then I found I was thirty years too late. She was an old lady of about seventy, but I saved her anyway. I carried her up the ladder and called the dock policeman. He wanted my name, but I wouldn't give it to him. Then I went ashore. My suit was of good quality, and I didn't get very wet carrying her. You see how it is best to be careful."

Ole spat into the distant cuspidor with an accuracy that could not fail. "The next day there was a story about it in the Liverpool papers, and I found she was a member of the Salvation Army. Well, she was a game old lady, anyway. I saved the story for a while, but only to remind myself to do everything carefully, even when

259

I thought I was going after something good. You see why it doesn't belong in my bible."

"I suppose it doesn't," Harry agreed. The story had upset him considerably. He remembered all the work he had to do, and got up from the bench. "Still, there are some good stories in the Bible."

"That is for hypocrites," the seaman maintained. He was annoyed that the Hebrew bible should be mentioned in the same breath with his own.

XIII

The Land of the Enemy

HARRY was giving the galley its weekly cleaning. It was no easy job. The lively desperation of the ship's movements slopped water from his half-filled scrub pail and played shuffleboard with everything loose. And the hulking cook took up a good deal of space, wedged in a chair between the range and sink. The cook had not shaved for weeks and his face was almost as shaggy as his head. Harry was sorry for his superior; he thought Ole was heartless for talking about him as he did. But he had to admit the cook was like an animal. He believed all people had come up from animals, through work and imagination, and maybe when they were strained past the breaking point they took refuge in becoming animals again.

The cook watched Harry scrub, with a sickly smile of self-pity. Sometimes he told the messman that he envied him, but more often he hinted that it was heartless of him to enjoy working while *he* suffered the torments of loneliness and privation. Harry had tried reminding him that the whole crew was in the same boat, but it did no good. The cook accepted it as a proof of his own superiority. He, alone, was sufficiently sensitive and urbane to suffer when he was away from civilization, and he therefore deserved the sympathy and pity of the whole crew.

While Harry scrubbed up and kept an eye on the bread in the oven, the cook regaled him with endless information about the process of putrefaction and the way of the worms with a corpse in the ground. His knowledge on the subject was so complete that he gave the impression of having been, variously, a corpse, a maggot and several kinds of a ghoul. The messman would have liked to shut him up, but he knew the cook did not talk to the other members of the crew because they were cold to his bids for pity. And the man might become dangerous if he talked to no one.

It was hard, though, having to hear such grisly rubbish, told with the cook's intimate leer. Harry was only able to stand it because he saw it was a little ridiculous. When the cook would have sacrified the lives of everyone else on board to get his feet on the ground, it was ridiculous for him to have such a dread of that same ground. Besides, he was rather going out of his way in torturing himself with the horrors of the grave when he stood a very fair chance of being buried at sea.

Harry stood it until he began making pies from the remainder of the dough and some septic-smelling meat. Then, the cook's recital became too suggestive, and he felt he was going to be sick.

"Why not go to your room and lie down?" he proposed gently. "I don't think you've been getting much sleep."

The cook gave him a clinging, accusing look. "You want to get rid of me!" His voice went up, hysterically. "And I thought you had some pity for me. Nowhere to go, nothing to see, nothing to do. Only you to talk to, and you want to send me away. O, Christ!" He put his head in his hands and rocked back and forth. "I feel so bad. Can't you see how terrible it is for me here? I want to jump overboard and end my misery."

The messman resorted to bribery. "I have a movie magazine for you," he observed, seductively, managing to get ahead with the meat pies while the cook was away from the grave. "You can have it if you go to your room."

"Is it a new one?" The cook's eyes were a mixture of suspicion and desire.

"Not quite. But it's one you haven't seen before, with lots of pretty pictures."

The cook changed to a tone of injury. "Why didn't you give it to me before? I suppose it's been here for months, and you didn't bother giving it to me. Didn't bother, when you knew it would give me a few minutes of happiness!" Tears started from his eyes.

Harry was exasperated. "I only found it this morning, when I was cleaning up aft. I couldn't have given it to you any earlier, when you were busy talking."

The shaggy giant looked forgiving. "I know you're sorry for me," he said generously. "Has it a picture of Wally Reid?"

A crafty look in the man's eyes stopped Harry from saying it had. If he said there was a picture of Wally Reid, the cook might say he had seen that one before, and accuse him of a cruel deception. "I'm sure I don't know," he answered. "I haven't time to look through magazines. But it's one you never saw. Do you want it, or not?"

The cook watched the messman work, seeming to forget about the magazine. "Do you know the first thing a worm does when it finds a corpse?" His voice was itching and confidential.

Harry knew, from the cook's say-so. He recoiled hastily from the meat pie. "Do you want the magazine or not?" he gulped. "If you don't, I'm going to give it to Mr. Gill. He likes to read."

"Don't let him have it!" The cook was in a panic. "You wouldn't take it away from me, would you? You know how I suffer, with nowhere to go and nothing to do. Give it to me, and maybe I can read myself to sleep."

Probably he would do just that. And after sleeping all day, he would keep the messman awake most of the night, telling about his itching desire for the earth, and his horror of becoming a part of it. But it was worth a lot to be rid of him. Harry led the cook to the cabin they shared and left him eating up the magazine with greedy eyes. He felt more kindly toward the cook as soon as he didn't have to listen to him. He had to stand a good deal from him, more than the other members of the crew realized, and for that reason was more considerate of him than anyone else.

When he was left in peace, the little messman no longer felt sick or lonely. While looking after the baking, and cleaning the galley, he told himself about the Sioux War, and his hero, Chief Crazy Horse.

It was a terrible story of the cruelty and greed and treachery of a white nation. It began in 1875, when gold was discovered in the Black Hills and General Crook was

264

sent to drive out the Sioux Nation. Seven years earlier, the United States had signed the Fort Laramie Treaty, agreeing that the Indians should have the Black Hills, unmolested, as long as the grass grew and the water ran. Nothing was known about the gold then.

Crook sent a message to the great Sioux leaders, Sitting Bull and Crazy Horse, ordering them to the Red Cloud Reservation, which would be theirs, under supervision, as long as the grass grew and the water ran—or until the land was found to be of some value.

Sitting Bull sent back his proud answer in the form of a question: "Are you the Great God who made me?"

Crazy Horse was too proud to answer at all.

The war ended in 1890, with the surrender of Big Foot at Wounded Knee—a fatal combination. The Indians found more disaster in surrender than they had in continuing a hopeless war. When the braves had given up all their weapons, the soldiers tried to disarm the two standing guard over their dying chief. One gave up his rifle and the other resisted. In the struggle, the rifle went off and a lieutenant was killed. The unarmed Sioux braves were mowed down, surrounded by five times their number of soldiers. Then the field guns were turned on the women and children, running away up a narrow gulch. Later, the soldiers followed them, mopping up. When they marched back, the gulch was strewn with huddled heaps of women and children and babies, butchered like rabbits in the snow. That was the end. Christian civilization had triumphed over the savage. The road was clear for billboards and Ford cars.

The messman blinked back tears of anger and shame,

and hung his head when he remembered he was a white man.

Afterward, he felt calmer, telling himself the story of Chief Crazy Horse.

Crazy Horse was the youngest and most famous of the Ogalala Sioux chiefs. Thirty-two when he met the first attack of General Crook; thirty-four when he was murdered at the door of Fort Robinson guard house by a timid soldiery that felt uncomfortable in the presence of the captive eagle. The honorable peace that had been promised in return for his surrender was to be a governmental kidnapping and life imprisonment on Dry Tortugas—and even that treachery was bungled.

Harry could think without sorrow of the death of Crazy Horse. It was best the way it happened. Crazy Horse had done himself a good turn by resisting the final trap and receiving a bayonette in the side. In thirty-odd years, he had lived a long time. When he was alone at the deserted camp on the Rosebud he discovered the meaning of life. He saw how it had been with people from the beginning, and he saw what would happen as long as there were people on the earth. The death he sought came soon after. It happened the way things do in stories: the one after other, so you can see the meaning; the unnecessary part between cut out.

There had been many contradictory opinions about Crazy Horse, among the whites. The only point they agreed on was that he was an ignorant, fanatical savage. Harry could not agree with them there. Crazy Horse had weighed two civilizations and chosen the better. He saw that a life of beef-doles and whiskey and air-tight houses was unsuited to his people. He consulted the written history of the Sioux Nation; a history that began before the Normans invaded England. He saw that the five tribes of the nation could continue their free, healthy life as long as they had their buffalo herds, which had not diminished in the nine centuries of their existence as a nation.

Crazy Horse cried to the invading white barbarians: "We have our herds. You can work if you wish. *We do not want your civilization!*

They called him a bloodthirsty savage, yet he avoided the whites and only fought when attacked. When Crook came to drive him out of the land the United States had given his people by treaty, Crazy Horse defeated him at the Rosebud. When General Custer made a suprise attack on his camp at the Little Bighorn and sent the women and children fleeing down the river in terror, Crazy Horse rallied his faltering braves with the cry: "Think of the helpless ones! To-day is a good day to fight; a good day to die! Brave men to the front, cowards to the rear!"

And when Crazy Horse crushed that wanton attack, the white people had the hypocrisy to call his act a massacre!

No, Crazy Horse was none of the things he had been called by people who plundered away his land and murdered him by treachery. The real Crazy Horse was quite different. There were pictures of the other Sioux chiefs, but none of the great Ogalala. When they wished to photograph him during his captivity, he refused. "Why should you try to save my shadow?" he said. "Nothing lasts but the earth."

267

There was no photograph of Crazy Horse, but from the many descriptions one could get a kind of picture. He was a slight, straight man of medium size, with a rather fair complexion and a thin face that was too sad for his years. His hair was reddish brown, something unusual but not unheard of for a full-blood Sioux. Of necessity, he was a warrior, and the most brilliant of all the Indian leaders, but he did not fight for personal gain. The spoils of war were divided among his people, and Crazy Horse kept nothing but his war gear, and his integrity. In the Dark Days, Crazy Horse became even greater. The days when the prairies were littered with the rotting carcasses of the sacred buffaloes. General Custer and his dapper officers had invented the buffalo game. They went out among the herds with relays of fresh horses and revolvers with endless rounds of ammunition. And they only stopped killing long enough to cut out the tongue of each buffalo as it fell. At the end of the day, General Custer, tossing back his yellow curls, recorded each man's score in his little notebook. The next day, a new rubber began.

The Ogalalas suffered as the herds were diminished and frightened away. When food was scarce, Crazy Horse ate nothing. When his friends brought him some of the precious food, he refused it. "I cannot eat," he said, "while one of my people is hungry."

Except among his intimate friends, Crazy Horse was a silent man. With the final darkness of civilization closing over his nation, he became more silent than ever. For days at a time he went about in such deep thought that no one dared speak to him. No one but the little children.

He was so great that they understood him and were not afraid. They crowded about him and brought him flowers and hung onto his hands and told him what they were thinking, and he was never angry or impatient with them. And sometimes the children would make him break his silence, and he would speak to some of his braves, repeating the first of his war-cry: "Think of the helpless ones!"

Sometimes Crazy Horse went out alone at night, and when he had been gone a long time one of his friends would go after him: the seven-foot Touch-the-Clouds, or the great-hearted Little-Big-Man, or the audacious Yellow Shirt. They would find their chief on the prairie, standing like a bowed statue in the wind and rain, or under the stars. Sometimes, they persuaded him to go back to camp with them, and sometimes he would not return until daybreak. His friends could not understand why. Harry understood. There was someone out there with him in the wind and rain; one who could not come into the tepee.

Crazy Horse was silent, it was said, and his eyes looked through everything because he lived most of the time in the spirit world. He didn't tell all that he saw, but he told one friend something of what it was like. This world, he said, is a world of shadows. The real objects of everything here are in the spirit world. Things here have weight and substance only because of their impurities. And it is because of their impurities that they change and break and wear out—the imperfect shadows of reality. That was only the fancy of a hunted savage, but the same savage fancy had come into the mind of the master of Aristotle in Athens, long before.

Crazy Horse never told anyone the circumstances of his vision of the final meaning of life. But the man who was with him during his three days and nights at the deserted camp on the Rosebud River told what he saw, and Harry discovered the rest. That was the story of Little Brown Rabbit.

Harry would have to tell himself that story, now that he had told about Crazy Horse. He could not tell that story often, even to himself, but he would have to tell it now. It helped a little that it was morning, and the galley bright and clean.

Little Brown Rabbit was the daughter of Crazy Horse, and his only child. He had wanted a son and was disappointed at first when it was a girl. Afterward, he was glad and would not have wished her to be any different than she was. Little Brown Rabbit took life in such good part and was so determined to do everything for herself that while she was still very small she was not a burden to anyone. She was as brave as any boy and a great deal wiser. A lovely, straight child with red-brown hair, like her father; a pink-and-brown face, big, dark eyes and a warm heart. Crazy Horse idolized her.

In the bad winter, when everything froze and the tribe moved to the Rosebud River where there was plenty of cottonwood bark for the ponies, Little Brown Rabbit never complained. Other children cried during the long journey through the snow, but the daughter of Crazy Horse took it in good part, as she did everything else. She sat very proudly in a pony drag, bundled up in furs so that nothing showed but her pink-and-brown face and eager black eyes. To the end of the desperate march, she smiled proudly at her father whenever he would ride back to see how she was making out. Even when her nose became white and frost-bitten in the great cold and he had to rub it with a handful of snow, she made a joke of it and whispered: "I only pretend to cry when Mother washes my face."

In the spring they were very happy. Crazy Horse and Little Brown Rabbit walked together on the flower-covered prairie and among the groves of sacred cottonwoods. Sometimes the child lagged behind, picking a fistful of flowers and scolding Crazy Horse a little for not waiting as long as she wished. After she had learned how soon flowers wither, she did not pick any more—only squatted down now and then to caress some lovely blossom. She had become a true savage and wished to leave everything as perfect as she found it.

Whenever Crazy Horse was away, his little daughter worked hard making something to surprise him, because she loved him more than anyone else in the world. Once, when he was away hunting, she spent two days on a dreadful little buckskin mask, with holes for her eyes and thongs to tie behind her head, and she would not let anyone help her. Crazy Horse returned suddenly, riding at the head of his file of hunters, and Little Brown Rabbit had to turn her back on him while she tied the strings of her mask. If he was not very much frightened when she faced him, it was because he was the bravest man in the world. Then the mask fell off and the chief saw who it was, and Little Brown Rabbit forgot all about the mask and everything else but her father's arms.

The summer when the child was four, there was trouble with the Crows, who ran off some of the Ogalala's ponies. Crazy Horse and most of his braves went after them. They expected to be back in a day or two, but the white soldiers had armed the Crows and put them up to trouble, and it turned out to be a long war. Crazy Horse finally got back the ponies, and many more. Then word was brought to him that the camp had been moved to the Tongue River, and the Crows had overrun the Rosebud Valley.

When Crazy Horse finally got back to his people, he learned that Little Brown Rabbit had died months before and was buried at the Rosebud River. She died of diphtheria. The slattern who was supposed to look after her while her mother was working—. The accounts didn't say what happened to her.

That night, Crazy Horse started back to the site of the old camp, seventy miles away, in the territory of the enemy. He had only one man with him and took no precautions against being discovered.

Crazy Horse never spoke during the journey, but when they reached the deserted camp on the Rosebud, he told his companion to hide. Then he climbed up on the burial platform and lay beside the remains of Little Brown Rabbit. He lay there for three nights—for three days and nights, without coming down to eat or drink. Parties of marauding Crows passed through the camp and down along the river; there was one night of icy rain, but no sign from the burial platform against the sky. The man in hiding did not know whether his chief lived or was dead.

On the fourth morning he woke at daybreak and saw Crazy Horse bending over him. "Come," he said. "I am ready." They went back to the Tongue River in silence, and the chief never told anyone where he had been.

But it was there that Crazy Horse had his vision and found the meaning of life—as much as anyone will ever know. He found it there on the burial platform, in the land of the enemy, with the body of the child he had loved too dearly lying beside him, and marauding Crows searching through the deserted camp—and far off, against the sky, the campfires of the American soldiers. The outposts of barbarian invaders who would wipe out the Crow and Sioux, the hunters and the hunted.

And beyond the distant campfires, across the grave starlit hills, in the infinite distance of the night, he saw the smoke and fire of still another race that would rub out the white invaders in their turn. And beyond those there were still others. But he could not see them, only knew they were rallying like shadows on the dark plain of the years to come.

Crazy Horse looked toward the west, and saw that the Sioux Nation had driven out the ancient men who were in the land before them, and they in turn had driven out the giants. He saw that nothing lasts but the earth. And people are like water on the earth, driven in waves before the Great Wind. He saw that the past and present are the same, and time is only an illusion—like the ripples that pass along a fluttering pennant that seems to have motion, without moving from where it is planted.

But he did not know how to make use of that part of his vision. And he saw that he was the leader of a doomed people, defenseless under the ancient stars, with his dead child in his arms . . .

For years Harry had believed in the vision of Crazy Horse, without being able to see who would be the next invaders. He thought, at first, it might be a long way off. Then it seemed to him that a people who speeded everything up must also speed their own end and perish through their own strength and ingenuity. During the last few days, his vision had become clearer, and now he believed in the idea he had only played with at first.

The machines were the new barbarians. They had come like other barbarians: a few at first, offering novelty and new intoxicants. Then they came in hordes, telling people they must change or perish. And after people had changed they found they must perish, anyway. The people were already being driven out, without knowing their country was invaded. They faced the same fate as the Sioux Nation, only blindly, because they did not recognize the invaders. The iron circle was closing, and the time was at hand when a few thousand great machines and a few thousand operators would do all the work of the nation. Machines that took away men's employment robbed them of their homes and children and future as certainly as the white invaders had stolen the Indians' land and destroyed their herds and sent them to their death.

The end, he thought, would be the same. There were already fewer children being born, and there would be still fewer. There would be little doles of money, and mean little reservations set aside for the dwindling members of a nation made homeless by the mechanical invaders. Innocent children would suffer and die, and the wise would despair. Then there would be another barbarian invasion, though he did not know where it would come from, or what it would be like. There was some comfort, though, in the thought that machines cannot suffer.

Harry was not sure, though, that the invaders would win, because machines tantalized people with the promise of ease and security they could never have. They could never have those benefits because of human greed. The greed that plundered the Sioux Nation, and then gnawed away their reservations and defrauded them of their dole; the greed that burned Clark's timber and drove him back to the sea; the greed that slaughtered the young Scandanavians in Ben's logging camps; the greed that had sold Harry into slavery for a few dollars and broken him. There was no help for it, no sanctuary. People must learn to take disaster when it comes. If only the children didn't suffer!

The lurching galley changed and opened away. There was a deep fog on the Rosebud, and through it came the hoots and whistles of barbarian invaders. He saw Little Brown Rabbit in the dusk of her father's tepee, playing with a bright tobacco tin. . . .

Ben, passing through the alleyway, heard but did not recognize the war-cry of Chief Crazy Horse: "*Think of the helpless ones!*" He started at the broken cry and looked through the open doorway, thinking the cook might be up to something violent. But Harry was alone, standing near the range, with a baking tin held aimlessly in his hands; the light of a vision shining on his wet frail face. His eyes were staring with such intensity that the young fireman felt their gaze pass through his body without seeing him. He hurried on to his cabin, but for a little while the ghostly feeling of invisibility lingered about him.

"Now the messman is going mad," he told himself.

XIV

Sunday on Board

For breakfast, the crew had the last of the raisins, boiled, corned beef hash, bread and butter and coffee. Ben held his nose with one hand, while passing the hash to Mr. Gill with the other. Allen, who sat between, declined the dish when Mr. Gill proffered it before helping himself.

"Thanks," he said. "I got the power of it as it went by." Allen was always clean, but he had just shaved and his face looked specially red and shiny for Sunday morning.

Ole looked across the clean-scrubbed wooden table, with disapproving eyes. "At sea," he observed, "you eat as long as there is anything, whatever it smells like."

Clark helped himself from the port dish. "Just the same, I'd rather take my poisons straight. With these mystery dishes, a man is likely to die of complications. When everything in it is bad, you wouldn't know what killed him."

"Think of me," the cook sighed, supping coffee noisily from a cup on the table in front of him. "I can't take anything but a little coffee, and it's been boiled too long."

Ben looked at the great, shaggy head bent over the

cup, with a sullen glow in his eyes. He had seen the messman's pathetic distress when the hash was being criticized. "If you don't like the food," he said between his teeth, "why don't *you* try cooking?"

The snubbing gear grunted in the embarrassed silence, and as the ship rolled a square of sunlight from the skylight popped into Ole's cabin and sat on his bunk for a moment. Oscar helped himself to butter, and looked down his nose at the rancid, greenish stuff, which the younger members of the crew had not touched for weeks.

"When I was a boy in Sweden, my Aunt Selma bought good butter for fifty *ore* a pound." His little eyes glanced about the table, suspiciously, as if he expected contradiction.

Allen grinned. "Do you suppose Aunt Selma could spare us a couple of pounds?" he asked familiarly.

The fat seaman's little eyes looked at the fireman, while his face looked down at his plate with a sheepish grin. "She's dead."

"Sure. What does she need with butter, now?"

Kidding Oscar was always contagious. Clark's somber face became boyish.

"Did you say she bought good butter for fifty *ore* a pound?" he demanded.

The sleek old seaman gave him a sly, sideways look. "I said so."

"How much did she pay in American money?"

Oscar looked down his nose, belching contemptuously. "She didn't pay in American money; that was in Sweden, and she paid in *ore*. I told you that."

Clark joined in the laugh. Everyone felt better except Oscar, who turned sulky and hung his head over his plate, muttering to himself. It was his misfortune never to know when he had scored. He believed the crew was laughing at him.

Mr. Gill came in to get the matter straight. "How much is an *ore*, Oscar?"

Oscar continued to hang his head. He had been suspicious of the old fireman ever since the night he collided with a mysterious figure in the galley. The figure claimed to be Mr. Gill, but Oscar had his sinister doubts. The fact that whoever it was had Mr. Gill's voice, made the circumstances all the more diabolical.

After a full minute of silence, Oscar half looked up. "A hundred *ore* make a *krona*," he said grudgingly. "What you tink?"

"Now we're getting somewhere," Clark observed, helping himself to coffee. "How much is a *krona?*"

"A hundred *ore*," Oscar muttered, after he had sulked a minute longer.

"We know something, but we don't know what it means," Ben commented.

"Well, how much is a *krona* in American money?" Allen wanted to know.

"How do I know?" Oscar grumbled through his drooping yellow moustache. "We didn't use American money in Sweden."

Clark set down his coffee mug with a despairing thump. "If we don't know, how can we tell if Aunt Selma was paying too much for her butter?"

Oscar's face was looking down at his plate, sheepishly,

while his glance scuttled about the hollow square of grinning faces. It seemed to be dawning on him that he was shipmates with a crew of lunatics. He got up, belching, and trundled aft, with a furtive look over his shoulder.

Ole rose, hitching up his breeches with a two-handed gesture, and went to his cabin. Ben finished his breakfast of unbuttered bread and coffee. Allen was already through and waiting for him. They got up together and went on deck, into the clear, cool gold of the morning sunshine.

"It's *threatenin'* to be a fine day," Allen said, mimicking the chief.

It was threatening to be a fine day. The sky was blown clear, and the wind had gone down the day before. Seagulls rode easily on the big blue and white seas astern, waiting for Harry to throw over the meager breakfast scraps. Against the dark green shore, beyond the white, bursting reef, a column of blue smoke rose toward the rising sun, as if some pagan rite were being celebrated. A big tug, with a hulk far astern, was coming up from the south—standing close in toward the lightship. A few miles out, a gray and white steam schooner was rolling down from the north. Off the blue, shadowy Cape, a big sailing ship waited for a tug—an improbable tower of white turrets reared above the sea. It was a blue and white and gold morning, Ben thought. The chill air and the power in the dying sea kept it from being pretty. It was beautiful, he thought, the way death is supposed to be beautiful. . . . White flashes astern. Blinding white against blue in the sunshine. The gulls rose and swooped with shrill, harsh cries as they fought for the breakfast scraps.

"It's like the old chanty," Allen's voice said. "One Day More."

"Ah, me byes, me byes!" Mickey O'Rorke stopped at the rail. His old cat's face was shaven and scrubbed clean and bright. He was wearing his blue coat with brass buttons. Only his eyes were faded and watery. Ben wondered if the chief saw everything like his eyes, faded and a little blurred. Then Ben saw him faded, like an old photograph of a child in a family album. A child in his Sunday suit, looking hopefully into the future while he is already fading into the past. . . . A shovel clashed on the floor plates below. Mr. Gill was getting ready to go off watch. Oscar thumped about the deck, softly on slippered feet, muttering through his yellow moustache and following his sleek paunch. . . . One day more, and how many more after that?

"Well, Chief, when do we get our coals?" Allen was asking the useless question.

"Tomorrow," Mickey said, "or tomorrow's tomorrow. Use the coals gently, byes, gently, until we get more. There's not much left. Just a dahsh now and then."

The tug with the hulk was going to pass close: a powerful ocean-going tug followed patiently by the hull of a steamer.

Mr. Gill came on deck, holding his old curved black pipe against his breast, like a ceremonial instrument. He looked about with mild, enduring approval. "It's a good day," he commented, "a fine day!" He took his place beside the others at the rail.

"Eight o'clock, Mr. Gill?" Allen asked. No bells were struck on the lightship.

"Eight o'clock, Allen." The watch had changed. After a while, for form's sake, Allen would go below and look at the banked fires, and maybe pump out the bilges.

The tug came abreast, close enough so the men could read her name: *Columbia*.

"She belongs in Seattle," Mr. Gill volunteered. "A fine old bulldog. When she was built she had a wheel aft, like a wind-jammer. Her captain disappeared one night out here, in heavy weather. After that, they gave her the wheelhouse. It's anchored to the keel with iron rods."

Allen grinned sarcastically. "I don't suppose the rods went deep enough to reach the captain."

Mickey was in a peaceful frame of mind, but he took up the cudgels. "Ah, well, Allen, there was more than one captain in the stable. And people learn that way." He drifted into silence, hitching his old shoulders in the grateful sunshine.

The *Columbia*, with her keel-anchored pilot house, drew ahead of the lightship and her tow came into better view: the slender iron hull of an old passenger steamer, with no more swank left, treading after the tug with dumb patience.

"Get that name?" Allen spoke to Ben, under his breath.

The boy didn't know what he was referring to. Then he saw the name on the bow of the hulk, *Mariposa*. He couldn't believe it at first. The *Mariposa* was the ship

Mickey had served in, forty years earlier. The ship he harked back to with such pride and surrounded with glamor. The great, beautiful packet he was always telling about. Here she was, a worn-out hulk, no bigger than the smallest coastwise steamer. Ben tried to reconcile what he saw with the famous *Mariposa*—flashing out through the Golden Gate, showing her heels to everything else in the Pacific. The *Mariposa*, like a gracious dream, gliding through the South Seas in an atmosphere of moonlight and music and famous passengers. *Lightship 167* was the ship Mickey had been faithful to since their marriage in the great gale, but *Mariposa* was the famous beauty of his life. And there she was, a battered little hulk being pulled about by the nose— brought up from the dead to give him the lie for having remembered things as being so much greater and grander than they were.

Ben looked at Mickey, cautiously. He could not tell if he recognized his fabulous *Mariposa*. The old cat's face was turned in her direction, blinking, but there was no sign of recognition.

"There's an old-timer," Mr. Gill observed, but did not comment on the name.

"Aye, an old-timer," the chief answered.

"I'll have a look at the fires," Allen said, and went below.

Still Ben couldn't make out if Mickey recognized his ship. In forty years, he might have yarned her out of his own recognition. Perhaps he only felt the presence of a ghost: the ghost of the unprogressive truth. Even if he saw, it would have been with different eyes. It wasn't fair to say that rust-eaten hulk was the *Mariposa*. It would be like confronting a man with the corpse of a famous beauty and asking if *that* was what he had loved.

A shovel clashed on the floor-plates. Use the coal gently, Allen, gently. There's not much left. The slender little hulk was drawing away, showing a still-graceful stern to the lightship. "It's a good day; we've fine weather at last." Mr. Gill booming softly. Water gushed from the sunken red side below. Allen was pumping out the bilges.

"Do you think the tender will be here tomorrow?" Useless question. It either would or wouldn't be. What anyone thought in advance had nothing to do with it—

"Holy Mither!" The chief burst the Sunday quiet with a howl. "That half-arsed Allen!"

"And now what's wrong?" Mr. Gill demanded, tolerantly.

"Wrong? He's pumping *oil* overboard!" Mickey scuttled below, like an old demon with something gone wrong in hell.

Ben had noticed the irridescent film spreading out from the side of the ship and soothing the waves astern, but he had only noticed it with his eyes, without considering what it meant.

Mr. Gill saw it now. "Someone was filling the oil measure, and let it run over while doing something else. Maybe a quart or two; a little oil goes a long way."

The boy's conscience was clear; he hadn't let the oil overflow since six weeks before, and he had been fired a time or two for that. But there would be time to clear himself when he was accused.

"Mickey's all right," Mr. Gill said indulgently, "only he gets excited. You mustn't pay too much attention to him then." He struck a safety match and lit his old black pipe, puffing gently. Showing Ben how to take the excitable little chief; how to take excitable life.

The boy nodded, smiling thoughtfully. He wasn't thinking about Mickey, he was thinking about Mr. Gill. For weeks at a time, the ponderous old fireman eased about so calmly and evenly that Ben hardly noticed him. Even when it came to calling the watch, he was either awake, with the lamp shining on his naked head, or sleeping so lightly that he opened his eyes at the first word. But whenever he took the trouble to notice Mr. Gill, Ben felt there was a great deal of meaning to him. Even his layers of fat seemed to have a meaning, as if he had put them on deliberately. They made him proof against heat and cold, short rations and hard knocks and flurries of excitement that wore other people out.

Ben was feeling thoughtful this morning, and Mr. Gill appeared in heroic size. He must have some secret power, to be what he was with the kind of life he had led. He had told the boy of stokeholds off Singapore and in the Red Sea, with the thermometer at 140 and men going raving mad; of furious weather in a little Bering Sea whaler, with a cable stretched across the fire room to save the stokers from being dashed against the red-hot doors; of coming up from that hell to subzero weather, where his sweat-soaked clothes froze like iron in a temperature that dropped 150 degrees in the minute between the fire room and a burst-in-door above.

That, and spells of whoring and drunkenness ashore

had been Mr. Gill's life. And he was everything that his life had not been. There must be some trick about it, or a secret. In heat and iron brutality, turmoil and violent change he had found coolness, gentleness, temperate calm that nothing seemed able to shake. Others had been killed or broken by that life, and Mr. Gill emerged from it with genial buoyancy, to look at the world approvingly and remark, "This is a good day." Perhaps some great integrity or innocence had led him, unhurt, through every earthly hell. . . .

Something in the nature of a hunt appeared to be going on below.

"There's some in the scupper!" Allen's voice called.

"It's here, too!" Clark announced, further forward.

"Where is it coming from?" Captain Lindstrom's voice demanded.

"Must be further for'ard."

"Here it is."

"Holy Christ!"

"Who did that?"

A tank resounded to blows, like an ominous drum.

Ben started, apprehensively, and Mr. Gill knocked the ashes from his pipe. "Well, Lad, there's something up. Let's go and see what it's all about." As they went below, down the smooth-worn iron steps of the companionway, he confided, with a heartening twinkle in his gray eyes, "It's wonderful how they manage to get excited over every little thing, when anything might happen."

They found the crew forward of the mess room bulkhead, looking like mourners at an oil drum that lay on its side, with the spigot open. The steel deck abaft the drum was wet, and the air reeked with kerosene. Captain Lindstrom stood nearest the drum, looking gravely perplexed and hurt. Mickey was in the background, grimacing. The oil had turned out to be none of his business, after all, and he took satisfaction in seeing the deck department in trouble. Ole squatted near the side of the heads, trying to fit together the ends of a severed lashing. Clark towered beside him with gloomy intentness, like a consulting undertaker. Harry was standing in the doorway of the heads, where he would be out of the way, twisting his apron with one hand and looking on with tragic eyes. Forward, the snubbing gear gave an indifferent grunt with the passing of each sea.

Allen edged over to Ben—the considerate man in the crowd who gives a newcomer the details. "It's the lamp oil," he explained. "Somebody cut the lashing and emptied it in the scupper."

"See, it went like this." Ole had reconstructed the lashing to his own satisfaction. The others shuffled closer. "That puts the chafed side next the drum."

"That's right," Clark agreed.

"And it was cut this way." Ole drew an imaginary knife toward himself, and away from the corner where the drum had stood. "The fibers are pulled on the outside. Whoever did it was no seaman. There's plenty of ways of getting hurt without cutting toward yourself."

"Don't be saying it was one of my men!" Mickey shoved forward, ready to die for his firemen—including Allen, whom he had fired on suspicion on the way down the engine room ladder. "There's more rigging done below than on deck, nowadays—"

"All right, Chief." There was a shade of annoyance in the captain's voice. "No one has been accused."

Oscar came trundling forward, and took in the situation with his blazing little eyes. "Rotten!" he growled. "Rotten!"

The captain looked at his crew, evenly. "I'm sorry this happened." His voice was quiet and natural. "I don't suspect anybody, but if one of you knows about this I expect him to tell me."

They stood silent and guilty-looking, after the manner of the innocent.

"Where is the cook? I want everyone here."

Harry went aft, limping quickly. The lightship grunted as she settled back on the snubbing gear. Ben stooped to dip his finger in the spilled oil, then straightened up, sniffing, to see if it really was oil. After having satisfied himself on that point, he was at a loss as to where he could wipe his finger. The whole scene was somewhat ridiculous, as if everyone sensed it was not the kind of situation intended for men made in the image of God.

The cook came forward, in the messman's wake, grinning foolishly and looking like a big, unkempt tramp.

"Georges, do you know anything about this oil?" the captain asked.

The crew started, realizing for the first time in five months that the man had a name. Georges—so that was his name.

"I never touched it," the cook declared. "I don't do anything."

The others guffawed, while he went on to explain himself. "I'm a sick man. I've had a terrible time here. If I could get ashore to a doctor—"

The captain interrupted him smoothly. "If anyone did this, thinking it would get us in from station any sooner, he showed poor sense. Whatever happens, we are here until the *Relief* comes. We have enough oil in the lamp-room for another two weeks. After that, there is the kerosene. It will burn in the lamps well enough and will last until Christmas if we use it carefully. We've been on station a long time, through no one's fault, and I don't want to punish anyone. But our first consideration is to give light to other ships, and we must be careful with what we have. Until we are relieved, or until supplies come, there are to be no more lights in the cabins. That is all I have to say."

The crew drifted aft, in pairs and singly. Ben and Allen went on deck again. The punishment the captain had devised was slight; it was hard to say if it was a punishment. Very possibly it was just what he said it was: a necessary economy and a reminder of their duty to others. But the stupid piece of mischief sickened Ben and spoiled the gold autumn sunshine. "Who do you think did it?" he asked.

"I'm not saying, because I don't know any more than you." Allen lit a cigarette, inhaling deeply. "Only, in my watch I'm going to keep an eye on the cook. A man in his right mind wouldn't have done a trick like that, and he's crazier than the rest of us."

Ben had the same suspicion. "I'm going to watch him, too."

Allen laughed, remembering something. "I tell you, I felt guilty for a minute, with Mickey rarin' down the ladder, firing me right and left! Look at the back of my head and see if I have any gray hairs."

But joking wasn't any good. The day had been spoiled.

Clark paused beside them. "It would have taken a strong man to capsize that drum without making a noise," he remarked.

"You're right, there," Allen agreed.

They stood at the rail a while longer. The tug and the ghost of the *Mariposa* were dwindling toward the. Cape that was like a lean blue finger laid on the sea. No tug had come for the great bark, and a current was drifting her farther from the land. A freighter had come up over the hill from Asia, trailing a sudden yarn of dark smoke. At a distance of twenty miles, one could tell, almost to the moment, when her firemen opened and closed the fire doors. The steam schooner from Alaska was drawing away toward the south. Bound for Portland, up the great river, or between Golden Gate Park and Sausalito, under the hills of San Francisco. From the lightship that went nowhere, even the slowest vessel seemed to pass with infinite speed.

XV

The Cook goes to the Movies

IT'S PUNISHMENT for him that poured out the lamp oil,"
Mickey O'Rorke commented the next afternoon,
when the tender hadn't come.

"Sure, and it's punishment for the hims that didn't,"
Allen answered sarcastically. He thought Mickey's god
was a good deal like Mickey—an irascible little Irish-
man who fired every angel in sight when anything went
wrong.

The chief was threading a short length of pipe,
clamped in the vice at the carpenter's bench. Ben, who
was supposed to be assisting him, stood by helplessly
with a squirt-can in his hand. Mickey did practically
everything himself and only kept a helper about to
scold. Allen and Clark sat on the bench, dangling their
feet and watching. Mickey grasped the die stock and
wrestled it round furiously. He did everything with
passionate energy. With his old cat's face set and his
disgraceful old pants about to fall off, he looked like
Puss-in-Boots turned pipe-fitter.

"A dahsh of oil, Ben!" he gasped. "A dahsh of oil.
Quick, now!"

The boy edged nearer, extending the squirt-can gingerly. One of the chief's flourishing elbows struck his

arm, deliberately it seemed, knocking the oiler from his hand. When he stooped to pick it up, the die-stock grazed his shaggy head.

"Ben, Ben!" the chief panted. "What are ye good for? A dahsh of oil, quick, before it burns up!" The old demon continued turning in a frenzy, making it impossible for the boy to carry out his order.

Allen kept his face straight, but Clark smiled openly, contemptuous of the chief's wild Irish methods. When the boy flattened himself against the bench for another attempt, the seaman, from his vantage point, took the squirt-can from his hand and shot oil on the die.

The moment there was no more danger of overheating, Mickey stopped, breathing hard, and examined his work. Then he took another turn, and spun the die stock in reverse.

"There we are, Ben," he said kindly, as if the boy had done most of the work. "Ben, me bye." (The Chief began mothering his firemen at the first sign of interference from the deck department.) He laid the stock on the bench and wiped fragments of steel from the end of the pipe with a piece of dirty waste. "A good job, Ben." He delivered a nipple from the back pocket of his sagging pants and tried it on the new threads. "Male and female." A creator admiring his handiwork. "A good job, Ben." He loosened the vice and removed the pipe.

"Bring the Stilson, me bye, and a dahsh of white lead, and we'll have it on in a minute." They passed below in a murmur of soothing words from the chief.

Clark looked after the odd pair, smiling wryly. "I'd

think it would drive you mad, working with that old lunatic."

Allen dusted the ash from his cigarette and swung his feet. "Sometimes I could kill him, if I weren't so fond of him. But then, I'm Irish myself, though Mickey would call me a 'far-downer.' "

"It's between Irishmen, I suppose." The seaman turned and looked out of the portlight above the carpenter's bench.

"Is the tender coming?"

"Don't see her." Clark continued looking, intently.

After a minute, Allen turned and looked out, with his bald young head close to Clark's iron gray one. There was nothing in sight but a steam schooner, bound north, standing far out under a slightly overcast sky. Then he noticed what had attracted the seaman's attention. Near the lightship, the sea was a heaving, blue-gray plain. A quarter of a mile west, beyond a sharp line of demarcation, it was rough and dark, like a ploughed field.

"Tide rip," Clark explained, "We're apt to get it this time of year. If you were on deck, you could hear it roaring. It'll swing over here and shake our teeth out for a while."

"What in hell is it, anyway?" The fireman was unpleasantly fascinated, watching the field of broken water eat its way toward the lightship.

"Currents fighting. There's a lot more to the sea than water. There won't be any wind, or any sea running, but plenty of motion."

"It would be like the tender to come when we were

busy hanging onto our false teeth," Allen observed with sour amusement.

The tender arrived two hours later. It was the *Magnolia* this time. A new steel craft, with a black hull and white superstructure. She was built on the general lines of the *Columbine*, but with more grace. By the time she reached the station, *Lightship 167* was well in the tide rip.

As Clark predicted, there was no wind and nothing that could be called a sea, but it was worse than the two combined. The broken, muddy-colored water roared and fought and jostled about the ship, buffeting her from every direction. She stumbled and jumped and fell and rolled insanely—every abominable motion at once. It was like some device in an amusement park, designed to make people sick.

The *Magnolia* managed to keep some of her dignity until she began to lose her headway, creeping up toward the lightship. Then she too behaved abominably. Neither vessel could have lowered a boat successfully if the fate of everyone had depended on it. There were no regular seas that could have been judged and no lee; nothing but incalculable fury and twisting blows from every direction.

Everyone was on deck but the cook. He had been asleep in his bunk with a worn copy of *Hollywood Follies*, and when Harry heard that the tender was coming, he closed the door quietly. He was deadly afraid of seeing the cook try to jump overboard again. That would be more than he could stand.

The *Magnolia* edged up toward the lightship's quarter,

moving a fathom up and down and to each side for every foot forward. When she tried standing on her head, she gave a fine view of her well-deck, colorful with red and black and black-and-white buoys of various shapes—to be laid like Easter eggs at suitable places on inland waters. Mothering lightships was only one of her many duties. Forward, a young seaman in new dungarees of crude blue leaned over the rail and was violently sick. One judged he had dined well.

"There's a boy for the lightship," Clark said. "Look what five minutes of it does for him!"

A strange captain was braced at the rail outside the wheelhouse, megaphone in hand. The two vessels fell away from each other, then bounced toward each other, dangerously close. The captain jerked up his megaphone, nervously, like a cheer-leader with things going badly for the home team. His voice came over faintly, through the angry roar of water. "No use . . . . come back tomorrow."

Captain Lindstrom raised his rarely-used trumpet. "Watch your chance. We can't hold out much longer!" His voice was urgent.

The other captain gestured soothingly and got his vessel under weigh again. It was hopeful that the *Magnolia* headed north. If she put in at Neah Bay or Port Angeles, she could come down to the station in a few hours.

"And let's hope they remember to come back!" Mickey said fervently when he and Captain Lindstrom had gone below. "It breaks me heart every time I hear a shovel on the floor-plates!"

"Or if the *Relief* would come—" The captain stood near the saloon table, fingering a letter which that vessel had brought on her disappointing visit, a week earlier. "If we were to get a snorter now, we would be caught with our pants down."

"Aye." Apprehensively, the little chief hitched up his dilapidated old breeches, which were always threatening to place him in that embarrasing position.

The night went slowly for Mr. Gill. His long habit of reading in his bunk had been disturbed by the captain's ban on lights. He slept little, and never deliberately. He was used to having oblivion overtake him in the company of his pipe and magazine and lighted lamp, and he could not fall asleep in the dark. He tried thinking of things; going over his past, but he didn't have the knack of making it exciting. The past was so definitely over and settled. Things had happened the way they had happened. He had done what it was his nature to do and taken the consequences. They hadn't been bad, considering.

What he remembered was mostly about firemen in stokeholds at sea, and firemen in saloons and brothels ashore. He never had much luck getting away from his profession. The *George W. Elder* business was a sample of that. He bought a first-class passage from San Francisco to Seattle, and for two days he went about on deck, as good as any of them. He met some nice little women, too, and he heard one of them refer to him as "a gentleman."

But in the end his profession found him out. A green

fireroom crew went to pieces in heavy weather and the gyrations which had earned the ship the nickname of *George W. Roller*. When they were in an uncomfortable situation off Destruction Island, with bare steerage way, Mr. Gill gave up trying to be a passenger. He left the comforting of the nice little women to others, and descended the familiar iron ladders to help get up steam. And in the end, he went ashore in Seattle, in ruined clothes, with the three members of the crew who really were firemen. Mr. Gill was supposed to take his examination for a third assistant's ticket, but the four of them went on a bender, and Mr. Gill ended up at "Honest Kate's" with a dark and lively girl from Idaho. It set a kind of precedent. Thereafter, whenever Mr. Gill was in danger of taking his examination, he went on a bender instead.

In the darkness, Mr. Gills' pipe and tobacco tin had found each other on the bunk shelf, like old friends, and were clicking together, talking in a kind of Morse Code as *167* stumbled about the tide rip. . . . Footsteps on the companionway, and Ole's voice: "Start the bell." As the footsteps died away again, the bell started beating its number in the sea. No, not much luck keeping clear of the sweat and grime below. . . . When was that, and where, and who was the little woman in the evening? It was a memory with no coal dust on it, and not much else. Something he had only seen out of the corner of his eye and would not have remembered at all, except for having to lie awake in the dark, years afterward.

Mr. Gill remembered walking with a girl at dusk by the shore of the sea. He could not recall her face distinctly, because he only remembered it in connection with the twilight, and he had no recollection of seeing her before or afterward. Only he remembered her as someone fine, and he had the impression of a pleasant land in the dusk. And it seemed she had seen him as someone much finer than he ever was. And she had said something, the sound of which he only half heard, and he did not hear the meaning at all. Something unexpected which he missed because it was unexpected, and because of his own inattention and the sound of the sea. He only remembered the whiteness of her hands in the dusk, and the caress of her voice—saying something that was lost on the way to his mind.

It wasn't much to remember: a shadow that had once been himself and an unknown shadow. The shadows of a man and woman, the ghost of a story. And he couldn't say how they came to be walking together, or what sea they had walked by, or on what shore. Not much to remember, but better than something certain and settled. It was all so vague and light and far away that he thought of it without any feeling of responsibility or loss. Nothing but wonder that he should remember so little, and remember that so persistently.

The lamp was burning low in the forward end of the messroom and its light came to the edge of the darkness of Mr. Gill's cabin, but did not enter. There were footsteps on the companion-stairs again, and Ole's wooden voice: "Start the whistle." After a little, the engine grumbled into motion and the cavorting lightship was shaken by the iron roar of the whistle. It went on at two-minute intervals, with the beat of the muffled bell in the sea filling the time between. Mr. Gill was used to sleeping to those sounds and when he let his eyes close, he could almost fancy that the lamp was shining on his head. Sleep came over him lightly.

Voices dug through Harry's sleep of exhaustion, down to where he was hiding from the world. Someone struck a match and lit the forbidden lamp.

"You see, there isn't anything." Ole's voice.

"I thought he might have left a note." Ben sounded aggrieved because some pet theory hadn't turned out.

"Why should he leave one?"

"Think we ought to ask Harry?"

"Let him sleep. The cook gave him enough trouble." Mr. Gill's voice.

"Yah, he was no good." Oscar's spiteful voice.

"Did you ask Harry?" The captain's voice, from the alleyway.

Harry opened his eyes, blinking, and saw the little cabin invaded. He sat up, wide awake. Something was very wrong. "What is it?"

"The cook is gone, Harry," Mr. Gill explained.

Gone . . . Gone? What did that mean? "Where did he go?"

"To the movies, I suppose," Ole observed cooly. "Where does he keep his shoes?"

"Shoes?" Were they laying the cook out for burial, or had he jumped overboard, as he often threatened, and was Ole going to throw his shoes after him? Harry struggled with a shocking desire to laugh at the scene he pictured: "Cook's Wedding with the Sea. Inset: Ole (last name unknown) Throwing Customary Old Shoes."

The seaman was holding up a big, disreputable pair of dress shoes, with their toes turned up, suggestively. "He left these at the head of the companionway. The last man who went overboard did the same thing." He gave the information for what it was worth, with no undue emphasis. It didn't explain everything, but at least set a precedent. Ben backed away from the relics, held up before him, but Ole only saw them as a pair of shoes to be put in their proper place. He had no respect for the cook, alive or dead, but he was scrupulous about the property of others.

"They go in the for'ard locker." The messman had begun to tremble. He didn't feel like laughing, now; he only wanted to cry. It was too much for him, the terrible neatness with which the sea could remove a man and leave nothing but a pair of empty shoes. Before Harry fell asleep, some time around midnight, the cook was lying in his bunk, talking about what was going on ashore, and fretting because of the darkness. And while it was still dark he was gone, body and mind and voice, and that was the end of him. The sea did things with such final, unimaginative neatness—Like Ole, only on a larger scale.

"Did anyone see him—go?"

"I heard footsteps on the companionway when I was calling the watch," Ole explained. "And when I went on deck I stepped on his shoes."

"Are you sure it was the cook?"

"Everyone else is here."

Harry began pulling on his clothes. "He might be hiding somewhere," he suggested hopefully.

"We looked everywhere," Mr. Gill said gently.

Ole adjusted his oilskin bonnet impatiently. All along, everyone had been saying that one of these days the cook was going to jump overboard. Now that he had done it, there was no end of surprise and disbelief. What did they, want, anyway?

Captain Lindstrom came in with his blue coat buttoned over his pyjamas. "I'm afraid he is gone," he observed regretfully. "I don't like to lose a man." He stroked his beard thoughtfully, looking from the empty berth to the gray little messman, dressing in the berth above. "When did you see him last, Harry?"

"Twelve o'clock, Sir. He was in his bunk when I fell asleep."

"How did he seem?"

"About as usual, Sir; talking about what he would do if he was ashore."

The captain smiled faintly at the repeated "Sir." Having the respect of his crew, he demanded no formalities, and in the presence of death he did not feel superior to anyone else. "There is nothing you could do, Harry. Better get some sleep; you've had a hard time."

The messman sat on the edge of his gyrating berth, buttoning his shirt with trembling hands. "I couldn't sleep," he said earnestly, "not until I've looked around, to make sure."

"Very well. The rest of you might turn in, all but the watch."

The captain did not take his own advice. He dressed and went on deck. Clark met him at the head of the companionway, a tall shadow in rustling oilskins.

"He couldn't possibly be hiding anywhere on deck; I've looked in every corner."

"I expected that."

The sea fought and snarled about the tumbling ship; the bell clanged monotonously and the whistle bellowed, raising a white plume of steam between the flourishing lights. Oscar's fat shadow stumped up and down, forward, and spray hissed on board. It was beginning to blow up.

Captain Lindstrom paced the deck, trying to put some profound excitement into words. He stopped beside Clark. "Death isn't a defeat, except for the individual." That seemed as far as he had thought, and he paced forward again. At the companionway, he turned quickly and walked aft, passing Clark without speaking. The whistle bellowed again. When it died away, the seaman heard Harry's strained voice calling through the ship: "*Georges, Georges!* Where are you?"

"Is the messman going, too?" he asked when the captain paused beside him again.

"He might, if we don't get relieved soon. Anything breaks with enough strain."

He walked up and down again, five minutes by the whistle blasts, with the muffled bell tolling under the sea and Harry calling, "*Georges, Georges!*"

"The race will triumph through the defeat of the individual." The captain had stopped beside Clark. "We change through defeats. How stable and permanent is the human form and the human mind? We know we came out of the sea in the beginning. None of us have got far from it. You and I are right in it, but that isn't material. Actually, we aren't any nearer or farther from the sea than people living in the middle of the continent. All of us are tied to the sea, which was our mother and our first home. On the surface, we have got away from it a little, but our blood and sweat and tears are still salt. Our blood is nothing but an ebbing and flowing tide of sea water, with one-celled animals—the first life—swimming in it. White corpuscles to eat the intruders and red ones to nourish us. Did you ever think of that? When a man loses a quantity of blood, the doctors pump sea water into his veins and it turns to blood because the heart remembers the sea. When the fluid is lost from the eyeball, the doctors put in sea water and sight is restored. Anything else would cause blindness. The eye remembers the sea. We don't catch cold in salt water because it was our first home. The body remembers the sea." He walked forward, and back again, giving the whistle time to have its say.

"I don't mean we will never get away from the sea," he went on. "Only we have come such a little way for having changed so much. And in going further we will change so much more. We don't know what shapes we had in the past, when we swam under the sea; and we don't know what shapes we will have in the future, when we fly through the air. We don't know how the human mind will change, or how our opinions and judgments and thoughts will be changed and modified. We are too new to our present conditions—fish just pulled out of the deep sea. We only know that we are not what we were, nor yet what we will be. In enough millions of years, we will have immortal souls. Not all of us, of course. One or two at first, then more. That will be the final change."

Clark didn't understand much of it. But he saw his captain's need for talking, and he knew the necessity of an audience, however uncomprehending. He listened on. . . .

Toward morning, the captain was explaining how the cities would be redeemed by their skyscrapers. There were to be roof-gardens, with flower gardens and fruit trees; bird sanctuaries; fish ponds, and swimming pools—all in an atmosphere as pure as mountain air. "If I had grown up in such a city, I would surely have learned how to swim," the captain said.

Clark was weary and restless, but he listened faithfully because of his master's need. He had run out of tobacco, and could not borrow any, since the captain didn't smoke. When he saw that relief was still far off, he took out his knife, secretly, cut some of the dark, caked drug from the heel of his pipe and put it in his mouth—as he had seen old seamen do in great extremities.

The darkness went gray at last and the vessel emerged substantial in a high, chill sunrise. When Oscar was lowering the after lights into the lamp room about the mast, he glared at the two with undisguised and hostile suspicion. There was no telling what devilish shapes they had assumed in the darkness, or what mischief had been wrought by the night-long ritual of the Russian Finn captain.

XVI

The Voyage Home

BY NIGHT it was blowing hard, with a big sea rolling in from the west. The threshing tide rip was gone and the lightship had her old motion, tremendous but regular. Each time she surged back on her mooring, the crash of snubbing gear sounded like a piece of artillery fired from the bow. Early in the afternoon, Captain Lindstrom had warned the crew to keep away from the forepeak, as recoil springs had been known to let go. Harry cried because the vegetable bin was in the forbidden triangle, and he had counted on the last of the potatoes for supper.

Actually, the rank corned beef was served with potatoes, which the messman claimed to have found in the galley. He thought the cook had put them there, though everyone knew the cook had done nothing useful up to the night he jumped overboard, as Ole expressed it, leaving his shoes for someone else to put away.

During Mr. Gill's afternoon watch, Ben and Allen held down the settee in the wheel house, while Ben read *Hamlet* aloud. It was Allen's final concession to monotony. He had been enthusiastic over all the other books, but shied away from Shakespeare. Having heard the playwright mentioned in the same breath with the Bible, he reasoned that they were two of a kind, pious and stuffy. Even with Ben's stilted reading, he changed his mind at once and became as excited as a first-nighter at the Globe.

"If I'd known what I do now," he said during a pause, "I'd have taken a run over to Elsinore when I was in Copenhagen. The Danes are fine people, though they go in more for butter and eggs than sadness, like this young Hamlet. But his father was the real thing, looking out that the wind didn't blow down the queen's neck. They're like that, considerate and gentle. And I can see this Horatio. I was shipmates with a little Dane named Nelson, on the Blue Funnel Line. He was just that quiet, faithful kind—a friend who would stick with you when everything else went to hell. Want to read some more? I don't usually care about detective stories, but this play they're cooking up ought to be good stuff."

Failing daylight sent them below, with Ben holding the stout volume under his sweater to save it from the driving spray. "Hamlet has his seagoing cloak about him," he thought.

They read a little more under the mess room lamp, after Harry had cleared away the remains of a wretched supper. But they were under restraint because of Clark and Ole, playing cribbage for matches at the other side of the heaving table. Ole was ill at ease, after the manner of a sober man engaged publicly in a frivolous pastime, and the hopeful glances he cast at the book only distracted the readers.

When Allen went on watch, at eight, Ben played a game of cribbage with Mr. Gill and then turned in, all standing. In the dark little cabin, he courted sleep deliberately. Neither Allen's new-born enthusiasm for Shakespeare nor Mr. Gill's reassuring, spectacled gaze across the cribbage board quite shut out the growing noise of the sea and the increasing motion of the ship, with their grim possibilities. Nothing less than oblivion could do that, and he stuck to his bunk with a stubborn determination to sleep.

In five months of the lightship, Ben had developed a technique for staying with his mattress. Depending on his posture, he could hold on with some combination of shoulder-blades, heels, knees, elbows, shoulders or chin. By scowling, he could exercise considerable holding power with the region about the top of either eye socket —literally hanging on by his eyebrows, which were becoming remarkably muscular. With the present motion of the ship, which rocked him violently while alternately half-standing him on his head and feet, he clung to the mattress with the aid of one elbow, one knee and his chin. Holding on was a matter of self preservation. Each time the ship rolled to port, a steel locker drawer under the bunk slid open, and with each starboard roll it banged shut. There were no padlocks, and even an oak peg, wedged through the staple and hasp, was soon chewed away. Ben had a persistent dread of falling on the drawer, which was automatically open whenever he was in danger of being thrown from his bunk. That had happened to another fireman, a few years earlier, and the sharp steel corner of a drawer entered his spine and killed him.

The sea raced and thundered outside, the locker banged in and out, and the boy dug deeper with his chin, elbows and knees as the bunk rose steeply under him. At the top of the wave, the ship was struck by a treacherous cross-sea. At the broadside crash of water, Ben brought his fingers and toes into action, dug his chin still deeper and caught an added grip with one scowling eyebrow. The ship fell over on her starboard side, shaking everything with her violent quivering, then tumbled crazily down the back of the long sea, threshing and bucking as if she would never find her balance again. . . .

Ben slept, half-waking to cling more tightly during an occasional convulsion of the ship. In one, he heard the *thump*, *thump* of two men thrown from their bunks at almost the same instant. Presumably, they had not developed their eyebrows—an accomplishment of which Ben was proud, but they must have been successful in securing their lockers. There were no cries for medical attention.

"It's a sea of troubles, all right," Allen observed when he called the watch.

The information was hardly necessary. Ben could hear it rushing and booming outside, and the crash of gear forward rang through the iron ship like an explosion. The motion had increased, too, and he had to hook one arm about the bunk stanchion while putting on his shoes in the dark.

Allen went with him as far as the galley. "You know about going easy on the coal," he said. "Just a 'dahsh' now and then. It gives me a nightmare when I look at the few tons left. The Old Man should have put out the lights below, too."

"I'll go easy, all right."

They parted, and Ben went into the dark galley. When he was stirring his coffee, he saw Ole, in silhouette, giving his breeches a two-handed hitch as he came in from the reeling alleyway. Then the seaman became another dim shadow, reaching down a cup from the hooks above the sink.

"Getting rough," the boy observed.

"It will be, before we're through." Ole unhooked the coffee pot from the back rail of the range. "You will see," he predicted, pouring, "there is no God. If there was, we would have got our coal before this hit us."

Ben held onto the sink with one hand, drinking his coffee. He didn't want to get into any religious argument.

"There is no power for good up in the sky," Ole went on, harshly. "The only power for good is in the hearts of people doing their duty. That is better than God."

"I suppose it is," the boy mumbled.

"It is bad to count on God, and then find he isn't there. I was caught that way, once. It takes the guts out of you. A man behaves much better when he knows what to expect."

The boy sensed that the seaman was trying to compose his mind for possible death. He did not like the implication, and finished his coffee hastily.

Below, the motion of the ship was not so bad, and the clamor of the sea dulled. Ben looked at the modest, banked fires and decided that while they stayed alive he would disregard the steam pressure. Then he lit a little whale-oil hand lamp and made his famous inspection of the bunkers, in the hope of finding some forgotten pocket of coal. Half-way through, he began to consider the possibility of finding the cook, dead or raving mad, in one of the gloomy, ringing iron chambers. It became so real that when the unprotected lamp went out he scratched matches in a frenzy. And before going through the starboard bunkers, he took down a machine hammer from the tool board. Intelligence told him it would be poor treatment for a man in need of hospital care, but fear drove him and he carried the hammer, shamefacedly, but ready for instant use. In the end, his relief at not finding the cook quite made up for not discovering any miraculous pocket of coal. He hunched up on the wooden box near the deck pump, feeling he had done rather well, and dozed asleep.

Once he had a nightmare to the effect that he was on deck in a great storm, where he saw the earth-rejected body of the cook carried past the ship, with its long hair floating out like seaweed. As a final touch of horror, the shoeless corpse wore gray socks with black heels and toes. He woke on the reeling box, and saw Ole peering down from the head of the ladder. "Start the bell."

Ben sprinkled a little coal on the fires and went above, where the bell machine started sluggishly with the low steam pressure. The rush and boom of seas was loud in the dark outside, and the ship fought like a wild horse on a tether. He was below again, slicing one of the fires, when Ole reappeared, in shining oilskins.

"Start the whistle."

The seaman was gone when the boy reached the 'tween deck, but his wet footprints and a trail of water remained as if Neptune had passed that way, a moment before.

With the periodic bellow of the whistle added to the

sound of the sea, the watery clank of the bell and the crash of snubbing gear, Ben settled himself on the box again and tried to stay awake. He dozed off almost at once, waking to find Mickey O'Rorke prowling about the main engine. Guiltily, he looked at the fires, and found that both had been sliced and fed. Then he went and stood near the chief at the engine.

The chief ignored him while he loosened the jamming lever with a sledge hammer, spun the great hand-wheel which controlled the drag links, and tested the throttle lever. When he turned from the engine, his old cat's face was grim with displeasure, but not at the boy this time. "Ha, Ben." he murmured, not unkindly. "Go open the main stop." As the boy was going up the ladder to the fidley, he called after him: "Gently, Ben, gently!"

Ben cracked the great valve and opened it slowly, gently, indeed. He remembered the chief's story of the green coal-passer in one of his ships, who set an all-time record for opening the main stop. The first rush of steam condensed into a water-hammer in the cold pipe; the steam behind drove it straight ahead, where the pipe called for a bend, killing the first assistant who stood at the cross-head, and everyone else in the engine room.

After taking a good five minutes to open the stop, the boy descended. The air pump and circulator were going, and the old chief was warming the engine.

"Give her a *dahsh* with the bar, Ben."

Ben had just pried the crank off dead-center, when he saw Captain Lindstrom at the head of the ladder, bareheaded, in somber oilskins, with his long black hair and beard setting off his fair, gentle face. If Christ had given up everything and followed the fishermen, instead of the other way about, he would have looked like that, the boy thought.

"Chief, are you ready?" the captain called.

"Everything but coal," Mickey answered spitefully, with his hand on the throttle.

"Put her at slow ahead."

"Slow ahead," Mickey answered, and under his breath: "Don't be blaming *my* department when we run out of coals." He opened the throttle craftily, coaxing the engine into its stamping, one-legged rhythm "the first dahsh out of the box."

Captain Lindstrom vanished from the ladder. Ben opened the dampers and began stoking the fires, taking care to do his firing when the ship was rising to a sea. He had just started, when the chief took the shovel from his hands.

"Ben, Ben, you're wasting the coals that way!" He took a modest shovelful and spread it evenly over the white-hot bed, with a deftly-arrested swing of the shovel which only Mr. Gill could have equalled. As usual, he forgot he was giving a demonstration and continued until he had coaled both fires.

Ben was discouraged. If this was the beginning of another great gale, he wanted to show what was in him. And how could he do that if the old chief insisted on being both engineer and fireman?

Altogether, he was relieved when it was twenty minutes to four, and he made his way to the darkness of Mr. Gill's cabin. The patriarchal fireman breathed peacefully in his threshing bunk. All the furious motions of the lightship were not enough to overcome the initial stability of his mighty bulk.

"Twenty to four," Ben said quietly.

"Right, my lad." Mr. Gill's naked head rose from pillow to zenith, like a ghostly moon. Another moment, and it disappeared under the black cloud of his padded cap. "I hear you have the engine turning over," he boomed softly.

"We started it about an hour ago."

The fireman's big shadow eased down from the high berth. "So? Well, it wouldn't do, breaking loose on a night like this." He followed Ben as far as the galley. "I'll be down when I have my cup of coffee."

He came easing down the ladder at ten minutes to four, and gently took the shovel from Ben's hands. If it wasn't one expert, it was another. "Easy," he said. "Give an old-timer a chance. Turn in, Lad, and get some sleep." Mr. Gill exhaled peace and homely comfort.

Ben went up the ladder with the certainty that everything was in good hands. Pausing at the half-doors, he looked out of a portlight at the sea, pitch black and bursting white, raging past the ship. He was in the thick of an impersonal duel, fought between the brain of a naval architect, long dead—and the sea that was older than life or death. Once the boy shrank back and steadied himself against the carpenter's bench, as a cross-sea blotted out the portlight and threw the ship on her starboard side. But the mathematical cunning of the dead architect, and the experience-bred cunning of boatbuilders from ancient times, shook the vessel, put her back on her feet and set her to fighting again. The minds of the dead fought the more confidently because they had no human hearts to be dismayed.

The boy's sympathy was all with the ship at first. Then he forgot it by degrees, as the intoxication of the gale went through his blood. Watching and listening at the portlight, he unconsciously built up from the passing seas a picture of the sea itself: an age-old man of ebon blackness, with snow-white hair and eyebrows and beard, stark mad and raging through the night with maniacal strength. He forgot and was lost to everything else in his admiration for the tremendous malediction of the sea.

"Thoughts black, hands apt, . . ."

He found himself chanting the words he had read to Allen the day before. Nothing else could have been as appropriate.

"Thoughts black, hands apt, drugs fit, and time agreeing;
Confederate season, else no creature seeing;
Thou mixture rank, of midnight weeds collected,
With Hecate's ban thrice blasted, thrice infected,
Thy natural magic and dire property,
On wholesome life usurp immediately."

Ben turned from the portlight, with the excitement of the gale and the marvelous incantation upon him—and found Oscar's fear-paralyzed face within a foot of his own.

The sleek seaman started back, with a gasping cry of horror.

"What's the matter?" the boy asked, in all innocence.

"You, you . . ." Oscar choked. "What you doing?"

"Nothing."

"*Who was you talking to, out there?*" Oscar's thin hair was bristling out in a halo, and his little eyes blazed with superstitious dread and hatred.

"Why, I wasn't talking to anybody!" By degrees it dawned on the boy that he had given the old seaman the supreme fright of his life. His looks and the working of his hands suggested that only fear of the supernatural prevented him from throttling the boy for conversing with the powers of darkness. "I wasn't talking to anybody," he repeated.

Oscar shuffled away, glaring hatred and disbelief over his shoulder. "You, you lie to me! You talked to *him* out there!" He did not take his eyes from the boy until the curve of the fidley came between them.

Ben knew he could never make it up to Oscar. Shakespeare's words and the music of the sea had established a reputation for sorcery he could never explain away.

Thoughts black, hands apt, . . .

If only Shakespeare could have seen that proof of his power! Perhaps he did see it—on that night of natural magic, when the cunning of dead men rose up and fought for the living against the age-old sea.

When Clark went on deck at eight, he sensed the game was about up. It was blowing a full gale, and the lightship leaped and bucked and rolled her boats under in the great seas that marched out of the west, thundering and smoking as they came. The engine was turning over at half speed, taking some of the strain from the cable, but the shock was tremendous each time she brought up.

Sooner or later, he thought, something would let go. Captain Lindstrom had made his choice between running the engine at half speed, on the chance of riding it out or breaking loose with enough fuel to reach shelter—or running at full speed until the coal was gone, and then going adrift for a certainty and piling helplessly on the reef.

The everlasting reef. Clark turned his face aft and saw the departing seas boil over the half-tide grinders and spout against the higher fangs. Wild white horses and geysering whales sporting on hell's bathing beach. The boil and leap and fall of white water down the long reef was soundless because of the gale from seaward, and the noise about the ship. Closer, the bellowing would be terrible. But if that was going to come, it would come. Clark turned his face seaward and did not look back again.

He cared and did not care about what might happen. His mind had admitted its defeat long ago, but his body was still powerful and terribly alive. It would go on fighting with strength and cunning as long as it had the spark of life. His body was already scheming; his muscles rehearsing the motions of fastening him to this or that flotsam if the ship foundered or broke up. They would be unerring in seizing the best chance; if anything living got through the reef, it would be Clark's body. And all the time his mind was scornful of the fight it would put up against destruction. His mind was quite ready to knock off and call it a day.

The lightship wasn't much of a life. At best, it preserved him, like salt junk, in brine. And it wasn't preserving him for anything in particular. He got ashore, sometimes, on liberty and when the ship was in drydock at Eagle Harbor. And he was tired of his search for prostitutes who were like Virginia. That was another defeat his body had never admitted. Wherever there were women, his body was trying to find her. After all these years, he couldn't make it understand she was dead. She had given herself to him so completely that she had taken him completely. His body could still feel her in every fiber and hear her sweet, ringing voice. It thought it had only to reach out and touch her. His body was like a great dog, too stupid and faithful to understand about death, searching for its lost mistress. Like the Great Dane after Mrs. Walters died. Like that, and his mind was chained to the brute; dragged after it, protesting against the ridiculous, tragic search.

In his mind, it was all over and done with. He wanted to forget Virginia as much as possible. That was the best thing to do. Sometimes he even cursed the unfair hold she had on him. She should have lived, or taken that wild, penetrating sweetness with her. He wanted to shake it off, but the terrible fidelity of his body defeated him. . . .

The sea was swept clean, except for one steamer. Those gray, smoking seas looked as if they could sweep everything clean, and start over again. One of the Commodore Line steamers from San Francisco, with passengers. Little single-screw tub, making heavy weather of it. She was standing out now, taking it on the nose. A long beat seaward, then she would run in for the Straits with a quartering sea. Handling a full-powered steamer like a sailing ship. She wasn't making much progress, though. None, it seemed. Hove-to, maybe, waiting for better weather. That would be a long wait. Better get more sea-room, Captain. She was four miles further from the reef than the lightship, but she was miles too close at that.

The lightship wasn't taking much solid water on board, riding high and empty, but she reared and bucked and rolled madly in the seas that came down on her like mountains gone adrift. Every now and then, one of the boats, double lashed to its spar, would be pushed clear under. Then it would flourish up against the sky, red and shining wet, as if newly painted. The snubbing gear was a big gun, fired at regular intervals. No gear could stand that forever.

"How is it, Clark?"

Harry, with his dirty apron on, and his game leg, came toiling up the companion stairs. Like a hopeful child going up to bed in a house with the roof blown off.

"Middling bad," Clark told him. "But we're holding on."

"Bad? I was afraid it would be. But isn't it wonderful!"

Clark was startled. Wonderful? He hadn't thought of it that way.

"It's very beautiful."

Harry hadn't expected death to come this way; to come on deck from peeling the last potatoes, with his apron still on, and see the gates opening in awful grandeur. He couldn't fight against it because the thing was so much greater than himself. He couldn't even be sorry, down in his heart where he was afraid. He was very tired, and while he had come near getting a great deal out of life, he had missed. He had worn himself out and didn't have much of anything to show for it. He didn't mind being broken up. In the morning, he thought, the Indians would find his body on the shore. There was a mysterious comfort in that. His body would be a sacrifice for the wrongs done by his arrogant race. He offered it gladly.

"God, look at her roll!" Clark's great voice called him back.

"Where?"

"Just off the port bow!" Clark shouted. "Come up here, and you can see her." He opened the iron companion door, and the messman stepped out on deck, where the wind slashed through his thin clothes and moulded his apron to his legs. "See her?"

The coastwise steamer had swung back on her course for the Straits, sluggishly, taking the sea directly on her beam. They saw her whole hurricane deck, with a row of toy lifeboats on each side, as she rolled to leeward. Then everything but the masts disappeared as she sank in the trough.

"They'll never hold that course," the seaman declared. "A few like that will do for her!"

The two watchers lost the steamer altogether as a great graybeard bore down on the lightship, shutting out everything to seaward. Rising, they saw her again, still a point off the port bow. Her position was unchanged, except that she was taking the sea more on the quarter.

"What are they doing?" Harry shouted, bewildered at the aimless manouver.

"Broken down, by God! Tell the captain there's a ship out here in distress—and better get a coat before you come on deck again."

Within a minute, everyone but the chief and Allen was on deck. The steamer had swung still more and was approaching them head-on. The men ignored the wild motion of their own ship, and only cursed the sea when it rose, smoking, between them and the approaching vessel. It was a nice source of speculation as to what was wrong.

"Maybe a broken tail-shaft," Ben suggested boldly. He had once read about that happening to a ship.

"That's one thing she hasn't got," Captain Lindstrom answered firmly. "The drag of the propeller is what keeps her stern up to the sea."

"Maybe they got no coal," Oscar said. The joke was too grim and personal for anyone to smile.

"What will we do if she comes here?" Harry wanted to know.

"What could we do?" Ole demanded cooly.

"We must do something!" the messman cried passionately. "There are women and children on board. Think of the helpless ones!"

The captain looked at him, anxiously. "We're doing all we can by being on our station, Harry." The snubbing gear crashed heavily, and he turned his face toward the steamer again as the spray-lashed ship rose with the sea. "Her master knows his exact position, and how long he has to make repairs—if they can be made."

"Ha, me byes, what have we got here?" Mickey

O'Rorke's gray, grimy cat's face popped up from the companionway. Ben moved nearer Oscar, making room for the chief, and Oscar shrank away from the boy, glaring.

"Well, Chief, it looks like a job for her engineers," the captain observed.

For the moment, Mickey ignored the gentle railery against his department. " 'Tis their circulator," he decided, "or else a main bearing."

The steamer was looming big as she bore down on the lightship, a thin banner of smoke driving before her.

Mickey hitched up his disgraceful old pants, on the very point of falling off. "They're all on their knees by now, praying to the engineers," he said with relish.

"Let's hope their prayers are answered."

The lightship leaped up and fell, floundering, ducking her boats under, with the crash of snubbing gear striking through the noise of the sea and gale. Ole sheltered a little round tin in his hand, and put a pinch of snuff in his cheek, without taking his cool, shrewd eyes from the steamer. "It's the *Paul Jones*," he said.

"What a half-arsed world," the chief commented. "They have fuel and no engine, and we have an engine and no fuel!" He blinked at the disabled craft, with piratical intent. If there were only some way of plundering her as she went by!

"Big one coming!" Ole called sharply.

At the same instant, Clark broke through the group about the companionway and lunged toward the wheelhouse.

"Ring full speed!" the captain roared after him, while the little chief scuttled below.

To Ben, the chance sea that alarmed the others did not seem much different from the ones that preceded it. Then, as it loomed nearer, he changed his mind and took shelter in the companionway. As the lightship sank in the trough, the gong clanged faintly in the engine room. The sea blotted out the horizon, all the other seas that followed, and even the masts of the *Paul Jones*. There was nothing yielding or liquid about that sea; it was like a solid mountain range, gray-green, flecked with dirty snow, booming and smoking with volcanic power. The lightship rose to it with gallant desperation, steeper and steeper. . . . Then the crest exploded over her bow in a great burst of white that swept aft like a snowstorm. The sea passed, thundering by in the white darkness, and the air cleared.

In the relative silence following, a new sound came from forward, something bumping and grating, painfully.

Mr. Gill put his hand on Ben's arm and stopped him as he was following the captain and Ole below. "Stay on deck and get some air while you can, Lad. We'll soon be on our way home, with no chance to come above."

"Do you think so?"

The portly old fireman was positive. "The chain stopper is breaking up," he said, "The first solid jerk after the springs are gone, and we'll be steaming hell-for-leather for the Straits."

"Do you suppose we'll make it?" the boy asked anxiously.

"We'll make it, Ben. We know a trick or two yet. Look how close she is."

The *Paul Jones* was coming down from windward, hardly a quarter of a mile away, heading close for the lightship.

"I'll give her until she gets abreast of us to make her repair," Mr. Gill announced, puffing comfortably at the pipe he had just lit in the shelter of the companionway.

"I do hope she makes it," Harry said fervently.

"She'll make it, Lads."

Captain Lindstrom and Ole came from below. The captain held a piece of the three-inch spiraled steel that had been driven through the side of the vegetable bin, denting one of the iron hull plates. The wonder was it hadn't gone clear through.

Mickey came up and looked at the fragment of spring. "How long will the other be lasting?" he wondered.

"Not long, with a real stress." The captain swept back his long, wet hair with one hand. "Steaming to our mooring like this, it should hold until we see what happens to that ship, God help her."

"And then God help us!" the chief answered.

The steamer was coming down fast. When a sea burst white against her stern, she yawed badly but was pushed along faster toward the reef. The light banner of smoke, whirled forward from the stack, showed she was still breathing; alive but unconscious. There was no one in sight but one oilskin figure, motionless on the high bridge. Below decks, there would be a crew of thirty or forty, and a hundred-odd passengers—to spill out horribly at the last moment, when the ship burst on the reef.

The lightship bounded and lunged and staggered, rolling her boats under, rolling them up against the gray, racing sky. Forward, the broken gear gnawed at her hold on life, grinding, tearing—something felt rather than heard. Harry had known something like it before: the ends of the broken bone in his leg working together as he dragged himself across the deck of the *Bloody Harvester*, after the mate had knocked him from the main yard. The grind and bump of broken gear went to his maimed leg, hurting it acutely.

The *Paul Jones* rolled abreast, fifty yards to port, drifting on toward destruction like a sleepwalker.

"God help her engineers!" Mickey said—and went below to look after his own engines.

"Wake up!" Ben shouted, as if the ship might hear and head up before it was too late.

Harry looked about, wildly, for some means of helping the disabled steamer. "Think of the helpless ones!" he cried, working his hands together. He was knocked down by a vicious roll of the lightship, and when Oscar helped him up, disgustedly, he was still shouting, "Think of the helpless ones!"

They had to look aft, now. The steamer was passing them. Her stern, thrown up by a sea, showed the rudder and four-bladed propeller, unbroken but lifeless. Three miles ahead, the white water of the reef leaped and spouted and beckoned: wild white horses and tall sirens, dancing their unholy welcome. A breaking sea exploded against the steamer's counter. It seemed to Ben that the thick, high-flung spray took the form of women with veiled white limbs. Impatient sirens who had swum out from the reef and were pushing the ship toward their rocks in triumph.

The crew turned until they were looking dead aft, staring after the ship as if their lives depended on her fate. She seemed to be closing with the reef more rapidly now. Beyond the veil of dancing white water, there were the hills and forests of the land, but they floated in grayness, cloudy and insubstantial, like the coast of another world. It was another world, since one would have to die to reach that shore.

"They're gone to hell," Oscar muttered. "It's rotten; everything is rotten!"

"Only one piece of machinery is rotten," Ole answered, impatiently.

Ben was wet through with spray, shivering violently.

"You should go below and warm up," the captain told him.

But he stayed on deck, doggedly, with chattering teeth.

The *Paul Jones* became a dark, receding bulk, outlined against bursting white. She looked like a ship steaming confidently toward a safe harbor. Now, it was hard to say how far she was from the reef. She appeared to be on top of it, but might have been half a mile away. At most, though, it could only be a matter of a few minutes. Time was measured by the heave and roll of the lightship, the boom of seas and the gnawing of broken gear.

"She's struck!" Oscar croaked.

The steamer's progress appeared to have stopped. Her stern swung toward the reef until she was broadside on. Then she rolled to leeward, farther and farther, until her superstructure disappeared.

"Holy Christ!" Allen had come above, with a sweatcloth about his neck, and was staring at the doomed ship.

Harry turned forward, clinging to the side of the companionway, unable to watch the white curtain of death fall over the ship. "Think of the helpless ones!"

"It will be quick," Ole said.

"*She's under weigh!*" the captain roared out.

The others held their breath, uncertain of the outcome. Harry took courage and looked. The steamer was turning still more, staggering wildly as she headed up.

"They're the boys!" Mr. Gill boomed, patting the surprised Oscar on his souwestered head.

The steamer's sharp bow divided a sea, head-on, in a great burst of snow. Black smoke raced aft from her stack. She was forging ahead now.

"Hooray for the engineers!" Mickey crowed, popping up from the companionway. A moment later, he spied the deserter from the fireroom. "Allen, Allen! Get below, ye tourist! You're fired! Do ye hear me, you're fired!"

"We'll be under weigh next," Mr. Gill confided to Ben, recognizing the familiar sign. "'Ray for the old *Paul Jones!*"

Allen gave a final look and went below, grinning broadly under a shower of abuse from the chief.

The steamer was drawing away from the reef, rearing and diving and reeling under the blows of the sea, but forging ahead.

Captain Lindstrom drew Mickey out of the hearing of the others.

"How long will the coal last at this rate, Chief?"

"Two hours, at most."

"At half speed?"

"Short of five hours."

The captain's mild eyes narrowed. "You can stand by," he said. "When the *Jones* passes, I will ring for half speed."

"The gear will never stand it!" Mickey's old face was grim.

"It will have to stand it, or carry away."

"We've hung on so long we can't afford to be breaking loose!"

The captain smiled gently, still able to appreciate irony. "We can't choose the moment of our freedom," he said. "The best we can do is gamble for a little more time. I will ring for half speed."

Mickey knew it was useless to argue with him when he had that mystical smile. And it was just possible he might be right; his understanding of things wasn't bad, for a captain.

The *Paul Jones* was heading to pass to starboard, and the crew shifted to that side of the companionway. They would have strung out along the rail, only the sea wouldn't have left them there for long.

The steamer's bow overlapped the lightship's flourishing stern. The figure on the bridge waved, in a more expansive mood than on the trip to the reef. Mickey gave the engineers a cheer. The man on the bridge had stood there like a bold hero, after the manner of deck officers, while the engineers made their repairs in the midst of blood and sweat and burns—and brought the ship back from the mouth of hell. He gave them another cheer, and went below. It spoiled things a little that the steamer's safety should be the signal for the lightship's mortal danger.

The lightship leaped and twisted and fought, tearing at her mooring as if she too wanted her moment of freedom. The spray-drenched crew was unconscious of her antics, with their eyes fastened on the *Paul Jones*. She battled abreast of them. Not yet. . . . A door on the upper deck opened a little, slowly, and a woman came out. A tall young woman in a gray coat and a small hat. She kept one hand on the knob of the door, which the wind had forcibly shut behind her, and raised the other to her throat, with a quick, compassionate gesture. Startled, perhaps, at finding the sea-battered lightship so close.

The steamer was drawing ahead, passing. A disordered cheer went up from the crew and was dashed away by the wind and lost in the thunder of a breaking sea. The lightship's whistle wheezed croupily, then changed into a roar as Clark hung on the cord. Good-bye, and good luck! An answering burst of steam swirled about the stack of the *Paul Jones*. The tall girl was waving now, throwing kisses with impersonal ardor. The mellow blast of the whistle reached them, faint but pleasantly.

Ole waved to the young woman, with the others. She was the kind he had never known. If he had been good-looking or fortunate, he might have been with a woman like that for love, and he would have known what she was like. But it hadn't happened that way. He had only been with whores and paid for what he got. Beyond quick necessity, women hadn't played much part in his life. It was stupid of him to know so little about them, when men and women were going to work together to make the new world. Ole removed the quid of snuff from his cheek and waved respectfully to the woman he had never known.

Mr. Gill took off his padded black cap and brandished it gallantly at the end of one big arm, wishing the little woman good luck. While he was still waving, he recognized her: the girl he had once walked with at dusk by the shore of the sea. Beyond that, he still didn't know who she was. Distance and driven spray blurred her face, as the twilight had done then. But he remembered her white hands, and he could still hear the caress of her voice, telling him a secret that was lost through his own preoccupation and the sound of the sea. He was flattered to think that she remembered him. If he could only recall a little more of their other meeting. . . . It came to him that she might be Death—he had been close to that lady before—and if that was it, he would know her better before long. Whoever she was, it was pleasant to see her again. Good-bye, and good luck, and no regrets! He had kept his own integrity and had a good life.

Harry waved frantically, with his voice calling: "Jibby, Jibby!" At first, he didn't know why he said that. Then he remembered. The *Paul Jones* was from San Francisco, and it was natural Jibby should be on board. The conscious part of him hadn't recognized her at first, because he had only known her as an irresponsible child. But that was years ago, and perhaps she had grown up; she would be about that age.

Jibby was a playmate Martha invented when she was three: she wore "a shirt, and then a bunnit-hat," and she lived in San Francisco. But Jibby had no regard for distance. Sometimes she pattered into Martha's room in the evening, and kept her awake and hilarious when she should have been sleeping, and sometimes she descended recklessly on a rare sunbeam. Jibby got into a great deal of mischief, and even drew pictures on the title page of Catlin's *North American Indians*. Often, Martha had to drive her away with angry little shouts and much stamping of feet, but when she didn't appear for a few days the flat was lonely. Harry never quite saw Jibby, but she had always been very real to him. Now, he was seeing her at last. She had grown up, tall and lovely, and was leaving San Francisco. If she went to New York, she would see the Village—it had become a kind of show-place, Harry understood. When she walked along Greenwich Avenue, would she remember the red tenement, near Jane Street, and the fifth-floor flat where she used to fly in at the window? Thank you, Jibby. You did your best. Good-bye, and good luck!

Ben had grown bold and was throwing kisses. His mind was clear and he felt sure of himself at last. The beautiful young woman on the steamer had done something to him. She had answered the questions that tumbled about in his mind for so long. The tumbling pieces had come to rest, fitting in a perfect pattern, and he saw how it was. Women weren't all either cold angels or degraded prostitutes. No woman was either of her own choice. They were warm-hearted human beings, eager for life, and he should have known that before. Everyone would know, only religion and education told men and women lies about each other to keep them apart. Often, the lies worked because people tried to live up to them. When that happened a man and woman didn't find each other, even though they lived together.

That was what the tall girl on the steamer was telling Ben. "We're warm and human, and we're coming into our own. The ones who treat women as something more than human beings wrong them as much as those who treat them as something less."

Ben waved frantically, to say he understood and would remember.

Only Oscar did not wave. And he found it hard to refrain, with so many waving hands and caps about him. He didn't think the woman on the *Paul Jones* was a whore, but her behavior strengthened a dark suspicion in his mind: the suspicion that at heart, all women are whores. Her waving and throwing kisses showed what she was under her fine clothes and fine manners. She had practically offered to come on board the lightship.

Oscar looked down his nose, to where his paunch made an expectant bulge in his spray-drenched yellow slicker. He felt dreadfully ashamed, standing there among those waving, cheering men. His embarrassment grew until he became afraid to look up and see the woman, flaunting the dirty secret of life. And at the same time he wanted, terribly, to have another look at her.

Clark was in the wheel house, waiting for the lightship to go adrift, and watching the *Paul Jones* battle her way seaward. As he pulled the whistle cord, wishing her good luck, his body told him that the graceful, tall girl was Virginia. And his mind half believed it. She was very like that, and she held her head that way, and there was something about her waving. . . .

He remembered the day after their swim in the starlit creek, when he was afraid she would never come back. Then he came out of the woods, and the flames shot through him when he saw her beside the cutter. She was mending the storm trys'l, with her hat beside her on the grass, turned so she would see him as soon as he appeared at the far end of the meadow. She had waved to him like that, dear and proud, to tell him that for her there was no turning back from love.

The girl was throwing kisses now, and the flames were going through him, telling him that for his body there was no turning back, either. Virginia was on the *Paul Jones;* she would be in Seattle before him. It couldn't be Virginia, that was impossible. But was it? No one knew what happened, afterward. There might be some way of escaping the backwaters of death. Maybe one learned how, after a while.

The *Paul Jones* drew away from the lightship, rolling and pitching, shouldering the gray, smoking seas into bursting white. Her stern was thrown up and the wet blades of the propeller spun madly in unsubstantial spray. They sank and took hold of the sea again, driving on toward safety. The ensign, inverted at the head of the mainmast as a signal of distress, descended, jerkily, on an invisible halliard. The steamer was confident of making her own way.

Captain Lindstrom went below to cut down the revolutions of the engine. Better to tell the chief, quietly, without using the gong. It was a great load off his mind to see the *Jones* clear of the reef. A close call, and a nice problem for her master. Another situation where letting go the anchors would have been the wrong thing. Perhaps commanding a lightship prejudiced a man against all anchors.

Anna. He mustn't think of her now. That young woman on the steamer had the making of a sailor, coming on deck in such a storm. Probably the stewards were too seasick or scared to stop her. A fine, healthy type. She reminded him of Anna. Not Anna, the woman, in childbed. He mustn't think of that now. Anna at twenty. Remember that last night in Finland? Pine and birch logs roaring in the fireplace. The cry of violins, loud-singing balalaikas and the stamping feet of the dance. Outside, the fields under snow; forest black in the iron cold, and the moon going down into Russia. Anna standing beside him, tall and strong and healthy, like that girl on the steamer. Flushed pink and gold, with the blue fires of her eyes flickering through him with countless meanings.

"Carl, we are going to the Promised Land!"

She had said that a hundred times before, always with thrilling wonder. Half her wonder was because he had been there before. People on the Oregon side of the

Columbia River didn't know they were living in the Promised Land. Clark hadn't known, living there, when he planned to search for it in the South Seas.

Now Anna knew the Promised Land better than he, and the children didn't know any other. Young Carl was doing well in the fifth grade; Richard was in the third, and at the end of Anna's last letter Walter had ground out in great, lumpy letters: "I love my Daddy." Three fine, healthy children growing up to be Americans, and the fourth waiting to be born, or born already. Or would it be born the moment the lightship crashed on the reef? Mustn't think of Anna and the children now. Not until the ship was safe—if there was any safety. Until then, he belonged to his other family, the crew. They needed him—those hopeful, heartbreaking bastards the sea had brought him.

The lightship went adrift at 12:41. It took her over an hour to break loose after the engine was throttled down. It happened so easily they wondered why she hadn't thought of doing that before, days before, when they had enough coal to reach the Straits. One sea, no bigger than the one before it, the feel of something letting go, and a new buoyancy in the forward part of the ship. Ole, at the wheel, rang for full speed. They had gained their doubtful freedom and were at liberty to go.

"We're going home, Lad!" Mr. Gill told Allen.

"Not saying which home," the bald young fireman answered, ducking below to companion slide to light a cigarette.

Freedom wasn't much different from imprisonment.

The lightship rose and fell with the great, roaring seas, expending all her energy in going up and down. She had been moored so long she couldn't get the idea of freedom through her head, and stayed on out of habit. At the end of half an hour, it was impossible to say whether she had gained or lost. A shovel rang steadily on the floor-plates below; black smoke crowded over the rim of the high stack and was spun away toward the white, spouting reef; the engine stamped out its one-legged rhythm—but it was a treadmill process, leading nowhere.

"Yah, we should start the whistle and bell," Oscar said, contemptuously. "She don't know anything else!"

Clark grumbled, shamefacedly, because there weren't any life-preservers. They had all the machinery for saving others, but the matter of saving themselves had been overlooked.

In the plunging engine room, Ben stood by, disconsolate, while Mickey nursed the engine and stoked the fires. The chief remembered his great one-man show of twenty years before, and wanted to duplicate it. But he couldn't do a dozen things at once with the same devilish glee; his old cat's face was grim when he thought how he had been trapped. He and the engine were old, and the ship was old and foul, but twenty years hadn't taken the fight out of them. Mickey could do it again, alone, and be damned to everyone, if he had the coal. Seventy years be damned! Years had nothing to do with it. He had been caught by a dirty trick of circumstance, and his department would be held up to ridicule.

"Ben, leave the fires alone! I'll stoke them when

they're needing it." He took the shovel from the boy, who had gingerly opened one of the doors, and sprayed precious coal over the even, white-hot fire—ignoring the motion of the boiler, which hung over him as the ship rose to a sea, and dived away from him as she slid down the other side.

"Ben, Ben," he growled, closing the door with his shovel, "why are ye standing there like a tourist? Go tell the captain we have coal for only an hour. Only half an hour, tell him. And find out what kind of song and dance is going on above."

Ben, too, heard the sound of axes and crowbars. The crew was gutting the vessel.

Captain Lindstrom received the message without surprise. "All right, Ben," he said gently. "Tell the chief there will be wood when the coal is gone. We'll begin passing it down when he says the word."

Clark was demolishing the sacred carpenter's bench. His old blue sweater hung on one of the half-door hooks, and his great shoulder muscles bulged and tightened as he swung a flashing axe. He looked like a woodsman working in the forest.

Oscar was chopping up the unhinged cabin door, with the face of a small boy doing something wicked. Each time his axe bit wood, he gave a loud "*Hah!*"

Allen and Mr. Gill were working with the same crowbar, prying planks from the cabin bulkhead. Allen was straining, with his face red and set; Mr. Gill was letting his sheer weight do most of the work, and saying, "Easy, easy," as if there were nothing in the world worth any panic of exertion.

When the breach in the bulkhead became sizable,

the captain looked pleased. "There isn't any more for'ard or aft," he commented. "It's all one ship."

Oscar had finished the door and was hacking the cabin table to pieces. The solid oak would make a nice bit of fuel. Clark was chopping things up forward, while Harry brought the proceeds aft. There was already a splendid stack of wood beside the fidley. The captain had given orders against smoking, and was sprinkling kerosene over the wood to give it more power. Oscar saw the idea was good, and brought the mattresses from aft, lashed in tight rolls with marlin, to be soaked in oil.

"They'll warm her heart for a minute," the captain said, approvingly.

A great sea threw Harry half the length of the fidley, with his load clattering about him, and he picked himself up to beam joyfully at the growing mountain of fuel. He was like a pirate cook, gloating over a great treasure.

Oscar unearthed another kind of treasure. After doing for the cabin table and armchairs, he attacked the chief's cabin. (His heart had been full of hatred ever since the chief laughed when he and Clark were nearly lost going after the box.) When he smashed the lockers under the berth, a roll of the ship poured out odds and ends of metal, until he was standing ankle-deep in ancient pipe couplings, valves, nuts, bolts, broken tools, and even tin cans. Mickey was known never to throw anything away, and at Eagle Harbor he sometimes led his disgusted firemen on foraging expeditions among the dumps, picking up things that might come in handy

337

some day. Oscar took savage joy in scattering the treasure of the old pack-rat.

They went on, gutting the ship, wetting the wood with oil and passing it below to Ben, whose energy seemed limitless. Now that he had work to do he was strong and sure of himself, and he never doubted that the ship would reach a safe harbor.

When the kerosene began to run low, Captain Lindstrom sent Clark above for the oil that had once been sacred to the lights. Now it was sacred as fuel, and before wetting the wood they put it on mattresses from forward—so when they were burned nothing would be lost.

The captain made the process of destruction orderly by dropping an occasional suggestion in a reassuring voice. He was well pleased with his crew. Clark worked alone and silently, like a giant, destroying bulkheads and freeing timbers. Oscar showed unexpected genius for finding wood in odd corners. Allen worked grimly, shrewdly, a devil of determination, while Mr. Gill exhaled calm as he boomed softly, "Easy, Lads, easy," and did a man's work. Harry alternated between carrying wood from the wrecked cabins forward, and making the rounds with a pot of coffee which no one had time to drink. There was a gently-fanatical light in his eyes, and sometimes he encouraged the others by crying: "To-day is a good day to fight; a good day to die!" He was going a little mad, but remained faithful to his human loyalties.

Alone, in the pilot house, Ole steadied the wheel and nursed a pinch of snuff in his cheek. He felt, rather than heard, the ship being gutted under his feet. The others were doing all that could be done. Gray-green and dirty white, the solid, wind-driven ridges swept down on the lightship, and she rose through the spray as lightly as an empty tin. She wasn't much more than that by now. The seaman got a rough bearing on a notch of land toward the shadowy Cape. It was two hours since the ship went adrift, and she was still on her station—eating her heart out, unwilling to go on the reef and unable to leave it. When the fuel was gone, though, unwillingness wouldn't matter.

If it came to that, Ole thought, they should use the last breath of steam to head down for the reef. He would rather face the thing than have it overtake him from behind. If he had the chance, he would suggest that to Captain Lindstrom. At the last, with the ship slipping back on the reef, sternfirst, the best of men would go to pieces. It would be better to tell everyone they were going to try for the passage through the reef. There was a kind of passage, though not even a fish could make it in the sea that was running. But they might get through a little way, and the men would go on hoping until the ship struck. After that, it would be too quick to matter.

Ole remembered the passage such as it was, and the landmarks ashore. He would at least have a shot at it, when the time came. He remembered the last time he had been there, when he killed the white calf, and the old Indian told him he couldn't come back until he was washed up, dead, on the beach. It looked as if that might happen. And he had planned that expedition so carefully and did everything so neatly—and it all turned out badly because of his ignorance.

Ole hated sadness. But now, for a little while, he felt sad that after coming such a long way on a rough voyage he had learned so little. Then his heart freshened with the thought that some day, a long time off, perhaps, people like him would find the meaning of life and come into their own. Then, the rest wouldn't matter. For himself, he didn't expect anything. With him things were the way they had been with the lightship toward the last. He didn't mind having lived in darkness if others could have light.

Three hours after they went adrift, Ole told himself plainly that *167* was still on her station. Possibly she was fifty fathoms north of her original position, but no farther from the reef. There was only one change of which he was certain: the ship was making water. Up to a point it was an advantage: she was not riding so high and crazily or offering so much resistance to the wind. But leaks are not made to order and before long this one would be too much of a good thing, like drowning to a thirsty man.

The ship reared on another great sea and Ole was perplexed by the sight of Clark's muscular figure dangling in the sky. The crest of the wave burst over the bow and Clark disappeared in a geyser of white spray, then reappeared, sliding down the forestay. He made something fast and vanished aft, past the wheel house. Ole shifted his quid of snuff and looked grave approval at the halliard which Clark had brought from aloft. He doubted if it would do any good; what they were attempting might drown them all a little sooner, but it was the only thing left to try and there was comfort in knowing that he was shipmates with sailors as well as donkeymen.

The starboard door was forced open and Captain Lindstrom loomed beside him. "Keep her right into it, Ole, until we bend the forestays'l."

Ole nodded. He had been doing that since the moment he saw Clark descending from the sky. "Making water fast, isn't she?"

The captain seemed positively gratified. "You noticed it? The chief is filling the shaft-alley tanks to give us a little ballast." He stroked his wet beard with one hand while holding on with the other. "God knows how she'll behave; not even Oscar has ever seen her under sail. But we must try to ratch her off."

Solid green water came over the bow when the sail was being bent. Captain Lindstrom and Oscar were carried floundering past the pilot house, but not swept overboard. When the spray cleared, Clark's body was left twisted about the forestay. After a moment it came to life and went on fastening the hanks to the stay. His desire to live had made him almost superhuman.

The ship steadied and hung in the wind, and Ole knew the main trys'l had been set. Presently the dripping captain looked into the pilot house. "You can bear a hand with the forestays'l," he called. "Oscar is standing by aft."

Ole was not superstitious, but it seemed to him that their luck might change when they began to steer like a sailing ship instead of a steamer. As he and Clark swayed on the halliard the sail burst from its spunyarns and rose jerkily on the stay, shaking and thundering in the wind which was made visible by driving spume.

It had been Clark's idea that the ship might be ratched off with the assistance of some canvas. He had a passion for small sailing craft, and it was he who remembered the riding sails, which had been renewed but never used in the memory of the oldest seaman on board. The captain was still sceptical, but it was a time to try anything rather than do nothing. He had hoped for something from the tide, which should have been favoring them for the last hour. But the wind had piled up the sea and the tide might be delayed another hour, or drowned altogether.

He let Clark relieve Oscar at the big wheel aft. That, too, had never been used in the memory of man—except when Ben and Allen, firemen, had posed beside it, taking pictures of each other.

The engine was stamping and shaking below. It was now or never. Neither sail nor steam alone could do them any good. Captain Lindstrom let one grandfather of the sea pass under and around them, then nodded to the helmsman. Clark tightened his lips as he put up the helm. The flattened scraps of sail swelled out and became as rigid as boiler plate as the ship fell off. Clark gave the wheel another spoke, then held it hard, his shoulder muscles swelling through his torn blue sweater and his eyes blazing. The lightship lay over, more and more, until short Ole and Oscar were looking far down on Clark from their anchorage at the weather rail.

Below there was the ringing crash of fireroom tools going down to leeward. Captain Lindstrom was braced against the side of the wheel box. "Just keep her stack out of the sea!" he shouted cheerfully.

Clark luffed up to meet the breaking crest of the next sea. It took them on the weather bow and blotted out the universe in flying water. The men had expected to drown with the ship, but now it seemed they would be drowned on deck. As they started down on the other side of the wave Clark was already flogging the ship onward, through the valley and up the next incredible hill of green and foaming water.

Since they did not capsize at once, the seamen began adjusting themselves to the new conditions. They were used to the ship falling over on her side repeatedly and it was a simple step to accustom themselves to her lying over on one side and staying there. After enough duckings they even got used to living half their time in a roaring twilight of spray. When they were in the comparative stillness of a valley between seas they felt the stamping of the engine below and knew that Mickey and his firemen were doing their part.

Near the crest of one sea Ole saw white water spouting high on the reef. It seemed to him they had gained nothing off shore, but they were making northing. He encouraged the sulking Oscar by offering him snuff.

"Rotten!" Oscar shouted to him, looking over the poised weather rail. "She's making nothing but leeway!"

Ole studied the broken water swirling away from the red side of the ship, then turned his back to meet the blast of spray from the crest. Oscar was right; they were making leeway, mostly, but a little more of it would carry them north of the reef, and if anything failed after that they would at least pile up on an honest shore.

Captain Lindstrom had uncovered the binnacle and was taking bearings in the moments when such a thing was approximately possible. After a while he went back to the wheel box. "The tide is favoring us now!" he shouted. "That set toward Vancouver—if we keep driving her we should make the Straits!"

Clark knew the set of that current; it had almost done for him once, when he and Oscar went after the box. He nodded his wet, iron-gray head. His somber eyes were fixed on the hard scraps of sail and the smoking hill of water that was bearing down on them.

When Oscar and Ole simultaneously offered to relieve him at the wheel he made no sign that he had heard, but there was no mistaking his refusal. He towered above them, savage and unmoving, with his eyes fixed irrevocably on the sails. His passionate urge to live would not let him entrust his salvation to other hands.

When the captain had said they should make the Straits, he had forgotten for a moment about fuel. They had left the reef behind when the companion hatch slid open a few inches and Allen's cheerful red face popped up. Captain Lindstrom went forward to him. The fireman's bald head was bleeding from a three-inch gash, which he did not seem to notice. Spray and chunks of water flew over them; the wound was washed clean, then began bleeding again.

"How is it below?"

Allen grinned. "Mickey sends you his compliments and wants to know if you have any wood up here?"

"How much is left?"

"Enough for two hours, the chief says. That probably means more. He's ladling in the spare oil to help along."

The captain glanced about the steep, spray-tormented deck. "We haven't much wood, but tell him to pass up two axes and we'll do our best for him."

"All right, Captain." The fireman still lingered.

"Anything else, Allen?"

"Mickey said to tell you if we do pull out of this don't go saying it was your half-arsed sails that did it!"

Captain Lindstrom looked annoyed. Then his face relaxed into an appreciative smile. "I hope we can discuss that later!" he shouted. Another sea burst on the weather bow and the companion slide closed. While he was still in the darkness of flying water he was planning how they would chop up the boat spars and chocks and the boats themselves and pass them down the companionway. He didn't know what the lighthouse inspector would say, but it was a nice philosophic thought that a man must burn his boats in order to reach port.